Beasts of New York
a children's book for grown-ups

BEASTS

---

of New York

A CHILDREN'S BOOK
FOR GROWNUPS

---

by Jon Evans

Wood Engravings by Jim Westergard

The Porcupine's Quill

Library and Archives Canada Cataloguing in Publication

Evans, Jon, 1973 –
    Beasts of New York: a children's book for grown-ups / by Jon Evans;
wood engravings by Jim Westergard.

ISBN 978-0-88984-341-7

    I. Title.

PS8609.V337B43 2011   C813'.6   C2011-900834-3

1   2   3   •   13   12   11

Published by The Porcupine's Quill. http://porcupinesquill.ca
68 Main Street, PO Box 160, Erin, Ontario NOB 1TO.

Represented in Canada by the Literary Press Group.
Trade orders are available from University of Toronto Press.

We acknowledge the support of the Ontario Arts Council and the Canada
Council for the Arts for our publishing program. The financial support of
the Government of Canada through the Canada Book Fund is also gratefully
acknowledged. Thanks, also, to the Government of Ontario through the
Ontario Media Development Corporation's Ontario Book Initiative.

Canadä

Ontario
Ontario Media Development
Corporation

Canada Council   Conseil des Arts
for the Arts   du Canada

ONTARIO ARTS COUNCIL
CONSEIL DES ARTS DE L'ONTARIO

To Susan

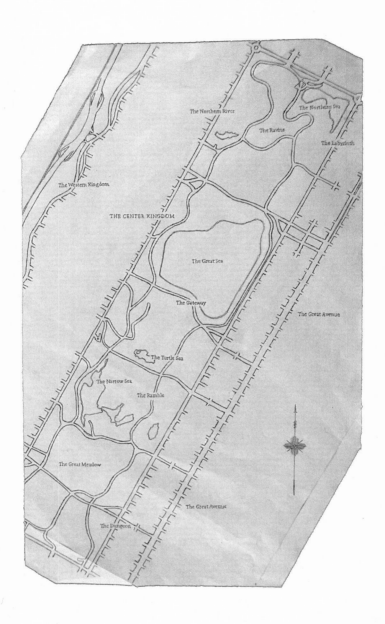

CONTENTS

PART ONE

I. THE CENTER KINGDOM

THE MISSING ACORNS

 long time ago, when humans still lived in cities, on a cold morning near the end of a long, cruel winter, in magnificent Central Park in the middle of magnificent New York City, a young squirrel named Patch was awakened very early by the growls of his empty stomach.

A squirrel's home is called a *drey*. Patch's drey was very comfortable. He lived high up an old oak tree, in a hollowed-out stump of a big branch that had long ago been cut off by humans. The entrance was only just big enough for Patch to squeeze in and out, but the drey itself was spacious, for a squirrel. Patch had lined his drey with dry leaves, grasses and bits of newspaper. It was warm and dry, and on that cold morning he would have liked nothing better than to stay home all day and sleep.

But he was so hungry. Hunger filled him like water fills a glass. The cherry and maple trees had not yet started to bud; flowers had not yet begun to grow; the juicy grubs and bugs of spring had not yet emerged; and it had been two days since Patch had found a nut. Imagine how hungry you would be if you went two whole days without eating, and you may have some idea of how Patch felt that morning.

Patch poked his head out of the drey, into the cold air, and shivered as he looked around. Clumps of white, crumbly ice still clung to the ground. Gusts of cold wind shook and rustled the trees' bare branches. The pale and distant sun seemed drained of heat. He took a moment to satisfy himself that there were no dangers nearby, no hawk circling above or unleashed dog below. Then Patch emerged from his drey and began to look for acorns.

But what marvels, what miracles, what mysteries are hidden within those simple words!

Squirrels are extraordinary creatures. Think first of how they climb. When Patch left his drey, he went up, not down. He passed the drey of his friend and neighbor Twitch, climbed to the northernmost tip of his oak tree's cloud of barren branches, and casually hopped onto the adjacent maple tree, home to his brother Tuft. To a squirrel, every tree is an apartment building, connected not only by the grassy thoroughfares of the ground but by sky-roads of overlapping branches. Tree trunks are like highways to them, even branches thin as twine are like walking paths, and they leap through the sky from one tree to another like circus acrobats.

When he reached the last of the thick grove of trees, Patch paused a moment to look around and consult his memory. His memory was not like yours or mine. Human memories are like messages written on crumbling sand, seen through warped glass. But squirrels have memories like photograph albums: exact and perfect recollections of individual moments. Patch, like every squirrel, had spent the past autumn burying hundreds and hundreds of nuts and acorns, each in a different place. And he had stored all of those places in his memory book. The winter had been long, but Patch's memory book still contained a precious few pages that depicted the locations of nuts not yet dug up and eaten. He climbed to a high branch, stood on his hind legs, and looked all around, seeking an image from one of those memories.

If you had looked at Central Park that morning with human eyes, you would have seen concrete paths, steel fences, a few early-morning joggers and dog walkers, all surrounded by fields of grass and ice and bare trees and rocks, and beyond them, Manhattan's endless rows of skyscrapers.

But through Patch's eyes, through *animal* eyes, there was no park at all. Instead Patch saw a city in itself. A vast and mighty city called the Center Kingdom. A city of trees, bushes, meadows and lakes; a city scarred by strips of barren concrete; a city surrounded by endless towering mountains. All manner of creatures lived in this city. Squirrels in their dreys, rats and mice in their underground warrens, raccoons in the bushes, fish and turtles in the lakes, birds fluttering through the trees or resting in their nests. At that hour on that day, very early on a winter morning, the Center Kingdom was almost abandoned – but soon spring would come, and the city would bloom into a thriving maelstrom of life and activity. All Patch needed to do, until that blessed time arrived, was find enough food for these last few days of winter.

He saw in the distance, near the edge of the densely wooded area he called home, a jagged rock outcropping familiar from his memory book. He was so hungry he paused only a moment to check for dangers before racing headfirst down the tree trunk and toward the rocks. In his memory that same outcropping was just *there* – and the nearest human mountain visible over the treetops to the west was *there* – and a particular maple tree, which had been covered in orange and scarlet leaves on the day Patch buried the acorn, had been exactly *there*, and *that* far away.

Patch found his way to the exact spot where all those landmarks fell into place, so that the place where he stood and the page from his memory book matched perfectly, like a picture and its tracing. Then he began to sniff. He knew as an undeniable fact that in the autumn he had buried an acorn within a tail-length of where he stood. And squirrels can smell perfume in a hurricane, or a dog a half-mile upwind, or a long-buried acorn.

But Patch smelled nothing but grass, and earth, and normal air-smells.

His heart fell. It seemed to fall all the way into his paws and seep out through the tips of his claws. Patch let out a little murmur of awful disappointment. There was no food here. This acorn was gone, already gone.

This was not unusual. Squirrels often found and ate nuts buried by other squirrels. But the same thing had happened with every nut Patch had tried to unearth for the last two days. And that was unusual. It was such an astonishing run of bad luck that Patch had never heard of such a thing happening before.

He dug anyway, hoping that maybe this acorn had no smell, or that his nose was not working right. But he found nothing. And at the next burial place, again there was nothing. He ran to the next; and the next; until finally there were no more pictures left in Patch's book of memories, no nuts left to try to unearth. And he was so hungry.

By this time other squirrels too had emerged from their dreys and begun to dig for food. Patch knew all of the half-dozen squirrels he could see around him, and the dozen more whose presence he could smell in the cold wind. All were of his tribe.

Squirrels are social animals, they have family and friends, clans and tribes and kingdoms. Patch's tribe, the squirrels of the Treetops, were not like the Meadow tribe, who lived near the city's grassy plains, or the Ramble tribe, which inhabited its rockiest wilderness, or the red Northern tribe. The Treetops tribe was more a group of individuals than a community. If they had had a motto, it would have been 'Take care of yourself.' None of the squirrels around Patch were of his clan. It would have been a terribly low and shameful thing for Patch to go to one of them and ask for even a single bite of an acorn. But while pride is important, it cannot be eaten, and hunger is more important still. Patch was so ravenous he would have begged for food.

But there was no one to beg from. For not a single one of the squirrels around him had found a nut. All of them were digging for nothing.

Patch sat and thought.

He was, you must remember, a squirrel, an animal, a creature of instinct. Thinking did not come naturally to him. He had to sit for a long time while he thought, in a little fenced-in patch of grass near one of the concrete-wasteland human trails. Around him there was little to see. In winter most birds flew south, rats stayed underground, raccoons hibernated. There were only the other hungry squirrels, a few fluttering pigeons, and the occasional passing human.

At one point an unleashed dog came near, and Patch had to interrupt his thinking to watch this threat. It was a very strange dog. If it was indeed a dog at all. It *looked* like a dog, but it was unaccompanied by any human, and it had a rich, feral scent like no other dog Patch had ever encountered. The dog-thing said nothing, which was also unusual, but it watched Patch with a leery grin full of sharp teeth for what felt like a long time. Patch was very glad of the fence that surrounded him. When the dog-thing finally moved on Patch sighed with relief. He could have escaped to the safety of a nearby tree if necessary. But he was so hungry that the effort of running away, combined with the terrible strain of thinking, would have left him weak and dizzy.

By the time Patch finally finished thinking, he had drawn one conclusion and made two decisions.

The conclusion was that something was very strange and wrong.

14

It was not Patch alone who had lost all of his food. That would have been bad enough. But the same thing seemed to have happened to every member of his tribe. That could not be mere ill luck. Something more, something worse, was happening. There were dark stories told in whispers among squirrels, ancient legends of winters that had out-lasted all the Center Kingdom's buried nuts, famines in which nine of every ten squirrels had died of hunger, and the few survivors had been forced to eat the bodies of the dead in order to live. But there were no legends in which all buried acorns had vanished uneaten from the earth. This was something new.

The first decision he made was that he would seek out his family, to see if they had any food. Patch was solitary by nature, and had not seen his family or indeed spoken to any other squirrel for three days, but he knew they would help him if they could, just as he would help them.

His second decision was that if his family did not have food, then ... he would try something else. Something very unusual, for a squirrel. Something very daring and dangerous indeed. But by this time hunger was growing stronger in Patch than fear.

PATCH'S FAMILY

atch's mother was named Silver, because the high sum-mer sun made her fur shine that color. She had a mar-velous drey high up a spruce tree, carved out long ago by a woodpecker, and since extended into a two-chambered home full of bright things. The journey along the sky-road to her drey did not take long. When Patch looked inside, he saw a hundred colors glittering in the sunlight, shining from the bits of metal and glass set into Silver's walls and floor. But his mother was not there.

He could tell by the faintness of the smells that no squirrel had been here in some time. There were two distant traces of scent, sev-eral days old: that of Silver, and that of another squirrel, a musky scent that Patch did not recognize. A scent that made his tail stiffen as if danger were near.

Patch stared into his mother's empty drey for a moment. It

wasn't normal for a squirrel to abandon her drey for days, not in winter. And he hadn't seen Silver for three days. Not since all the acorns had disappeared from the earth.

Patch ran back to his own tree, and then to the maple tree next door, to his brother Tuft's drey. He ran very fast. He was hungrier than ever, and he was beginning to be very worried. He was relieved when he looked into Tuft's drey and found it occupied. Tuft himself was not present, but Brighteyes was, and their babies, and it was clear from the smells that Tuft had only just departed.

'Hello, Patch,' Brighteyes said weakly. 'Would you like to come in?'

Patch entered. Brighteyes was curled up with her babies in the drey's deepest, warmest corner. The last time Patch had visited, seven days ago, this had been a den of noise and chaos, with all of Brighteye's four babies running and jumping and playfighting. Today they lay weakly beside Brighteyes, and the once-shining eyes from which their mother had taken her name were dim and clouded.

'Uncle Patch,' the littlest baby said, in a piteous mewling voice. 'Please, Uncle Patch, do you have any food?'

The other children looked up at Patch with hopeful eyes. As hungry as he was at that moment, if he had had an acorn, he would have given it to his nieces and nephews. But he had nothing.

'I'm sorry,' Patch said, ashamed. 'I haven't found any food for days.'

'No one has,' Brighteyes said.

'Have you seen Silver?'

'No. She hasn't come to visit since the food ran out.'

Patch considered. 'Is Tuft out looking for food?'

After a long moment Brighteyes said, very quietly, as if she were admitting something terribly shameful, 'Tuft has gone to the Meadow tribe.'

'The Meadow tribe?' Patch asked, confused. 'What for?'

Brighteyes said, in a voice hardly louder than a whisper, 'To accept their offer.'

'What offer?'

Brighteyes stiffened with surprise. 'You haven't heard?'

'Heard what?'

'You spend too much time on your own, Patch. If you talked to others more you wouldn't always be the last to know.'

'The last to know *what?*'

'The Meadow tribe has offered food to Treetops squirrels. But only if we join their tribe.'

'Join their tribe?' Patch looked at her, perplexed. 'Join the Meadow? That's not possible. We're of the Treetops. We can't become of the Meadow.'

'They say if we swear an oath of allegiance to the Meadow tribe, if we swear by the moon, then we will become of the Meadow, and then they will give us food.'

After a long moment, Patch asked, his voice now as hushed as that of Brighteyes, 'Swear by the moon?'

This is not the place to explain what the moon means to animals. Suffice to say that an oath sworn by the moon is even stronger than an oath sworn on blood. Such an oath can never be broken or unsworn.

'Yes,' Brighteyes said, looking away from Patch.

'Tuft has gone to swear by the moon to join the Meadow tribe?'

'Yes. We will all go. We will all swear. Tuft will bring back some food for the children, and when they are strong enough they will go and swear themselves.'

'You can't do this,' Patch said, shocked. 'You can't leave the Treetops. You can't give your children to another tribe.'

'We must. We haven't any *food,* Patch. You see how weak my babies are. No one else can help us. Silver is gone. Jumper is gone.'

'Jumper is gone? Gone where?'

'No one knows. No one has seen him in days. Like no one has seen Silver. Or any of the other clan leaders.'

'The king,' Patch said. 'We'll go to King Thorn.'

'The Ramble is too far. Even if the King sends help, it will never reach us in time. My babies are starving, Patch. My babies are *dying.* The Meadow is our only hope.'

'No,' Patch said. 'There is another. If I had known things were this bad –' He hesitated. 'I know another place to get food.'

'Then why are you hungry?' Brighteyes asked.

'It's dangerous. It's in the mountains.'

17

'In the *mountains?* Are you *mad?*'

Patch was saved from answering by the appearance of his brother, Tuft, at the entrance to the drey. Tuft held two acorns against his chest, but he looked perilously thin, and weak, and tired.

'It's done,' Tuft said. His voice was grim. 'I have joined the Meadow.'

Tuft carried the food in to his family. As the children devoured one acorn, Brighteyes and Tuft and Patch stood around the other, staring as if it glowed.

'This one is for you,' Tuft said to Brighteyes. 'The Meadow gave me one for myself when I was there.'

Patch knew Tuft was lying.

Brighteyes said, 'We'll share it. All three of us.'

Patch wanted a bite of acorn so much that his whole body trembled with desire. 'No,' he said faintly.

Tuft and Brighteyes turned to him, amazed.

'I will go to the mountains,' Patch said.

Right away, before the acorn's temptation became too great to deny, he turned and fled from his brother's drey, and ran straight down the maple trunk to the ground. From there Patch ran north and west. His hunger was a searing flame within him.

PATCH AND THE BIRDS

t was not entirely true that Patch knew there was food in the mountains. He had never been to the mountains. No squirrel in all the Center Kingdom, as far as he knew, had ever been to the mountains. For between the kingdom and the mountains, surrounding the kingdom on all sides like a moat around a castle, there lay a blasted concrete wasteland, as wide as fifty squirrels laid nose to tail, and horrific death machines roared up and down this wasteland at terrifying speeds, all day and night. What's more, humans and dogs often crossed between the mountains and the kingdoms; and sometimes the dogs were unleashed. A squirrel would have to be very desperate indeed to dare the wastelands.

It was Toro who had told Patch about the food in the mountains. Toro was Patch's friend. And that itself was extraordinary.

Patch had always talked to birds. The drey he had grown up in – Silver's old drey, before she became leader of the Seeker clan – had been only a few branches away from a nest of robins. Once, in early spring when he was still a baby, Patch had crawled out of Silver's drey and into the robin's nest, and had spent a whole day among the chicks before Silver returned home and retrieved him. The robin mother had been unamused by Silver's profound apologies, and even less amused when Patch returned to her nest the very next day.

Eventually Silver taught Patch to leave the robins alone, but not before he had learned how to speak Bird. Most squirrels of the Center Kingdom could say and understand a few simple things in Bird, but Patch could actually hold conversations. And so, one autumn day when a bluejay swooped past and stole an acorn out of Patch's paws, Patch shouted angrily at the thief in Bird to bring it back; and the thief, intrigued, wheeled around in midair, perched on a branch above Patch, and looked curiously down at the irate squirrel.

'Thieving feather-brained no-nose hawkbait!' Patch shouted up.

'Stupid blind furry groundworm!' the bluejay retorted, and began to peck at the acorn.

'Your mother should have dropped your egg onto a rock!'

'I must say,' the bluejay said between bites, 'you speak Bird remarkably well, for a thick hairy slug with a mangy tail.'

'Thank you, you moldy-feathered sky-rat. Now give me back my acorn!'

The bluejay considered, while he finished eating half of the acorn. And then, rather incredibly, he let the other half drop to the ground.

'To tell you the truth I wasn't very hungry,' he said. 'I just enjoy taking acorns from squirrels. I didn't know you spoke Bird. What is your name?'

'My name is Patch.'

'My name is Toro.'

Patch didn't know what to say. He had never been introduced to a bluejay before. Like all squirrels he thought of bluejays, the Center Kingdom's most prolific eaters of nuts, as dire enemies. Patch looked around to see if any other squirrels could see him talking to a bluejay. Fortunately none were nearby.

'If you're looking for acorns,' Toro said, 'the wind has been strong today on the other side of those rocks, and many there have fallen.'

After a moment Patch said, stiffly, 'Thank you.'

'Anytime,' the bird said carelessly, before flying away.

That was the beginning of their secret friendship. It had to remain secret, for other squirrels would have been enraged by the thought of Patch befriending Toro, and other bluejays would have looked askance at Toro befriending Patch. But the two had much in common. Both were lone explorers. And when they saw one another in remote corners of the Center Kingdom, as they often did, they stopped to talk. It was during one of those conversations, in the depths of the winter, that Toro told Patch of what his sharp bluejay eyes had seen in the nearby mountains.

IN THE MOUNTAINS

atch stood beneath the tree that marked the absolute edge of the Center Kingdom and stared, horrified, at the wasteland between himself and the mountains. Death machines hurtled past in both directions, roaring and snarling, zooming by at speeds so great that Patch could feel the wind of their slipstreams. Sometimes they stopped for a few moments to gather in packs; then they all leapt into motion at once. On either side of the wasteland, metal tree trunks protruded from the concrete, and from their glistening branches hung ever-changing lights. Patch knew from previous experimentation that he could not climb these metal trees. Even a squirrel's claws found no purchase on their smooth and shining bark.

At least he saw no dogs, and only a few humans. But from where he stood his intent seemed not just dangerous but actually insane. Surely it was better to abandon the Treetops and swear allegiance to the Meadow than to leap into the certain death of the wasteland. Patch turned around and took a few steps back toward Tuft's drey.

Then he stopped, turned, cocked his head, and looked once more at the wasteland. He had just realized there was something rhythmic about the way the death machines moved. There was a *pattern*. The same pattern as that of the changing lights in the sky.

He thought of what Toro had told him. Heaps and rivers of food, waiting to be eaten. Patch couldn't smell any food. He could hardly smell anything over the foul belches of the death machines. The death machines that stopped when the lights changed, maybe, just maybe, long enough for a squirrel to scamper across the wasteland.

Hunger plays tricks on the mind. By the time Patch realized he was actually running for the mountains, and not merely considering it, he was already halfway across the wasteland. The concrete beneath his paws was hard and cold. The several humans on the mountain side of the wasteland had ceased their motion and turned their heads to look at Patch. That wasn't good. But he had gone too far to turn back. The death machines would crush him if he did. His only hope was to keep running. He ran so hard and so fast that after crossing the wasteland he very nearly ran headfirst into the nearest mountain.

Patch stopped just in time and looked around, breathless, amazed at what he had just done. Having reached his destination he did not know what to do next. This was a new and alien world. The ground was entirely concrete; he couldn't see a single blade of grass on this side of the wasteland. The mountain before him was a perfectly vertical wall of rock that reared into the sky far higher than any tree. There was wasteland on two sides; behind him, the wide barrier he had just crossed, teeming with death machines, and to his right, a narrower offshoot that ran deeper into the mountains, occupied by stationary death machines along its edges. Patch wondered if they were dead or only sleeping. He hoped for dead. At least there were a few trees along the side of this narrow wasteland, although they were small and withered; their trunks were caged with bricks and they were spaced so far apart there was no sky-road. Between some of the trees, in the distance, Patch saw a few piles of what looked like big, shiny black rocks.

There were no other animals, only a few passing humans. But while these humans did not approach Patch, they seemed to be directing their attention toward him. This made him very nervous.

Humans were huge and unpredictable. Some humans who entered the Center Kingdom spilled food all around them, but the younger ones often tried to attack squirrels, and all of them smelled extraordinarily strange.

Patch sniffed the air. Beneath the thick acrid fumes of the death machines and the alien scent of humanity, he smelled danger. He smelled dogs. Upwind, to the north, across the narrow wasteland, three large dogs leashed to an old human were approaching. Patch hoped the wasteland would forestall them – but, as he watched, the dogs began to cross. And when the lead dog saw Patch, its eyes lit up like flames.

'Kill you and eat you!' it howled ecstatically. 'Kill you and eat you!'

The other dogs joined in. 'Kill you and eat you! Kill you and eat you! Kill you and eat you!'

Patch didn't stop to listen. Dog conversation was always the same. He scrambled for the nearest scrawny tree, and raced right up to its crown.

'Kill you and eat you, kill you and eat you, kill you and eat you!' the dogs shrieked at him, while they tried to pull their human toward the tree. But the human, although old, was still a massive creature, and to Patch's relief it pulled the murderous dogs along until they vanished behind the corner of the mountain.

Patch looked around. He stood atop a sickly tree, surrounded by mountains and wasteland. Beneath him, a death machine shuddered into motion and roared forward, and Patch realized to his horror that all those motionless machines were not dead, only sleeping, and might come to life at any moment.

Patch was starving, but worse, he was so terrified he could hardly move. He wished with all his heart he had never crossed the wasteland into the mountains. He saw and smelled no food here. And he did not dare descend from this scrawny tree. There was no safety below. Between the mountains and the line of death machines beneath him there was a slightly raised strip of concrete, in which the trees were set; but it was perfectly apparent to Patch that the death machines, with their terrible rolling feet, could easily rampage down this narrow strip too if they so desired. Nowhere and nothing in the mountains was safe.

atch!' a voice chirped. 'Patch, is that you?'

Patch looked to the sky and his heart filled with relief as a bluejay fluttered downward and settled on a nearby branch. Nothing dispels fear like the unexpected arrival of a friend.

'What are you doing here?' Toro asked, amazed.

'I came to get food,' Patch said. 'You said there was food here.'

'There is. Just down there.' Toro pointed with his beak deeper into the mountains. 'Inside those black things. Around them too, sometimes.'

'The rocks?' Patch asked doubtfully, but as he looked, he saw the skins of what he had taken to be rocks fluttering in the cold wind.

'Some of them are full of food. Food falls right out of them. Go on down, I'll show you.'

'Go on down,' Patch echoed, even more doubtfully.

'It's perfectly safe. Just follow me,' Toro said.

The bluejay launched himself into the wind, angled his wings into a slow gliding turn, and came to rest on the concrete, next to a heap of black things that stood beside one of the caged little trees.

'Easy for you,' Patch muttered. 'You're a bird. You just fly away from trouble.'

But the sight of his friend perched casually right next to a sleeping death machine, combined with the promise of food, was enough to bring Patch down to the concrete. He scampered toward Toro as quickly as possible, turning his head from side to side to look for danger. He found it everywhere. There were humans both behind and ahead of Patch, a row of sleeping death machines to his right, and to his left he smelled rats. Many rats.

'This is it!' Toro said when Patch reached him.

Toro sounded as proud as if he stood before a hill of acorns as high as a human, rather than a pile of huge, foul-smelling black things like seedpods, their shiny skins flapping like leaves in the wind. Patch looked skeptically at the trickled heap of decaying sludge beneath one of the seedpods, and said, 'You said there was *food*.'

'There's food inside them,' Toro promised. 'Just go inside. That's what the rats do.'

'It's rat food?' Patch asked, horrified. Rats would eat anything, the more rancid and disgusting the better.'

'Rats come here,' Toro admitted. 'That's how I found it, I saw them. But sometimes it's good food too. Once, right here, I found the most marvelous seeds I ever tasted. They were wonderful.'

Patch sniffed the air. He smelled bluejay, death machines, rotting sludge and rats. He smelled his own fear and hunger. But there was something else beneath all that. Like the faintest hint of wine in muddy water, or a musical phrase almost drowned out by a howling crowd, Patch smelled something so delicious that his mouth began to water.

'What is it?' Toro asked.

'It's here,' Patch said. He leapt up on the nearest black thing. Its material had a strange slick feel, made an alarming crinkling noise when he landed, and was so soft his claws tore right through it. Patch jumped to the top of the pile of huge black seedpods, and ripped open the skin of the uppermost one with a few bites. The wonderful smell was suddenly stronger. Patch hesitated only a moment. Then he dove headfirst into the hole he had made.

It was so dark inside the seedpod that he could not see. His snout encountered dry fluttery things, wet sticky things, even hard metal things. In his hunger he pushed them all aside, squirming deeper and deeper, following his nose toward the smell that made him dizzy with hunger. He found paper, like the newspaper with which his drey was lined. He tore the paper open with his teeth. And inside he found a whole mound of food like nothing he had ever tasted before. It was soft, salty, and delicious. There was enough to fill the bellies of a dozen squirrels.

Patch ate, and ate, and ate.

Until dimly, through all the debris that surrounded him, he heard Toro's high, harsh cry that meant *Danger!*

hen Patch finally found his way out of the seedpod, Toro was gone, and there were rats all around him. Some hid beneath the huge black seedpods, some scuttled in the shadows of the nearby mountain. Patch knew from their smells there were at least a dozen of them.

There was another smell too, mixed with that of the rats. The very same unsavory squirrel-smell he had detected in Silver's abandoned drey.

'What do you want?' Patch asked from his perch atop the mound of seedpods. He was concerned but not yet frightened. Rats and squirrels were neither friends nor enemies. Squirrels were bigger and stronger, but rats were far more numerous. There were legends of long-ago wars between the two species, but no squirrel Patch knew had ever been attacked by rats. Squirrels lived aboveground, in the sun; rats frequented the night and the dark underworld. Of course, squirrels found rats disgusting and disagreeable – but so did all other animals.

An unusually large rat climbed up to the top of a seedpod. It was almost as big as Patch himself. Rats usually avoided light, but this one stood unafraid beneath the sun, and demanded: 'Who are you?'

'I am Patch son of Silver, of the Seeker clan, of the Treetops tribe, of the Center Kingdom,' Patch said. 'Who are you that asks?'

'I am Lord Snout,' the rat replied. 'Why are you here?'

'I came to look for food.'

'This is our food. These mountains are ours.'

'Your food?' Patch asked, bewildered. There was no ownership of food in the Center Kingdom, not until it had actually been eaten. 'That's ridiculous. It's food. It belongs to whoever finds it first.'

'Then you belong to us,' Snout hissed. 'Because we are the rats who will suck the marrow from your broken bones.'

And from the shadows all around the heaped seedpods other rats arose and began to climb toward Patch at the top of the pile.

Patch didn't hesitate. He sprinted downward, running straight at one of the rats. His charge was so unexpected that the rat in question stopped and shrank away a little, just enough for Patch to scamper past him, toward the edge of the pile. Two more rats raced out from beneath the mountain, blocking any escape across the concrete. He was still surrounded, and rats were scuttling toward him from all directions.

From the very edge of the pile of seedpods, Patch jumped as high and as far as he could. For a moment, in midair, he was sure he wouldn't make it, he would fall to the concrete and be torn apart by the rats – but then his outstretched claws latched onto the bark of the little tree beside which the seedpods had been heaped. Moments later he stood atop the tree, looking down at the milling figures of more than a dozen frustrated rats.

'Come on up!' Patch cried out cheerfully.

He wasn't as confident as he sounded. Rats weren't near as nimble as squirrels, but there were many of them, and this was a very small tree. If all the rats climbed up, Patch wasn't sure he would escape. But at least he was up a tree, his belly was full for the first time in days, and Toro was watching from the next tree over.

'I will find you, Patch son of Silver,' promised the rat named Snout. 'I will find you and eat your eyes from your skull.'

Patch said nothing. He only watched as the rats scurried away. Most returned to the shadows at the base of the mountain. But Snout ran along the mountain's edge, until he reached a huge hole in its side. Humans had blocked the hole with a wire fence much like those in the Center Kingdom. Snout squeezed himself through a gap in the fence and disappeared into shadow.

'Did you find food?' Toro asked.

'Yes,' Patch said. 'It was wonderful.'

'I've never seen rats like that before.'

'Neither have I.'

'You should go back to the kingdom. It's safe there.'

Patch was afraid to stay in these mountains for a moment longer. He wanted to run back to the Center Kingdom, with his full belly and his wonderful story of adventure that no other squirrel would ever believe, and wait for spring to come. But he thought of his mother's empty drey, and the haunting squirrel-smell there – and the way that very same musty squirrel-smell had emanated from that biggest rat.

'Not yet,' Patch said.

he opening in the wire fence that Snout had squeezed through was too small for Patch to do the same. But it was easy enough to climb up to the top of the fence. From there, Patch could see all of the hole in the side of the mountain. It was like some enormous creature had taken a big bite from the mountainside. Beneath the wire fence, a sheer-walled pit plunged deep into darkness. The pit was full of metal and concrete shaped in the strange curves and straight lines that humans favored but that made animals feel queasy. The air was dusty and smelled awful. Patch shaded his eyes with his tail and squinted, but from the top of the fence, where the sun shone brightly, he still could not see into the darkness at the pit's bottom.

'I think we should go,' Toro said.

'Not yet,' Patch repeated. He watched the dust clouds in the pit, the way they moved. He didn't want to be upwind of the rats. They too had sharp noses. He ran along the top of the fence, as far downwind as he could, and then he took a deep breath and ran straight down its side.

The lip of the pit was hard concrete, no good for downclimbing, but a wooden plank descended into the shadows. Patch moved down this plank as quietly as he could; rats had sharp hearing too. It was strange to walk on wood with such a perfectly straight surface. The pit was as deep as a medium-sized tree. About halfway down the plank he moved from sunlight into shadow, and his eyes began to adjust to his new surroundings.

The center of the pit was jumbled full of huge, geometric human things. Its bottom was crisscrossed by pipes and planks and girders. The floor and one wall of the pit were rocky earth rather than concrete. But it was in a corner between two concrete walls, toward the inside of the mountain, that he saw the unmistakable scuttling motion of a rat.

Patch crept closer, staying behind human things as much as possible. He reached a metal pipe that ran near the corner, and followed its length until the pipe ran into the concrete wall, just a half-dozen squirrel-lengths from the corner. He was still downwind, he thought, although it was difficult to read the wind down here. When he stood as high as he could he was just barely able to look over the pipe and see into the corner of the pit.

In that corner Patch saw something very strange. He saw a dozen large rats standing in a circle, all facing outwards, with all their tails knotted together in a big tangled lump in the middle of their circle. Standing on this lumpy knot of tails was Snout, the biggest rat of all. And next to this bizarre clump of rats, Patch saw, to his great surprise, another squirrel, small and with reddish fur.

'Patch son of Silver,' the strange squirrel said, and Patch stiffened. 'I've heard of him. He's of the Treetops. He talks to birds and goes off alone for days. I'm sure he doesn't know anything. He just came to the mountains for the food.'

'That's not good enough,' Snout said. 'We will give him to Karmerruk.'

'But –' the squirrel began.

'We will give him to Karmerruk.'

The name meant nothing to Patch, but it seemed to frighten the other squirrel. 'You said you would show me Jumper,' the squirrel said hesitantly to Snout.

'Oh, yes, Jumper,' Snout said, and smiled, revealing jagged yellow teeth. Then, loudly, the rat commanded, 'Bring him!'

There was a dark hole in the corner of the pit, near where the rats and the other squirrel stood. Patch saw motion in that hole. He saw a squirrel's head emerge. He watched, shocked, as Jumper, Lord of the Treetops tribe, crawled painfully out of that hole, his motions slow and spastic, and fell clumsily to the ground. Jumper was bleeding in many places, and he pulled himself along with his forelegs alone; both his hind legs hung motionless from his body. Several rats followed Jumper out of the hole.

'Lord Jumper won't be jumping anymore,' Snout said, and laughed.

Jumper pulled himself up on his forelegs. Patch could see he was in great pain.

'Redeye,' Jumper said in a ragged voice to the squirrel who stood among the rats. 'How can you have done this?'

The other squirrel looked uneasy, and didn't answer. Patch was glad to have his name. It was Redeye he had smelled in Silver's drey.

'He did it for me,' Snout said. 'He has sworn to serve me, as I have sworn to serve the King Beneath. The king in whose name you and all your kind will die and be devoured.'

Snout stepped away from the knot of rat tails on which he stood. The knot began to squirm like a nest of worms as the rats untied themselves from one another. As they were released the rats formed a tight circle around Jumper. Snout joined the circle. So did Redeye. Patch knew what would happen next. He didn't want to watch. But it was too awful a thing to turn away from.

'No,' Jumper begged them. 'No, please. Not like this.'

'Yes,' Snout hissed. '*Exactly* like this.'

And then they swarmed the crippled lord of the Treetops. Jumper howled three times before he fell silent beneath the frenzied mass of biting rats. Redeye seemed more rat than squirrel as he tore at Jumper's body with his sharp fangs. In scarcely more time than it takes to tell it there was nothing left of Jumper but scraps, bones, and a puddle of blood. Even then the rats began to gnaw on Jumper's bones and lick his blood. They would leave nothing of him at all.

Patch retreated silently to the wooden plank that led out of the pit. He felt colder than he had on the worst day of the winter. The squirrel Redeye had betrayed Jumper to rats, helped to kill him, helped to *eat* him. And Redeye's scent had been in Silver's drey. Patch climbed numbly into the sunlight, over the fence, back to the concrete, heedless of the passing humans and the death machines. They held scarcely any terror for him now; all he could think about was what he had seen in the pit below.

'What did you see?' Toro called out from a tree. 'What was down there?'

Patch said, 'I have to go back to the kingdom.'

eturning to the Center Kingdom was relatively easy, now that Patch knew how to cross the wastelands. He was relieved when he once again felt snow and ice beneath his paws. But he was also very worried, and he immediately dashed for the maple tree next to his own. He was too late. Tuft's drey was empty; he and Brighteyes had already taken their children to swear to the Meadow tribe.

Patch considered a moment, and then he took the sky-road to his own tree, and descended to the drey of his friend and neighbor Twitch. He half-expected to find that Twitch too had gone to the Meadow. But Twitch was in his drey, and Patch was very pleased to find that he was not alone, but was with Patch's oldest friend, Sniffer.

'Patch!' Twitch cried out, excitedly jumping to his feet when he saw Patch at the drey entrance. 'Sniffer is here! Sniffer found me food!'

And indeed a chestnut and two acorns sat on the floor of Twitch's drey. It made sense that Sniffer, of all the Treetops squirrels, had been able to find food. Sniffer had the sharpest nose in all of Treetops, probably in all the Center Kingdom. It was said he could smell a buried acorn from halfway up a tree.

'I brought it for you too, Patch,' Sniffer said.

'Thank you,' Patch said, 'but I've eaten.'

Sniffer gave him a sharp look.

'You found food too?' Twitch asked. 'Where? How was it? Was it acorns? Was it chestnuts? Did humans bring it? Are the maples budding? Oh, I would love a nice fresh maple bud right now. I love nuts, you know I love nuts, but it's been only nuts all winter, I'd love a maple bud. Or a fresh grub, oh, a nice juicy grub. Or best of all, a tulip bulb, imagine, Patch, tulips! I just can't wait for spring. What kind of food did you find, Patch? Was it good? Is there more?'

Patch had to interrupt. It was difficult to get Twitch to stop talking about food once he had started. Patch said harshly, 'Jumper is dead.'

Sniffer and Twitch stared at him.

'He was eaten by rats,' Patch said. 'And a squirrel named Redeye. In the mountains. I saw it all. And Redeye was in Silver's drey, I smelled him there. Sniffer, do you think you can follow his scent?'

'Dead?' Twitch asked, still trying to understand. Twitch was bigger and stronger and could run faster than any other squirrel in Treetops, but he had never been able to understand things particularly quickly. 'Lord Jumper? Eaten by rats? In the mountains? You were in the mountains?'

'Yes,' Patch said.

'This is serious,' Sniffer said. 'This is very serious.'

Patch inclined his head in agreement.

'Did you say Redeye?' Twitch asked. 'I know Redeye. He's of the Meadow. He's Gobbler clan. One of his eyes is red and he's called Redeye. Just like you have that white patch on your head and you're called Patch. And I twitch a lot and I'm called Twitch. And Sniffer –'

'Yes, thank you,' Sniffer interrupted.

When Twitch wasn't talking about food, he often spent a lot of time restating the very obvious. But Twitch did have a very good memory for animals and their names. If Twitch said Redeye was a squirrel of the Meadow, then it was certainly so.

'I'll take you to Silver's drey so you can know his scent,' Patch said. 'And then we'll go to the Meadow. Maybe we can find him there.'

'It's a long way to the Meadow,' Sniffer objected. 'It's cold. It might be night before we can get back.'

'We can find a tree to stay in.'

Sniffer looked dubious.

'Please, Sniffer,' Patch said. 'Silver is missing. Jumper is dead. This is serious. You said so yourself.'

'Serious means dangerous,' Sniffer muttered. 'All right. Just … just let me go to my drey and get a little more food. Twitch can eat all this himself. Then I'll come back here and we can go to Silver's drey and to the Meadow.'

'Thank you,' Patch said, but Sniffer did not stay to hear his thanks. Sniffer's tail was already disappearing out the entrance to Twitch's drey. Sniffer did not usually move so quickly. Patch supposed he wanted to hurry to make sure they could get back before night.

'Tell me about the food in the mountains,' Twitch said eagerly.

'Not now, Twitch,' Patch said distractedly. 'You should eat. It's a long way to the Meadow. You need your strength.'

Patch was thinking about what might have happened to Silver, and at the same time, he was trying *not* to think about what might have happened.

Twitch looked at his chestnut and two acorns. Then he looked at Patch, and said, in a tense, strained voice, 'Would you like some?'

'No, thank you,' Patch said.

Twitch grinned with relief and fell to his lunch. By the time Sniffer got back there was nothing left of the three nuts but their shells.

They had a long way to go. In general, the Treetops tribe was spread across the western section of the Center Kingdom, the Meadow tribe was in the south, the Ramble tribe was in the center and the east, and the Northern tribe inhabited the kingdom's farthest northern reaches. There were exceptions, such as a colony of Meadow squirrels just north of the Great Sea, and those Treetops settlers who lived in the North; but Patch and his friends lived in the heart of Treetops territory. A journey to the green fields of the Meadow and back would occupy at least half a day. Much of the journey required ground travel rather than the sky-road, and that meant warily crossing concrete strips, avoiding dogs and humans, checking the skies for danger, and so forth.

But it was not while they were on the ground that danger struck. It struck instead when Patch, Sniffer and Twitch were in a dense cluster of cherry trees, traveling rapidly along the sky-road to the south. They did not hear a flutter of wings. They did not see a dark shadow streak along the ground toward them. The first they knew of the red-tailed hawk was when it seized Patch with talons sharp as broken glass, snatched him up from the cherry tree, and carried him screaming into the sky to be killed and eaten.

ANIMAL LANGUAGE

brief word is perhaps in order on the subject of animal languages.

I have already made it clear, I hope, that animals do not think in the way that you and I do. It should not surprise you to learn that they do not speak like humans either. In fact, sound plays little part in the language of most animals. Many animals speak mostly with their bodies, by moving their heads and limbs, and with pheromones, chemicals released by special glands that long ago withered away in humans.

There is of course no one animal language. There are as many animal languages as there are animal species. It is true, however, that the more similar the animal the more similar their languages. Squirrels, chipmunks, rats and mice are all rodents, and can understand one another very well. Dogs are not rodents, but they are mammals; a dog and a squirrel could have a conversation, if it ever occurred to the dog to say anything other than 'Kill you and eat you!' It is fair to say that, with a little effort, all mammals can speak Mammal to one another – except for humans, who have lost all their powers of animal speech, and the great apes, who understand sounds and motions but not pheromones, and so are half-deaf and half-dumb.

Birds are another matter entirely. Birds are the descendants of dinosaurs, more like reptiles than like mammals. Again, while all bird species speak their own language, it is fair to say all birds can speak Bird. But birds, like the great apes, do not use pheromones; theirs is a language entirely of sounds and motions. It is because of this that birds and mammals can usually communicate only a few basic notions. Patch's ability to speak Bird was quite rare. But since Bird is half body language, you can imagine how difficult it was for him to speak while his body was held by the hawk's strong and terribly sharp talons.

As for reptiles, there will be more to say of them in time.

A BARGAIN OF MICE AND WORDS

 atch squirmed and wriggled, fighting for freedom, trying to break free of the hawk's vicious talons. He had already been carried higher than the highest tree of the Center Kingdom; indeed he was higher than many of the mountains, and he knew a fall might well kill him; but he was small, and would not fall hard, and so escape from the hawk's claws meant at least a *chance* of survival, compared to the certainty of being eaten if he did not escape. So he struggled with all his might. But the hawk was too strong. All Patch managed to do was work the painful talons even deeper into his flesh.

Patch gave up and sagged limply. He was going to die. That was simply all there was to it. Every animal had a time to die, and this was his. He looked down at the Center Kingdom from high above. He had never seen it like this before, a lush rectangle set amid the gray mountains. The trees of the Center Kingdom looked as small as blades of grass. He committed the striking image to his memory book before remembering there was no point; soon he would be dead, and the dead have no memories at all.

It occurred to Patch that it was very strange for a hawk to capture a squirrel from a tree. Even in winter, hawks usually avoided diving into trees, for fear of branches that might tear at their faces and feathers. Hawks usually preyed only on animals in open spaces. Patch had been extremely unlucky.

This realization made Patch so angry at the unfairness of the world that he shouted out to the hawk, in broken sound-only Bird, 'Why take me from tree? Why not take squirrel on ground?'

The hawk was so surprised it nearly dropped him.

'You speak Bird?' the hawk asked, its voice rasping and imperious.

'Yes,' Patch said.

'You speak Bird,' the hawk repeated. It considered for a moment. 'Well then, my furry little lunch, let us speak a moment before I dine.'

The hawk changed course, headed for a conical turret atop one of the mountains, and swooped into a perfect landing on a small, circular, walled stone platform at the very top of the turret, a platform shaped a little like a bird's nest. It was only a few squirrel-lengths across, and its smooth vertical walls could not be climbed. There was no way for Patch to escape.

'What is your name, little squirrel?' the hawk asked, releasing Patch.

Patch stood to his full height, painfully, for he was bleeding from the talon wounds, and said, for what he expected was the very last time in his life, 'I am Patch son of Silver, of the Seeker clan, of the

Treetops tribe, of the Center Kingdom. Who are you that asks?'

'I am Karmerruk,' the hawk said proudly. 'Now tell me, what have you done to Snout, that he so badly wants you dead?'

Patch twitched with surprise. 'The rat,' he said, amazed. 'You serve the rat.'

Then he cried out as Karmerruk's talons slashed his face.

'I serve no one and nothing,' Karmerruk said, his voice low and very dangerous. 'I am a Prince of the Air, and I live only for myself, my mate, and my nestlings. The rat serves me. He finds me mice, morsels which, I must say, I far prefer to squirrels. And from time to time, I deign to capture other creatures that Snout would like eaten. As I will soon eat you, insolent little squirrel.'

'I'm sorry,' Patch said, trembling. 'I didn't mean to offend you.'

'You're just a groundling, you couldn't have known any better,' Karmerruk said dismissively. 'But for a groundling you do speak Bird remarkably well. Answer me. Why does Snout want you dead?'

'Because I saw him kill Jumper.'

'Jumper?'

'An important squirrel,' Patch explained. 'A lord. Snout and his rats and another squirrel killed him.'

'And why would Snout do a thing like that?'

Patch racked his memory, and remembered: 'He said he served the King Beneath.'

Karmerruk looked silently at Patch for a long moment. Then he beat his wings twice, and used their lift to leap to the edge of the wall that surrounded Patch. Karmerruk turned his back to Patch, folded his wings, and looked down at the ground.

'There is no King Beneath,' Karmerruk said. 'The King Beneath is a myth.'

Patch did not dare speak.

'I hear such news of strange and terrible things below. This long winter, these terrible things, it must be a very difficult time to be a groundling. I think it will only get worse, little squirrel. I think I do you a kindness by eating you now.'

'Excuse me if I don't agree,' Patch said angrily.

Karmerruk paid no notice. 'Perhaps I have indulged this Snout long enough. But he takes such care not to be found. Where did you see Snout and this other little squirrel, this traitor to his own kind? And what is the traitor's name?'

Patch did not answer.

Karmerruk turned back and looked down at Patch with a hawk's terrible unblinking eyes. 'I asked you a question, little squirrel.'

Patch swallowed, and said in a very small voice, 'I won't tell you unless you let me go.'

Karmerruk was speechless at Patch's temerity.

'You don't want to eat me,' Patch said. 'You don't like squirrel. You said so yourself. Let me go and I'll tell you what you want.'

'You will tell me what I want *without* this impudent bargaining,' Karmerruk said, leaping right down at Patch, who had to back away quickly to avoid being caught beneath the hawk's talons. 'Your only choice is whether you speak in words or screams.'

He advanced slowly toward Patch until the squirrel's back was to the stone wall.

Patch said, desperately, 'I know where there are lots of mice. Families of them. Hundreds of them.'

Karmerruk stopped his advance. 'You lie.'

'I'm not lying,' Patch said. 'I swear by the moon I'm not lying.'

Something strange happened to Patch when he said those words. An odd shivery feeling came from inside him and spread right to the edge of his skin.

'You swear by the moon,' Karmerruk said, impressed.

'Yes.'

'And you offer me a bargain. If I let you live, you will answer all of my questions, and tell me where these mice are.'

'Yes.'

Karmerruk considered. 'I think I like you, little squirrel. You have the heart of a hawk. So I will strike this bargain with you.'

'Swear by the moon,' Patch demanded.

Karmerruk's laugh was a croaking cackle that made Patch shiver uncontrollably. 'Oh, I think not. The moon is more dangerous than you know. I will swear on the blood of my nestlings. That will have to be oath enough.'

Patch, who didn't really have much choice in the matter, said, 'All right.'

Patch answered Karmerruk's questions. Then the hawk leapt up to the wall and disappeared over its edge. The time that passed before he returned felt like most of a day, but must have been much less.

'Your words were pure and true, little squirrel,' Karmerruk said, as he fluttered back down into Patch's prison. 'I found both pit and mice, and filled my belly with the latter. Now it is time to fulfill my own oath.'

And Karmerruk reached out with his talons and once again seized Patch in their cruel grip. He beat his powerful wings and again carried Patch up into the sky. But he did not set a course for Patch's home. Instead he traveled due south, directly away from the Center Kingdom.

'No!' Patch cried out.

'I swore to let you live,' Karmerruk said, and there was chilling laughter in his voice. 'And so I will. But we can't have Snout knowing that, can we? Not before I find and dine on him. You will live, little squirrel. But a long way away from the home you once knew.'

ABOVE THE SKY-ROAD

he talons that gripped Patch's flesh seemed to stab at him with Karmerruk's every wingbeat; he was bleeding from those wounds and from his face, where the hawk had slashed him for his impudence; he was aghast that Karmerruk was taking him away from his home, apparently forever; he was terribly frightened by the thought of his unknown destination – but at the same time, as Patch hung from Karmerruk's claws and looked down at the world, he could not help but marvel at all the wonders he saw below.

Patch had never imagined that there was so much water in the world. He had never known that the Great Sea of the Center Kingdom was a mere pond, and that the Center Kingdom itself, and all its surrounding mountains, stood on an island in a sea so immense it seemed to go on forever. There seemed to be as much water as land in the world. And the Center Kingdom was not the only plot of green that Patch could see. Indeed it was not even the largest.

There were innumerable other curiosities. A shining metal thing flew through the air at a distance; it looked like a bird, but it was enormously larger, and its wings did not flap. Huge arching spans of metal connected the islands beneath him, crossing enormous sea-chasms like branches lying across streams. And Patch had never smelled air as pure and sweet as that of the high sky.

Karmerruk carried Patch south. They passed a green statue of a human that protruded from the midst of the waters, immensely larger than any statue he had ever seen before. They passed several human-built things drifting on the water, metal half-shells like the ones humans sometimes played with on the Center Kingdom's seas, but incomparably larger. They passed a hilly island even bigger than that of the Center Kingdom, where the human habitations were sparser and smaller, and then crossed the slender metal span that connected this island to an even greater landmass to its east. They flew so high that the death machines hurtling across that colossal thoroughfare looked like crawling beetles, and the strands of metal hanging from its two pale towers no more substantial than spiderwebs.

'You are very heavy, little squirrel,' Karmerruk said, his voice strained, as he swooped into a long, shallow glide toward the windswept strip of sand that hugged a tail-shaped shred of land that seemed to be the uttermost edge of the world. The hawk's wingbeats had become more labored and less rhythmic. 'It would have been much easier to simply have eaten you.'

Beyond the vast and empty field of sand and wind-stunted brush, the immense waves of the great waters stretched as far as Patch could see, gleaming red as blood in the setting sun. Karmerruk swooped downward, toward where land met water. The air was full of salt and spray.

'Where are you taking me?' Patch asked, frightened. 'What is this place?'

Karmerruk answered by letting him go. Patch tumbled through the air and fell hard.

Fortunately, or perhaps through Karmerruk's good graces, he landed not on the earth but in the water. It was shockingly cold, and the salt of the water shriveled his lips; but squirrels are strong swimmers, they can paddle with all four limbs, and use their tail as a rudder. Karmerruk circled three times as Patch swam to land, until he climbed groggily out of the water onto the sandy beach, and then the hawk soared up and away, back to the Center Kingdom, abandoning Patch to his fate.

'Good luck, little squirrel!' Karmerruk called out as he departed. 'May the moon shine on you!'

Patch scarcely heard him. He was cold and wet, he had no strength left, and the places where the hawk's claws had carved his flesh hurt like fire. He barely managed the short walk up into the thickets of tough grass that grew in the dunes above the beach. He had never been so tired.

As the sun disappeared behind the great waters, bringing that long, cruel day to a close, Patch curled up in a rough and stony hollow in the ground and tried to sleep. He had never slept on the ground before. He thought longingly of where he had slept last night, in his own warm drey in the Center Kingdom, lined with grasses and leaves and newspaper. His last thought, before he finally allowed exhaustion to carry him into sleep's dark embrace, was that he would never see his own drey again.

II. THE OCEAN KINGDOM

THE BEACH

atch was awoken by the rattling sound of wind in the dry dune grass. The sun on his face was warm, for the first time since winter had begun, and the beach was swept by a wind so strong that it lifted little tendrils of sand above the ground. The grass around him was like none he had ever seen before: golden and brown, wide-stalked, the roots of its blades matted and woven together like an enormous spiderweb sunk into the sand.

He was weak from his wounds, and cold, and starving, and desperately thirsty. But there was no food or water on the beach. All he smelled was salt air and dry grass. He walked inland, moving slowly, so feeble that it was difficult to ascend the sandy dunes. He had to rest for some time after climbing the small wire fence he came across, a fence he would normally have bounded over without thinking. Patch knew as he limped forward that if danger found him he would not be able to run away.

As he continued inland the grasses grew thicker and were joined by bushes and vines. He came across a vine with shining leaves and bright, tasty-looking berries – but its smell made his tail stiffen, and he steered around it. Where the sand turned into earth, the tall grasses were topped by clumps of seeds, and he tried to eat some from a fallen stalk, but after a few bites he realized they might fill his belly but they had no sustenance. Some patches were damp with dew, but it was not enough to slake his thirst.

Then the wind changed, and he smelled two things. Fresh water, and a cat.

Normally Patch would have avoided the cat-smell. Cats were bigger and faster than squirrels, and far more vicious and dangerous; and while birds, mice and rats were their preferred prey, squirrels were not so different. But there was fresh water near this cat – and, too, cats often lived near humans, and Patch thought he was more likely to find food in human lands than in this desolate wilderness.

He changed direction and moved upwind, following the smells, until he crested a bushy ridge and saw a blocklike concrete structure mostly buried in the next ridge of sandy earth. Part of its flat roof protruded, and in that corner was a depression full of rainwater that smelled stagnant but drinkable. The cat-scent was stronger than ever.

Patch approached with caution, but went unchallenged as he quenched his thirst. At first he supposed the cat had just left. But when he descended the ridge, he saw a large hole, human-made and big enough for a dog, in the side of the concrete block; and just inside, barely visible, the silhouette of a small cat.

Patch froze.

'Who are you that dares disturb me?' the cat demanded. Its fur was bristled, and it stank of rage and fear.

'I am Patch son of Silver, of the Seeker clan, of the Treetops tribe, of the Center Kingdom,' Patch said. 'Who are you that asks?'

The cat took two stalking steps out into the light. She was all black but for the two green eyes that stared at Patch with haughty contempt. 'My name is Zelina,' she said, 'and I am the Queen of All Cats.'

THE QUEEN OF ALL CATS

ay no heed to my unfortunate surroundings,' Zelina said. 'I have been tricked, abused, betrayed and exiled. My throne has been stolen from me. But a throne does not make a queen. I will die here in this broken shell of a ruin, but I will die a queen.'

After a moment Patch said, 'Is there any food near here?'

'No. Three days I have been without food, Patch son of Silver, ever since I was betrayed. I will starve here, and I will die.'

'But you can get food here,' Patch objected. 'You're a cat. You can catch birds. I've seen sparrows and starlings in the bushes.'

'Catch a bird?' Zelina asked, offended. 'And eat it with ... with feathers and bones and blood? I, the Queen of All Cats? Don't be ridiculous.'

'You'd rather starve to death?'

'I lived as a queen, and I will die as a queen.'

'I see,' Patch said, although he didn't really. 'Are there humans near here?'

'No.'

'Is there anything near here?'

'No.'

Patch looked at her suspiciously. 'Are you sure? I crossed a fence before. How much have you explored?'

'A queen does not explore.'

'Do you at least know where we are?' Patch asked, exasperated.

Zelina looked at him for a moment. Then she said, 'Follow me.'

Patch followed her up the ridge, and then up a thick bush atop the ridge. She climbed nearly as well as he did. Once they stood at the top of the bush, Zelina turned to the northwest, and said, 'See there.'

Patch squinted. His vision was not near as good as a cat's, but in the very great distance, past the waving field of grasses and bushes, he could see … something … rising above the horizon. Something gray and silver and glittering, and very far away. After a moment he gasped with recognition. What he saw was the mountain range that surrounded the Center Kingdom.

'There is the heart of the city,' Zelina said, her voice soft with longing. 'There is the Great Avenue. They left me close enough to see it, but so far away that I can never return. Oh, but their cruelty knows no boundaries.'

They descended from the bush. Zelina had to choose her way down very carefully, and once she almost fell. Cats were not near as good at downclimbing as squirrels. Patch moved without thinking, for his mind was in his memory book, trying to match what he had just seen to his vision of the world when he had hung in Karmerruk's talons, as if the Center Kingdom itself was an acorn he had buried and needed to find.

Until then he hadn't even thought about trying to go back home. The landmass he was on was gigantic, many times the size of the island that housed the Center Kingdom. No squirrel had ever made such a journey, unless you counted the dusty legends of the great migrations of the past. Furthermore, it would require the crossing of the great chasm of water that surrounded the island of the

Center Kingdom, a chasm far too wide and violent for any squirrel to swim. And, most of all, how could a tiny squirrel like Patch ever find his way across a land full of enormous human structures?

But while it was true that the Center Kingdom was a very long way away, it was also true that they were still near enough to see its mountains. Furthermore, the waters that surrounded the island of the Center Kingdom were spanned by several vast human-built crossings. And, most important, Patch was not like any other squirrel, not any more – for, unlike any other squirrel, Patch had seen the world from high above.

The idea struck him like a thunderbolt. He could use his memory book to find his way home. The same voyage that had carried him into exile could also be the key to his return. The journey would be arduous, certainly, and probably dangerous; it might well take several seasons, or even years; but it was not *impossible.*

The decision was an easy one to make.

'Thank you for showing me, Zelina, Queen of All Cats,' Patch said politely when they were back on the sandy earth. He turned to leave.

'Wait,' she said. 'Where will you go?'

'To the Center Kingdom,' he said simply. 'To my home.'

Zelina looked at him for a long and thoughtful moment.

Then she said, 'Of course I must not accompany you. I am a queen. I cannot demean myself even to survive. Even though my subjects need me, it wouldn't be right to reduce myself to a wandering scavenger, living off refuse, traveling with a ragged, filthy squirrel.'

'I am not filthy!'

She gave him a look. 'Your fur is all clumpy and you are covered with sand and dried salt.'

'Oh,' Patch said, chastened. 'Well, I almost died several times yesterday –'

'That is no excuse not to keep up appearances. Look at me. I expect to starve to death very soon, but see how neatly my fur is groomed.' And indeed Zelina's fur was clean, neat, and shining.

'I think I should be going now.'

'My subjects cannot demand of me that I become a vagabond, a tramp, a beggar queen. They cannot ask me to surrender my dignity, my pride, no matter how they suffer.'

'I understand. Now it's time –'

'But their needs are so great. A traitorous pretender sits on my throne. If I must abase myself, I shall. Because a true queen loves her people as they love her, and will make any sacrifice they require, even stooping so low as the shameful expedient of traveling with a squirrel.'

'But –'

'Lead the way, Patch son of Silver,' Zelina commanded. 'Take me back to the Great Avenue. If you serve me well you may be rewarded when again I sit on the throne.'

Patch did not want to travel with Zelina, even if she was Queen of All Cats. But he decided not to protest her decision. He was sure she would lose interest soon enough, or some event or obstacle would separate them. And he felt sorry for her. Despite her arrogant words, he knew by her scent that she was terribly frightened.

They passed near a small maple tree – and Patch came to a sudden halt. If his nose did not deceive him, and he was sure that it did not, a cool, sweet, enticing smell drifted down from the tree. A smell that meant the most wonderful thing in the world.

He climbed into this maple, out to the ends of its branches, and began to devour the sweet, delectable buds that had begun to sprout from its gnarled wood. When he raised his head again he breathed deeply of the air, and he smelled more maple buds, and hints of flowers, of new grasses, of a world beginning to awake from a long and dolorous sleep. Patch was sick and hurt, and in a strange land so far away from home that he might never see it again, but he smiled all the same.

Spring had come.

COMPANIONS

elina followed him north across the grassy wilderness. Patch began to catch the scent of death machines. He found a narrow, pebbly rivulet, and ate beetles from beneath its damp rocks, and tiny purple flowers that grew from its sides, as Zelina watched with fascinated horror. Patch was glad she did not want to eat this food; there was barely enough to take the edge off his own hunger.

As he picked beetles off rocks, a swirling gust brought a new scent to them, the scent of mice, and Zelina leapt to her feet.

'What is that?' she whispered, amazed.

Patch looked at her oddly. 'Mice.'

'Oh yes. I've heard of mice. They smell delicious!'

'You've never smelled mice before?' Patch asked, astonished.

'No.'

'What did you eat before you came out here?'

'Caviar. Cream. Sushi.'

The words were gibberish to Patch.

'Just wait a moment,' Zelina said. She advanced into the grass, following the mouse-smell, and soon disappeared.

When Patch had finished with his food, he moved on, toward the smells and now the sounds of death machines. He thought he had seen the last of Zelina. But as he reached a big, rusting wire fence, she reappeared from the thick grasses. There was blood on her mouth and whiskers, and she smelled of adrenalin and delight.

'It's a very *primitive* way of eating,' Zelina said. 'All that thrashing and screaming and blood. Of course it was disgusting. It was absolutely disgusting. But sometimes queens have terrible responsibilities. And I must say, it has to be admitted, there is a certain savage thrill in the hunt. And the kill. Especially the kill. I've never killed anything before, Patch son of Silver. It's really quite thrilling. I never understood before that queens must know how to kill. We must be revered with terror as much as with love. That was my downfall. I was well-loved, but I was not terrible. But that will change. Oh, yes, I see that now. When I return to the Great Avenue, my return will be the dawn of a day of blood and terror and vengeance!'

Her exultation in killing made Patch uneasy, and he said nothing. She followed him out through a large hole at the base of the wire fence, into a grassy field that was much more to Patch's liking than the tangled wilderness behind them, even though there were human buildings at the end of the field.

Like in the Center Kingdom, humans had erected metal tree trunks here, from which winking lights dangled. Unlike in the Center

Kingdom, they had not stopped there. For the endless winding strips of wasteland that carved these human lands were lined by trees. Real trees, green and growing – but also dead, severed tree trunks, perfectly straight. And these dead trunks were connected by an endless web of wires that served as a sky-road.

Those wires sagged beneath Patch's weight, their material felt strange beneath his paws, and sometimes they emitted a disturbing hum that made him feel ill and shaken, but they provided an easy route across the wasteland strips, high above the death machines. This sky-road had three levels, two high strands of thin wires, and a lower layer of thick wires intertwined into a cable as broad and strong as a moderate-sized tree branch. Zelina was small enough that she found it easy to follow Patch along even its thinnest wires.

They traveled east, through clusters of relatively small buildings divided at regular intervals by wasteland strips, with clumps of larger buildings here and there.

'I don't object to all this climbing of posts and wires,' Zelina said after a little while, 'it has a certain acrobatic appeal, and the views beneath are undeniably striking, but I do wonder, what is your objection to simply walking along the highways?'

'The what?'

She indicated the wasteland strip beneath them. 'The highways.'

'We can't walk on those! Those aren't roads. Not for us. Even humans don't walk on them. There are death machines.'

'Automobiles,' Zelina said.

'Excuse me?'

'They aren't *death machines*. There's nothing deathly about an automobile. In fact they're extremely pleasant. My attendants have taken me on highway automobile journeys on any number of occasions.'

'Attendants?' Patch said, even more confused.

'The humans who care for me.'

'The what who what?'

'Please do remember, I am the Queen of All Cats,' Zelina said. 'I have a human attendant who lives in my home to feed me and entertain me, and on certain occasions, such as automobile journeys, teams of other humans assist her.'

'You mean cats live with humans? Like dogs?'

'By the light of the moon, Patch, not like *dogs*,' Zelina said scathingly. 'Humans serve cats as dogs serve humans. And sometimes, I fear, as ineptly.'

Her invocation of the moon made Patch uneasy. But he was still curious. 'You lived with humans? In a human building?'

'I lived so high above the Great Avenue that if the window was open, and I went out to the metal stairs and looked down, the automobiles below looked no bigger than ants.'

'Where is the Great Avenue?'

'Quite near your Center Kingdom, I believe,' Zelina said. 'I never paid a royal visit to your king myself, having been constantly deluged with affairs of state, but that was the impression I received from the other cats who sometimes visited me on the stairs.'

'Did you ever meet squirrels there?'

'No. The only squirrels I ever previously encountered were on automobile journeys. But our words grow distant from the point I seek to make, Patch son of Silver, which is that I think it would be faster to simply walk along the highway.'

'I'm staying on the sky-road. You can do what you like.'

He kept walking. Zelina slowed for a little while, but she kept following.

'Where do you intend to sleep?' she asked.

'I'll find a tree.'

'I can't sleep in a tree.'

'You can sleep anywhere you want,' Patch said impatiently.

'Why don't we find our way into a house?'

Patch wished she would stop using strange words. 'A what?'

'One of those little buildings. A human home.'

'I'm not going into a human building.'

'Why not?' she asked, annoyed.

'I'm just not,' Patch said. 'Humans are dangerous.'

He expected her to laugh at this and to explain again how humans served her; but she only sighed, and said, after a few moments, 'You are more right than you know.'

Patch didn't understand, but at least she left him in peace after that. They made good time for the rest of the day, and in the afternoon the wire sky-road happened to lead right past a maple tree. Patch gorged on so many of its sweet buds that his belly felt a little unbalanced afterward and he had to be careful not to fall from the sky-road.

WATERWATCHER

ventually, when the sun was so low that long shadows spilled over the landscape below them, Patch decided it was time to find a drey for the night. He scrambled down the sky-road onto a patch of green surrounded by several of the buildings Zelina called *houses.* This greenery was subdivided into a dozen little plots by tall fences, for which Patch was very grateful, for two of these little plots contained dogs. The dogs did not notice the squirrel and cat, for they were upwind and distracted by what passed for conversation among dogs:

'I'm here! I'm here!'

'I'm here too! I'm here too!'

'This is my territory! Mine and my master's!'

'This territory is mine! I guard it for my master!'

'You can't come in here!'

'You can't come in here either!'

Patch climbed a wooden fence, leapt from it onto a tree, and found a bowl-shaped hollow at the top of its trunk. It was full of recent squirrel-smells. Patch considered a moment, then followed the most recent smells higher up the tree, until he came to a drey. There was a squirrel within.

'Who's there?' the squirrel inside asked.

'I am Patch son of Silver, of the Seeker clan, of the Treetops tribe, of the Center Kingdom,' Patch said. 'Who are you that asks?'

'I am Waterwatcher daughter of Shine, of the Runner clan, of the City tribe, of the Ocean Kingdom.'

'Would it be all right to sleep in your tree tonight?'

'Of course. My goodness, are you really from the Center Kingdom?'

Waterwatcher emerged from her drey and looked at Patch. She was beautiful. Her fur shone and her eyes were bright and inquisitive.

Patch was suddenly acutely aware of his own scarred, salt-stained, travel-worn, clumpy-furred appearance.

'Yes,' he said. 'It's been a hard journey.'

Then Zelina, from below, cried out, alarmed: 'Patch! Help!'

Her cry was followed by two sharp intakes of canine breath.

Then the dogs began to yammer: 'Cat! Cat! Cat! Cat! Kill it! Kill it! Kill it!'

'Did that cat call your name?' Waterwatcher asked.

'Yes,' Patch admitted, embarrassed. He considered abandoning Zelina to her fate. Then he sighed and said, 'Just a moment.'

The dimming red light made it difficult to see what was going on, so Patch ran back down for a closer look. He saw Zelina standing on top of the wooden fence that ran immediately beneath the sky-road, and divided the plot of land on which Waterwatcher's tree stood from the plot with one of the barking dogs.

'What's wrong?' Patch asked, over the din of the dogs. 'Just climb down.'

'I can't climb down a wall!' Zelina reeked of terror.

Patch remembered that cats couldn't downclimb. 'Then jump to the tree.'

'I can't!'

After a moment Patch understood. Zelina could go *along* the wooden fence, in the same way that she had moved along the sky-road all day; but unlike a squirrel, she was not nimble enough to turn, balance on top, and jump *away* from it. She could go along the wall to its end – but there was nothing at its end, it was the highest fence there.

'I'm sorry,' Patch said. 'There's nothing I can do.'

'Kill it! Kill it! Kill it!' the dog on the other side of the fence screamed, and Patch could tell it was charging as it howled. It threw its massive body against the wooden fence and Zelina began to rock back and forth like a branch in the breeze. Her claws lost their purchase on the fence, and she fell.

Fortunately for Zelina, she fell on Patch's side of the fence, rather than the dog's. Her fall was clumsy but she landed very elegantly on all four feet. Before Patch could say anything to dissuade her she had climbed the oak tree and stood beside him.

'I nearly died,' she said angrily. 'I could have died. I could have been killed and eaten. By a *dog*.'

'That's life,' Patch said.

She looked around the oak tree. 'Is this where you intend for us to sleep?'

'I was going to sleep here. But feel free to …'

'To think I am reduced to this. The Queen of All Cats reduced to sleeping in a tree, like a wild animal, like a common beast!'

Waterwatcher said from above, in a voice full of puzzled hostility, 'Patch, is this cat here with you?'

Patch looked up at the beautiful squirrel and tried to think of an excuse.

'This squirrel is guiding me back to my home,' Zelina said, 'and if he serves well and faithfully he will be justly rewarded.'

A few moments passed that were silent except for the yapping of the dogs.

Then Waterwatcher said coldly, 'Stanger, in the Ocean Kingdom we do not consort with cats. You may stay here tonight. But only tonight. And don't eat anything.' She disappeared into her drey.

Patch turned and looked angrily at Zelina.

'I'm very tired,' she said. 'I'll see you in the morning.'

DAFFA

hen Patch awoke, Waterwatcher was gone, and Zelina was still asleep. Patch stood over the cat for some time. He knew he had to abandon her and continue alone. Even if she was the Queen of All Cats, she was only causing problems and slowing him down. But it was with a little guilt that he took to the sky-road alone.

His guilt did not last long. Nor did his solitude. For before the sun had traveled more than a quarter of its way up the sky, Patch heard shuffling *tictictic* noises behind him: Zelina's claws against the wires of the sky-road.

'Very thoughtful of you to let me sleep,' she said brightly as she caught up with him.

Patch groaned to himself and kept walking.

The sky-road led east, as did the shore to the north. Another shoreline was visible farther north, across the great waters; and above that land, in the faraway northwest, rose the mountains of the Center Kingdom, so distant that they seemed like a memory of a dream. Patch and Zelina slowly approached a human-built crossing that stretched across the great waters to their left. When they were level with it, Patch gave that huge concrete span a single searching look, and then continued to the east.

'What are you doing?' Zelina asked.

'The great waters here are an inlet,' Patch explained. 'If we go straight, in time we can go around them.'

'We can go over them right now. There's a bridge right there.'

'We can't cross that. It's crawling with death machines.'

'Automobiles,' she corrected him. 'And not all of it. Look to the right.'

Patch looked again and hesitated. It was true that on the extreme right-hand side of the bridge there was a little concrete channel too narrow for a death machine. But the thought of traveling along it made his skin crawl. Concrete was wasteland, something to be avoided if possible and traversed if necessary, not something to be used as a pathway.

'No,' he said.

'Are you mad? This sky-road goes *away* from the city. The bridge goes right toward it.'

That too was true. But – 'No. It's a bad idea.'

'Why?'

Patch searched for an answer. 'There's nowhere to run. What if a dog comes? Or a hawk? It's a bridge for humans. It's not for animals.'

'I'm not afraid.'

'I'm going forward on the sky-road. You can do what you like.'

'And so I shall,' Zelina said. 'I shall cross this bridge.'

'Fine.'

Patch marched onward, alone.

He had seen much strange behavior since entering the human lands. Watching the concrete strips below, he had realized for the first time that humans actually rode *inside* death machines, and he wondered how the two species had struck such a bargain. He had seen humans run down the street, smelling of sweat and terrible exhaustion, although they neither chased nor were chased by anything. But what he encountered soon after leaving Zelina was far more peculiar than either of those things.

What Patch saw, as he sat bemused on a sky-wire, was a human with dark skin, who was standing alone on the flat top of a building, swinging a big broken tree branch around him in slow circles. As he did so, in the sky above him, a flock of hundreds of pigeons flew in circles around this building, in the same speed and direction as the human's branch. Indeed it looked as if that branch extended invisibly until it connected to the flock, and as if the human held them like dogs on leashes, controlling their motions. As they flew the birds chanted something that sounded like 'Kabooti, kabooti, kabooti.' Patch could only conclude that they had all gone mad.

One of the pigeons fluttered weakly away from the flock and came to rest on the wire not far from Patch.

'What are you doing?' he asked the pigeon in Bird.

'Oh my goodness,' the pigeon gasped. 'Oh my goodness, I thought I would die. I just went to watch but then I was in the flock. I thought I would die.'

'Who are you?' Patch asked hopefully. This pigeon did not sound mad.

'I'm Daffa. Who are you?'

'I am Patch son of Silver, of the Seeker clan, of the Treetops tribe, of the Center Kingdom,' Patch said.

'Good heavens, you're a long way from home, aren't you?'

'You've heard of the Center Kingdom?'

'I am of the Center Kingdom,' Daffa said. 'I flew here. How did you get here?'

'I don't suppose you know a hawk named Karmerruk.'

Daffa took two frightened hops away from Patch. 'Is he here?'

'No,' Patch said. 'I made a bargain with him, but he tricked me and left me here, and he flew back to the Center Kingdom.'

Daffa looked relieved.

'Do you know a bluejay named Toro?' Patch asked.

'I don't think so.'

'Are you going back to the Center Kingdom? Can you find him and give him a message from me?'

'Can you tell me where he is?' Daffa asked.

Patch considered. 'Not exactly. But you can ask around ...'

'I'm not very good at remembering things like messages,' Daffa admitted. 'Really I can only remember faces and places. I can go exactly to any place I've ever been. But I'm not good with messages. A big cat told me to take a message once. He'd learned Bird just like you. I forget what the message was. But I can go right back to the big cat any time I want.'

'A cat learned Bird?' Patch asked, intrigued. 'I thought cats ate birds.'

'This cat was different.'

'Why did you come here?' Patch asked.

Daffa looked down and sighed. 'I'm looking for my home.'

'Looking for your home? But I thought you could go exactly –'

'I don't understand it either,' Daffa said sadly. 'I used to have two homes. I would go to one, and the humans would tie a ribbon to my leg, and I would fly to the other, and they would take off the ribbon and give me wonderful food. It was so much fun. But one day I got carried away by a big thunderstorm. And when I came back I couldn't find either home anymore. The storm must have confused me.'

'When did this happen?' Patch asked. He didn't remember any recent storm.

'I don't know. I'm not good with time either. But whenever it was, ever since then I've been flying around looking for my home. That's why I'm here. Then I saw the flock and went to see what they were doing. But that whole flock is mad!'

'What are they saying? *Kabooti, kabooti, kabooti,* what does that mean?'

'It doesn't mean anything.'

'I'm going back to the Center Kingdom.' It occurred to Patch that a bird would be a far more useful companion than a cat. 'Do you want to come with me? We can look for your home together.'

'We can't go together. I fly, and you crawl.'

'I don't crawl!' Patch said indignantly. 'I walk and I run.'

Daffa shrugged as if to say he didn't see the difference. 'Besides, you're going the wrong way. You want to cross that bridge back there. If you go this way you'll come to the rocs' nest. That's not a place for anyone, bird or groundling.'

'*Rocs?*' Patch had never heard the word before.

'Giant metal birds as big as mountains. They make a horrible noise, they fly faster than the wind, and they eat smaller birds. Or anything else that gets in front of them. And they're always *terribly* hungry.'

Patch didn't like the sound of that at all.

'Well, good luck, little squirrel,' Daffa said. 'Maybe I'll come visit you sometime if I see you. What did you say your name was again?'

'Patch son of Silver, of the Seeker clan –' Patch began, but Daffa had already begun to soar into the sky.

THE HIGHWAY BRIDGE

atch continued onward; but he had not gone far before he slowed and stopped. Much as he hated to admit it, Zelina was right. This sky-road *did* lead away from the Center Kingdom. Daffa's rocs sounded like an obstacle far greater than a concrete channel free of any death machines. And while the risk of hawks and dogs on the bridge was real, it was also small.

Patch sighed, turned around, and trotted back. He caught up with Zelina just as she was performing an awkward and elaborate descent from the sky-road, a descent that involved two trees, a house, a wall, and several human-built things beneath the wall. Patch simply ran straight down one of the sky-road's dead tree trunks and joined her.

'I'm glad to see you have come to your senses, Patch son of Silver,' she said. 'Follow me.'

They had to cross two of the wasteland strips Zelina called *highways* to get to the bridge, but that was no trouble, there were few death machines and fewer humans about. Once at the edge of the bridge Patch wanted to wait and survey the terrain, but Zelina kept moving. After only a moment's hesitation Patch followed. He didn't want to cross this bridge alone.

He had grown accustomed to the feel of concrete beneath his paws, but his overwhelming urge was to get away from this wasteland, not to travel along its length. Once they were in the channel, with concrete walls rising from either side of the concrete floor, Patch felt terror begin to tear at his mind. The walls were too high to jump and too sheer to climb. All he could see or feel was concrete. His muscles shuddered with fear, he wanted to turn back and run for his life – but Zelina kept going; indeed she sauntered casually onward. Patch focused on her, on her sight and scent, and followed her trail exactly, breathing hard, trying not to panic.

The bridge arched across the waters like a rainbow. They were just past its peak when Patch saw and smelled two humans approaching. He squeezed his eyes half-shut and made himself continue. The humans stopped dead in their tracks, as if frightened. As Patch and Zelina darted past, the humans watched very closely and rumbled loudly to one another in their strange voices. Patch didn't think he had ever been so near a human before. At least they were not accompanied by a dog.

He was so focused on his surroundings rather than his destination that the end of the bridge came as a surprise. Suddenly the wall to his right was wire, not concrete, and green grass lay beyond. Patch immediately scrambled up and over. Zelina continued along the concrete, until, on opposite sides of the wire fence, they reached the end-post of a human sky-road.

At first his relief at having survived the crossing was a pure delight, unmatched by that of food or drink. But as Patch walked onward that day, he began to wonder how and why his life had suddenly become so extraordinarily desperate that he had found himself forced to traverse a wasteland bridge. He began to think of the Center Kingdom, and how it was that he found himself so far away from his home. And soon those thoughts turned dark and vengeful.

For he could not help but to draw a dreadful conclusion. He had been betrayed.

How else, he asked himself, could Karmerruk have found him and snatched him up from that cherry tree? Yes, a hawk's eyes could have spied out the white patch on Patch's forehead – but how would Karmerruk have known where to look? Scarcely any time had passed between the death of Jumper and the taking of Patch. Was it mere ill luck that Karmerruk had spotted Patch so soon? On top of the ill luck of all the nuts of the Treetops tribe vanishing from the earth?

The more Patch pondered, the more he realized that both of these mysteries could be answered and explained with a single name.

Sniffer.

Sniffer, who had disappeared alone before he and Twitch and Patch had set out to the Meadow. Sniffer, who never grew hungry in winter. Sniffer, who alone of the Treetops tribe had food enough to give to his friend Twitch. Sniffer, who could find buried nuts from up a tree ... and who could have, over the winter, led the squirrels of the Meadow tribe to all the missing Treetop's nuts. Sniffer, who could have led the rats to Jumper ... and to Silver. The idea of a squirrel conspiring with rats against other squirrels would have been unthinkable – had Patch not seen Redeye among the rats.

Patch knew he ought not to gnaw on what had passed. He should try to be thankful that Karmerruk had spared his life, and think only of his journey home, rather than brood about what he would do if he succeeded. But all he could think about, as he walked that wire sky-road, as the wind grew wild and dark clouds began to loom above him, was the awful betrayal that had ruined him, and his family, and his tribe; and about how much he wanted revenge.

STORM SHELTER

The sky-road progressed to the north, toward the mountains visible on the horizon, along a wide and busy highway, past houses and humans below. The wind grew so strong that Patch and Zelina had to take care not to be blown off the wire. The sky to the northeast was busy with human flying machines, the kinds with wings that did not beat, rising from and plunging down to the earth. Patch wondered if those were Daffa's rocs. They were certainly terrifying enough. The distant roars that followed them across the sky made Patch felt as if an owl or hawk were circling above, ready to pounce.

The sky grew dark; but the day was not yet over. This was the dark of storm clouds, not of sunset. Patch and Zelina had just left the area of human buildings, and entered a large wilderness cut in two by the highway below the sky-road, when the first huge drops of rain began to fall. It was soon obvious that they had to find shelter. This wind and rain would sweep them right off the sky-road if they stayed.

The wilderness below was like nowhere Patch had ever been. Its ground was damp and muddy, shot through with ponds, streams, and rivulets, thick with small, vine-choked trees and bushes. Rising above this dense undergrowth were trees he did not know, with peeling white bark, slender vertical trunks and a profusion of short, thin horizontal branches. These branches made it relatively easy for Zelina to downclimb, but they did not extend and overlap like the branches of elms, maples and oaks. There were a few other trees beyond the white ones, strange trees whose bark had mostly peeled away, revealing pale wood underneath like bones under skin; but these were few in number, and even if they had formed a sky-road, it would have been rendered impassable by the weather. The animals had to find shelter on the ground.

There were no leaves yet on the bushes to block the rain. As Patch and Zelina poked their way through the brambles and bushes, rain streamed off the branches and fell on them, and the ground beneath them grew wetter and muddier with every passing heartbeat. The rain caused animal smells to rise like ghosts from the earth, and as they ran, seeking shelter, Patch smelled mouse, chipmunk, rat, squirrel, raccoon, frog, turtle, innumerable birds, ... and something else. Something that made his tail stiffen. Something that was definitely predator.

The sky flashed with light, and there was a sound like a tree trunk breaking in two, and the air itself shook.

'Oh, this is terrible, terrible!' Zelina wailed.

'There's nothing here!' Patch shouted. He had to shout to be heard over the noise of branches flailing in the wind. By this time Patch was thoroughly miserable. 'We'll have to just stay under the bushes!'

'No! Look! Over there!'

Patch looked and saw nothing.

'Follow me!' Zelina cried, and set out at a dead run. It was all Patch could do to follow her, first through more bushes, then through a stand of huge clubgrass. He was convinced they were utterly lost, and half-convinced that the storm had driven Zelina mad, when they suddenly emerged on the edge of a pool of freshwater so big that Patch could not see across it. A huge fallen tree extended into this pool. And the ground beneath this tree's overturned stump was warm and dry.

There were three squirrels already sheltering beneath the stump, along with two large, ugly, foul-smelling birds that Patch did not recognize. He followed Zelina onto the blissfully dry ground. The other squirrels backed away from Zelina fearfully.

'I am Patch son of Silver, of the Seeker clan, of the Treetops tribe, of the Center Kingdom,' Patch said. After a moment he reluctantly added, 'And this is my friend, the Queen of All Cats.'

He expected full introductions, but the squirrels said nothing, only stared. Patch sighed and looked at Zelina, who was cleaning herself. He supposed she was the problem. But he wouldn't have found this shelter, or crossed the bridge, without her.

'Where do you come from?' one of the squirrels whispered, her voice full of fear.

'The Center Kingdom.'

She backed away a little farther, almost to the curtain of rain. 'But how did you get here?'

'From the Ocean Kingdom.'

'This is the Ocean Kingdom,' another squirrel said.

'Then from your southern lands, across the waters.'

'What do you know of the monsters?' the third squirrel demanded angrily.

Patch blinked. 'Monsters? What monsters?'

'The monsters who hunt near our homes,' said the first. 'They killed my mate. They carried him into the sky and killed him.'

Patch didn't understand. 'You mean hawks? Owls?'

'We mean monsters,' said the third squirrel. 'They grow among the trees and snatch us up from the ground with long metal claws like vines. They have driven us out of our dreys and into this swamp, where we must live like rats.'

'I don't know anything about monsters. I'm just trying to get back to the Center Kingdom. Who are you?'

A little less suspicious now, the squirrels introduced themselves as Hindlegs, Brokenclaw and Mudwalker.

'Beware the wasteland,' Mudwalker said. 'The monsters hunt near there. And there are foxes too.'

'What's a fox?' Patch asked.

'You don't want to know.'

Patch thought of the predator scent he had noticed earlier, and wondered if it had been fox or monster.

'You must stay out here in the swamps,' Brokenclaw said.

'We just came from the wasteland,' Patch said. 'Well, from the sky-road above the wasteland, and we didn't see any monsters. Or foxes.'

'You were very lucky,' said Hindlegs, the squirrel who had lost her mate to the monsters.

'Excuse me,' Patch said in Bird to the big, ugly, stinking birds. 'Do you know anything about monsters around here? With long metal claws?'

'Sorry,' one of them croaked. 'We're new around here.'

'Say, you speak good Bird,' hissed the other. 'Have you see anything dead?'

'Excuse me?'

'Dead bodies. Corpses. Fresh would be best, but we'll take maggots and rot if we have to, we've been flying for days to get here.'

'No, sorry,' Patch said.

The first bird peered at Patch quizzically. 'How about you? How are you feeling? Sick? Weak? Feverish? Dying?'

'I feel fine, thank you.'

'Pity. How about your friends?'

'I'm sure they're fine too.'

The birds sighed and turned back to the water.

Then a reptilian head rose out of the shallows at the edge of the pond. It looked like a growth on the end of a stalk, emerging from a large shell mostly hidden by the water.

'Pardon me, young squirrel,' the turtle said in excellent Bird, 'might you indulge me for a moment?'

atch had seen many turtles before, in the Center Kingdom, but never one as large as this, and never one who spoke Bird.

The turtle said, 'I may perhaps have misunderstood you – my Mammal is truly quite atrocious – but did you just say that you were Patch, of the Center Kingdom?'

'Yes,' Patch said.

'Most interesting. How long ago did you leave the Center Kingdom? Do you know of the war that rages across your home?'

Patch stared at the turtle. 'War?'

'War,' the turtle repeated. 'There is a squirrel – my reports name him Redeye – who has declared himself the true king of the Center Kingdom, and who leads the Meadow tribe, its numbers swelled by rebels, against King Thorn. There have been several small battles already these last few days, and dozens of deaths, and there are rumors of strange alliances.'

'Redeye calls himself king?' Patch was shocked. 'How do you know this? Have you been there?'

The turtle's laugh was dry and jolly. 'Oh, no, young Patch. In all my life I have never left these marshes.'

'Then how –'

'Conversation,' the turtle said. 'Birds fly to these marshes from the Center Kingdom, from the Kingdom of Madness, from the Hidden Kingdom, even from empires across the great mountains, even from empires across the ocean, and from time to time I speak with them. Why, one might even say that they bring me reports. And there is little that is hidden from the eyes of birds. Only the Kingdom Beneath. Of late, Patch son of Silver, the birds bring me news of strange and terrible things. They speak of a sickness that spreads among all the birds of the world.'

Patch was hardly listening. 'There hasn't ever been war in the Center Kingdom.'

'There has, but not for a very long time. Not since before the second coming of the humans, and the rise of the mountains.'

'The rise of the mountains? They have always been there.'

'Oh, no,' the turtle said. 'I remember looking westward from these marshes and seeing no mountains in the distance, young Patch. Once there was only the wild. And one day only the wild shall remain.'

Patch stared at the turtle. 'How old are you? Who are you?'

'Very old. *Very* old. Old enough that you may simply call me Old One. But I am not quite the eldest. There is another as old as I, one whom you have already met.'

'What? Who?'

'My oldest friend. My most ancient adversary. I believe you will meet him again.'

'I don't understand,' Patch said.

'None of us are meant to understand everything, young Patch. But I do have one thing to say to you that I hope you will understand. One solitary morsel of advice. Listen carefully. Always abandon your enemies, and never abandon your friends.'

'All right,' Patch said, even more confused.

'The rain is stopping,' the turtle said, and indeed it was. 'You and Zelina had best hurry. You have a long way to go, and little time in which to travel, if you are not to arrive too late.'

'Too late for what?' Patch asked. 'And how do you know her name?'

But the Old One had already disappeared back into the water.

MONSTERS

n the way back to the sky-road, Zelina found a robin's nest that had been blown to the ground by the wind, and as the mother robin looked on helplessly, the cat greedily shattered and devoured all the eggs. Patch thought of the robin babies who had accepted him into their midst and taught him Bird, and tried not to look. There were worms all over the ground, as always after rain, and he ate several. He didn't like their sludgy taste, or the way they squirmed in his mouth, but at least they filled his belly.

'Do you think there are really monsters near the highway?' Zelina asked, when they were finished eating.

'I don't know. But I know those squirrels were frightened.' Patch considered. 'Let's follow our own scents back, just to be sure.'

They retraced their trail back toward the highway.

Patch thought about the news that war had come to the Center Kingdom. It hardly sounded possible. Wars between tribes, squirrels killing squirrels, that just didn't happen – except it did; Patch had seen it himself, had watched, horrified, as Redeye and the rats had devoured Lord Jumper alive. But how had Redeye convinced all the other squirrels of the Meadow to go to war? There was no rancor between the Meadow and the Ramble, or between any of the tribes of the Center Kingdom. Tribes were like names; useful as labels, but not really meaningful.

Patch had never really thought about tribes, even his own, until he had learned from Tuft that it was possible to be moon-sworn to another tribe. He wondered why the notion had so appalled him. It had never really meant anything to him to be of the Treetops. He had always preferred to be on his own, until now. Now all he wanted was to be back among the squirrels he knew. It is one thing to prefer to be solitary when you know that you are part of a tribe. It is another entirely to be truly all alone.

The strands of the wire sky-road were in sight when Patch, leading the way with his more sensitive nose, suddenly and halted.

'What is it?' Zelina asked.

Patch said nervously, 'I think I smell fox. Or …'

He left the word *monster* unspoken, and took a couple of experimental paces forward. The sky-road was so close – but the predator-smell was definitely getting stronger. The wind was swirling in the aftermath of the storm, and Patch couldn't tell from which direction the scent came, except that it had recently been between them and the highway … and could now be anywhere.

'We'll go south, toward the human lands,' Patch said quietly. 'Keep your eyes and ears open, they're better than mine.'

Zelina agreed. The predator-smell diminished as they went south, but did not disappear. Patch tried going to the west toward the road again, but it intensified again. They continued south.

'There's something behind us,' Zelina said, her voice tense. 'Moving in the bushes. Something bigger than us.'

Patch knew the human lands weren't far away. If they could reach the fence on the southern border of the wilderness they would be safe.

'Run!' he said.

Both he and Zelina sprinted south as fast as they could. They ran so quickly that by the time Patch smelled the sharp scent of metal beneath his paws it was too late.

The next thing he knew, he was dangling upside down in midair, and his left hindpaw was encircled in a ring of agony. The earth was above his head, bouncing dizzyingly closer and then farther away. Patch screamed with pain, fear, and confusion. When he looked down he saw his hindleg ensnared in a tight loop of glittering wire. The wire hung from a branch bouncing slowly up and down. 'Help!' he cried out to Zelina. 'Help me!'

Zelina looked north, toward the rustling sounds then south, where the fence that marked the wilderness boundary was visible through the trees.

'Oh, I'm sorry, Patch,' Zelina said, her voice quivering with emotion. 'I don't know how. And there is something dreadful coming. I can smell it.'

'Please,' Patch begged her.

'I'm so sorry,' Zelina said, and took two steps south – and a branch flew high into the air with a silver flash of metal, and Zelina too dangled upside down from a wire noose, helpless and screaming.

Patch tried to struggle, but any motion only tightened the wire around his leg. The pain was awful. Blood dripped down his leg onto his body. Being upside down made him feel sick, and he could barely understood the things he saw. He saw motion, something pushing through the upside-down trees, but it was only from its smell that he understood that this was the fox.

'Oh happy day of dangling delights,' the fox said, and there was laughter in his voice, and his mouth was full of viciously sharp teeth. 'Oh loyal monsters, oh faithful gravity, you have done your work so well.'

'These aren't your monsters,' Patch managed to say, though it was hard to talk upside down. 'This is human work.'

'This is human work,' the fox agreed, 'but it works for me. They bring traps, and I frighten into them panicky rabbits, stupid squirrels, and foolhardy cats. And then my dinner hangs in the air before my eyes.'

'Let me go!' Zelina cried out. 'I am the Queen of All Cats!'

'Are you indeed, oh little morsel swinging in the breeze? Well, your majesty, I am most graciously honored to make your ever-so-brief acquaintance. Allow me to introduce myself as well. I am Talis the hungry fox, and I bear the sad news that between royalty and hunger, there is really no contest.'

'You are a vile beast who should have been fed to your brothers and sisters,' Zelina hissed. 'You are so repulsive the moon weeps to see you, if ever you dare turn your loathsome face to the sky. You conspire with rats and reptiles, you copulate with cockroaches, and when other foxes smell you they drive you from their dens!'

Patch saw a gleam of metal from the ground between the fox and the cat, and he understood.

'Right,' Talis said, 'you die first.'

He ran at Zelina; and a branch leapt upwards, trailing a wire in its wake; and suddenly Talis too dangled in the air, hanging from his foreleg, yowling with shock and pain. Through his own dizzying agony Patch felt a certain deadly satisfaction.

But by the time the humans came that satisfaction had long since dissipated. By then it was night, and Patch could no longer feel his own paw.

III. THE HIDDEN KINGDOM

CAGES

he human grasped Patch with a hand wrapped in thick material that smelled faintly of dead animal skin. Patch was too weak and delirious to struggle. He only trembled as his trapped paw was released from the snare and he was thrust into a small wire cage. Zelina and Talis were treated similarly. The humans, there were three of them, took extra care with Talis, and spoke to one another for a little while after caging Zelina.

Patch's cage was large enough for three or four squirrels. It was made of a fine mesh of strong wire. The wall that had opened to allow him entry had afterward been clamped shut by some small human device made of metal, but it rattled a little as Patch was passed over the wire fence to another human, who in turn put Patch into the back of a sleeping death machine. The interior stank of animal pain and fear.

The cages were stacked, Zelina atop Patch atop Talis. After some time the death machine stirred and began to move. Patch curled around his wounded leg and licked the blood from his paw. He couldn't think, his mind felt trapped in mud, he had no sense of time or place, only of terror. A little sensation began to seep back into his paw, but that sensation was agony.

At some point the death machine stopped, its back was opened, and humans took a dozen empty cages from it. Shortly afterward the cages were returned. Most now contained rabbits, but there were also two squirrels, and one imprisoned a dog so small it was hardly more than a baby. The dog whined and bleated for the rest of the journey. The other animals remained silent.

Patch didn't so much fall asleep as fall away from the world. When he next became aware of his surroundings, he was no longer in a death machine. He was inside a huge, dim space that smelled overpoweringly of blood. There was no sky above, only metal and brick. There were dogs in the shadowy distance; their voices were terrible, but he could not make out what they were saying. Patch's cage was part of a wall built three or four cages high and he did not know how long. All the cages were occupied by small animals – mostly rabbits, but amid the thick miasma of blood and pain and fear-smells, he made out the scents of at least half a dozen other squirrels. Zelina was now below him, and Talis above.

'What happened?' he whispered to Zelina. 'Where are we?'

'I don't know,' she whispered back. 'Oh, my leg hurts so much I can't even stand.'

Patch tried to stand, and discovered that he could – but the pain of doing so was so excruciating that he quickly slumped back down onto his belly. He began to lick the blood from his paw and leg, trying to clean the wound.

Something moved near the cages. A rat.

'Soon we will sup on your blood too,' the rat said to the animals in the cages, and chittered loudly with laughter.

Other rats, dozens of them, emerged from holes in the walls behind the wall of cages, and scuttled around the cages and toward the center of the room, toward the strongest blood-smells.

'What is this place?' Patch asked weakly. 'What happened to the sky?'

'We're inside a building,' Zelina said. 'I've never been in a room this big before.'

Patch gasped as he understood. He was actually *inside* a human mountain. Like being in a drey inside a tree. Humans had captured them, caged them, and taken them into a mountain. But why?

The answer was not long in coming. Bright lights winked on across the ceiling, lights that flickered so fast that they soon gave Patch a headache. The rats fled into the darkness, out of the immense space revealed by the sudden illumination, a hollow so big that it could have encompassed several large trees – if they had fallen, that is, for while the length and width of the room were very great, the ceiling was lower than the height of a small tree. The nearness of this wall between Patch and the sky made him even more unnerved and frightened.

There were more cages far away on the opposite side of the room. But these cages were much larger, and they contained snarling, slavering dogs, except for one that held … something else, something very large. In the middle of the room, rows of benches surrounded a circular wire fence. This fence in turn enclosed an open space from which the blood-smell rose. The blood was actually visible, smeared in dark patches on the ground.

Humans began to enter, many of them, until the benches were full. Two of them went to the dog-cages and brought out two of the dogs, holding them with leashes made of solid metal. The dogs snarled at each other as they were led to the middle of the room:

'Beg! Whimper! Bleed! Die!'

'Taste your flesh! Eat your heart! Drink your blood! Gnaw your bones!'

Once released inside the fence the dogs fought each other until one was badly hurt and the other almost dead. During the battle the humans jumped about, shouted to one another, and cried with exultation. Finally humans separated the combatants and dragged them back into cages.

Another dog was brought forth from the cages. This one was the largest dog that Patch had ever seen, as big as the two humans that conducted it into the killing space. It strutted confidently among the bloodstains, shouting, 'I kill! I kill! I kill! I kill!'

And then suddenly the big dog went silent.

The two humans had opened another cage door, the one that led to the strange thing that was not a dog. It was, incredibly, a cat. Patch had never dreamed that there were cats so immense in this world. The biggest animals he had ever seen were the horses that sometimes pulled humans through the Center Kingdom; this cat looked nearly as large. Its teeth were as big as Patch's head. Its fur was orange and black. As it stalked across the room with musical grace, its scent wafted through the air, a burning, feverish scent of wild rage. It was utterly unlike anything else Patch had ever smelled – except, possibly, the scent of that strange dog-thing in the Center Kingdom, on the day he had traveled into the mountains.

'Oh my goodness,' Zelina breathed, below him. She was standing in her cage to see better, the pain in her leg forgotten. 'Oh, he's beautiful as the moon!'

When the cat-thing entered the killing space, the huge dog

whimpered and cowered onto the ground. A human touched a stick to the huge dog, and there was a crackling sound and the smell of lightning. The dog leapt to its feet, screaming with pain and rage, and the battle began. The shouts and howls of the humans did not last long. The cat-thing tore the huge dog's throat out, settled down in the killing space, and began to eat. The humans watched this as intently as they had watched the battle.

Eventually most of them filed out of the room. The two that remained walked over toward the small cages, and many of the animals inside began to howl and thrash with terror, and all the cages trembled with their desperate fear. The humans took many of the cages, maybe a fifth of them, and carried them across the room; and as Patch watched with speechless horror, the smaller animals were deposited into the dog-cages. Most of the dogs wasted no time killing and eating their rabbits and squirrels, but several seemed to have learned to enjoy tormenting their victims, and drew out their deaths for some time.

The humans caught the cat-thing with steel leashes and led it back to its cage. Then they divided up the blood-soaked rags of flesh that were all that was left of the cat-thing's adversary, and fed those remains to the caged dogs. After they left the room the lights went out. Patch was alone in his cage, in the dark, surrounded by the terrified whimpers of the animals around him, and the distant growls of dogs.

THE DEVICE

omorrow you die,' a rat whispered from the darkness, waking Patch from a long and nightmare-laden sleep. 'Tomorrow all of you die and we gnaw on the shards of your bones.'

'Shut your mouth and go away, filth-eater,' Patch muttered, almost without thinking.

'You shut your mouth, squirrel. You are lucky to be in a cage, or in the name of the King Beneath, we would kill you now ourselves.'

'There is no King Beneath,' Patch said, remembering and echoing Karmerruk's words. 'The King Beneath is a myth.'

Gasps of furious dismay echoed from dozens of rat voices in the darkness around the cages.

'For your blasphemy you should die of the blackblood disease!' a rat said angrily. 'You should have your skin torn away while still you live!'

'The King Beneath is as real as your death tomorrow,' another said cleverly, to general rat approval.

'How do you know?' Patch asked. 'Have you seen him? What does he look like? What does he smell like?'

At first there was no reply, and Patch thought he had won the argument.

Then a rat said reverently, 'Lord Snout has seen him.'

Patch twitched with surprise. 'Snout of the Center Kingdom?'

'There is no Center Kingdom. The Center Kingdom is a myth,' the clever rat said. The other rats hooted with approval at her wit. 'There is only one kingdom, the Kingdom Beneath, and its roads and rivers run beneath all of the shell you call the world. Soon our armies will rise from the Kingdom Beneath, and no squirrel will ever speak of the Center Kingdom again, for there will be none left to remember that name!'

The rats cheered. Patch fell silent and began to once again lick his wounded paw, which had healed a little overnight. There was no point arguing with rats. What he had to do was figure out how to escape. It was true that escape seemed impossible. But if he did not find a way, before long he and Zelina would be fed to savage dogs.

A little unnatural light spilled and spread into the room from the ceiling, enough to illuminate the wire mesh of his cage. One end of his cage, the end that pointed away from the wall and toward the killing space and the dogs, was slightly loose, and rattled when Patch pushed against it. This loose wall was also adorned with the small human thing made of metal. Patch pushed harder, but it was clear that force alone would not break the cage. Patch sighed and looked around for other animals. Maybe a bird would come in, a bird strong enough to carry a cage in its claws. It wasn't much of a hope. But it seemed to be all they had.

'We must find a way to open the device,' Zelina said.

Patch looked down at her. 'What device?'

'The device that holds the cage shut. That metal device.' She indicated the little metal thing that perched on the loose wall of her cage as well. It looked just like the one on Patch's, right on the corner between two walls. 'There is some way to open it. That's how the humans put us in and take us out.'

Patch's paws were just small enough to fit through the cage's wire mesh. The device was like a metal loop from which a small metal bar extended. The bar was connected to one of the pipes that formed the frame of the cage, and the loop encircled part of the wire mesh, preventing the cage from opening. A tiny knob protruded from the bar. Patch prodded the device with his paws, and it moved a little, but would not detach. He sniffed it, but there was only the sharp, pure smell of metal. He didn't understand Zelina's claim that it held his cage shut, but she had lived among humans, and knew their ways.

'You will need to use both paws,' said a voice from above.

Patch started with surprise and looked up. A fox's sharp, inquisitive eyes looked back down at him, and at the device on the wall of Patch's cage.

'Use one paw to hold it still,' Talis explained, 'and with the other paw, hook the little bit that sticks out and pull it away from the rest.'

Patch didn't understand. Talis repeated what he had said, and Patch tried very hard to understand, but his brain just couldn't turn into pictures and then motions what Talis had described in words.

'You'll have to do it yourself,' Patch said.

'I can't. My paws are too big to fit through the cage. Cat, do you understand?'

'Perhaps,' Zelina said doubtfully.

She reached through the bars of her cage and tried to manipulate the device. There was a scraping sound, and a gap suddenly appeared in the metal loop, and Patch stiffened with excitement – but then, with a loud click, the gap vanished.

'That's almost it!' Talis said. 'Once it's open, you just have to pull it away from the cage. Do it again!'

Zelina did. She did it at least a dozen times. She repeatedly managed to slide open a gap in the metal loop, but that occupied both her paws, and as soon as she tried to do anything else with the device, it snapped shut.

'It's hopeless,' she said, frustrated. 'Humans have ten fingers. I have only two forelegs. One holds, one opens, but I would need to grow a third foreleg to pull it away from the cage. There is no hope.'

'Wait,' Patch said.

He advanced to the front of his cage, and after several attempts, following the visual example Zelina had just set, he managed to grasp the device's metal loop with one paw, reach his other paw over the metal protrusion, and pull the protrusion away from the loop, opening up a gap.

'Admirably done, but now what?' Zelina asked. 'You too have only two forelegs.'

Patch answered by waving his long, proud tail. Then he curled up his body as much as he could, arched his tail over his head, and just barely, shuddering with the strain on his tail muscles, he managed to use the tip of his tail instead of his paw to hold the metal loop in place.

'Excellent!' Talis cried out.

Patch opened the loop with one paw, and reached out with the other – but did not know what to do with it. He could see the device where it was, and he could imagine it where he wanted it to be, outside the cage rather than with a strand of wire mesh caught in its loop, but he could not picture the required motion.

'I don't know what to do,' Patch wailed.

Talis said, 'Close your eyes.'

Patch did so.

'Now pull the device back a very little. That's it. Now to the left. A little more. Now push it forward.'

Patch lost his grip on the device, and it snapped back shut, and he cried out with dismay as he opened his eyes – and his cage door yawned open.

'Oh, Patch, well done!' Zelina cried.

And then, all around him, dozens of voices gasped with surprise, hope, and anticipation. Many of those voices belonged to the animals in the cages. Many more belonged to the surrounding rats.

he light was so dim, and the animal- and blood-smells so thick, that Patch could not count the number of rats around the cages; but he knew it had to be dozens, and perhaps more, perhaps an entire rat army. The opening of his cage door no longer seemed like a brilliant victory. Rats could not climb like squirrels or cats, but given time they would find a way up and into the open cage. And if Patch tried to escape, or if he descended to open Zelina's cage, they would swarm him and eat him alive.

'Release me, squirrel,' Talis said, 'and I will protect you.'

Patch looked up at the fox above him. Talis was crammed into his cage. He was as big as a small dog, and had a predator's sharp teeth. It would take a brave group of rats indeed to charge a fox, and rats were not known for their courage. But it would take a very stupid squirrel to release a fox that had already tried to kill and eat him.

'Swear by the moon that you will protect me,' Patch said. 'And that you will never attack a squirrel again.'

'That's outrageous!' Talis cried out.

'Or a cat,' Zelina suggested.

'Or a cat,' Patch agreed.

'I will not swear that or anything else by the moon!' Talis said.

'Then the dogs will have you.'

'Then the rats will have *you*.'

'They will have me anyway if I let you go without a moon-oath,' Patch said.

Talis frowned. Patch said nothing. It took considerable self-control to say nothing, as several rats had already clustered outside Zelina's cage, immediately beneath his, and were chittering as they probed at the wire mesh, trying to find a way up into Patch's open cage. Fortunately they were still mostly getting in one another's way, but Patch knew it was only a matter of time before they figured out how to reach him.

'You're a sharp bargainer, for a squirrel,' Talis said.

'Thank you.'

'I don't even know your names.'

'My name is Patch son of Silver,' Patch said, 'and my friend is Zelina, Queen of All Cats.'

Talis sighed, long and loud.

Then he declared, 'I swear by the moon that I, Talis, shall protect Patch son of Silver and Zelina, Queen of All Cats.' His eyes shone and his body shuddered as he spoke, and all the animals in the cages, and even those rats surrounding the cages, and even the dogs across the room, fell silent and stopped moving. 'And I swear by the moon that I will never again attack a squirrel or a cat.'

It was Patch who broke the awed silence. 'Then let's get you out of here.'

He pushed his cage door open and climbed the wire mesh onto Talis's cage door. He had to brace himself with his hindlegs, and the pain from his wounded paw made him whimper, but with desperate strength Patch managed to open the device that sealed Talis's cage. He very nearly fell off the door when it swung open, but scrambled up it and onto the top of Talis's cage. His wounded hindleg ached like fire.

Talis burst out of the cage like water erupting from a fountain. The air filled with the terrified squeals of rats as the fox began to maraud among them, killing with fangs and claws. If the rat army had worked together, they could have swarmed Talis and reduced him to a skeleton in heartbeats – but the first wave of assailants in such a swarm would have been killed by the fox before Talis was over-whelmed, and no rats were willing to sacrifice themselves for the good of their companions. Instead they fled into the walls, into the hidden crawlspaces and tunnels of the Kingdom Beneath.

As Patch released Zelina, a chorus of pleas began to rise from all the other caged animals: 'Save us! Outside, please! Free us, open our cages!'

Patch's leg hurt badly, and he knew that climbing onto all these cages and opening them would be a great strain, but he could not leave fellow squirrels here to be eaten by dogs. One at a time, slowly and painfully, he pried open the devices that held squirrels captive, and let them out into the room.

Rabbits thumped against the walls of their cages, saying, 'Out-side, please, please, please! Outside, please, please, *please!*' Patch had never thought much of rabbits, who were neither very bright nor very eloquent. He felt sorry for these ones, but he did not have the strength to free them all.

To his surprise he saw Talis at a ground-level cage, playing dexterously with the device that shut in a rabbit. The cage opened, the rabbit bounced out with a cry of glee – and Talis promptly killed it and began to dine on its remains. Patch winced with sympathy. The other rabbits gasped with horror.

'I never swore not to attack rabbits,' the fox said between bites.

'We should go,' Zelina said. 'The humans may return. The rats may return with a leader.'

'She's right,' said one of the just-released squirrels.

'Just a moment,' Talis said through a mouthful of rabbit meat.

Then a deep, throbbing voice echoed through the room. It came from its other side, from the big cages, and it drowned out the dogs who had begun to snarl with dismay.

'Please,' it said. 'Please, if you have any mercy in your hearts, help me.'

SIVA

 elina began to run across the room.

'Zelina, what are you doing?' Patch cried out, appalled, but she did not stop.

After a moment he raced after her, intending to intercept her before she reached the big cages. But to Patch's surprise she could run much faster than he. By the time he caught up with her she was standing in front of the cage of the immense cat-thing, which lay coiled miserably on the ground.

'Who are you?' Zelina asked. 'What are you?'

'My name is Siva,' came the reply, 'and I am *tiger*. Who are you?'

'My name is Zelina.'

Patch, hanging back a little behind her, approved of her diplomatic omission of 'Queen of All Cats'. It did not seem right to imply to a terrifying cat-thing big enough to eat a human that it was in any way a social inferior, even if it was in a cage made of steel bars the size of tree branches and sealed by several devices far larger and more solid than those that had imprisoned Patch and Zelina.

'I beg of you to carry a message for me,' Siva said. 'I beg of you to find my human brother and bring to him a ball of glass. That will tell him that I live.'

Patch was amazed by this extraordinary request, but Zelina seemed to take it in stride.

'Where can we find your human brother?' she asked.

'All I know is he will be among animals, for he is a great *kabooti* man.'

'A great what?' Zelina asked.

The word triggered a memory in Patch. 'Did you once ask a pigeon to find him? Named Daffa?'

Siva turned his gaze on Patch, and Patch quivered beneath its strength and immensity.

'Yes,' the tiger said. 'From time to time pigeons find their way into this room, and I charge them with my mission. I learned to speak Bird long ago, in the jungles in which I grew. But I fear they forget my words as soon as they find the sky.'

'I think I have seen your human brother, in the Ocean Kingdom,' Patch said. 'Is his skin dark? Do flocks of pigeons follow him?'

Siva leapt to his feet, hissing with excitement, and Patch shrank back.

'Yes!' Siva said. 'Yes, that is him! You must find him again! You must bring to him a ball of glass!'

Patch said, 'I can't go back to the Ocean Kingdom. I have to go home. I'm sorry.'

'Please. Please, little squirrel. I beg you. *Please.*'

Patch swallowed and said, 'When I can, after I get home, I'll try to have a bird carry your message. That's all I can tell you. I'll try.'

After a long moment, Siva said, 'Thank you, little squirrel. Your words give me hope. I have been so long in this place of cages and killing that even hope is a gift beyond measure. Please remember, little squirrel. Please remember and do as you say you will.'

'I'll try,' Patch said again.

He was relieved when they finally left the tiger in his cage, rejoined Talis and the freed squirrels, and began to search for a way out of the mountain.

he way out was through the shattered corner of a piece of glass set about human-high into a brick wall. Zelina called the glass a *window*. The bricks of the wall, and especially the mortar between the bricks, were just crumbly enough to give purchase to a squirrel's claws, and just strong enough to hold a squirrel's weight. Zelina too was able to climb to the window. But Talis had to remain behind, trapped on the ground.

'I'm sorry, Talis,' Patch said. 'We'd help you escape if we could.'

'Don't you feign guilt to me, Patch son of Silver,' Talis grumbled. 'As well to have cut off one of my legs as to have made me swear that oath. Don't you worry about me. None need ever worry about foxes. We survive. I know from the smells what door the humans will enter. When they come in, I will run out. And in the meantime there are rabbits to eat.'

'Don't forget your oaths,' Zelina said.

The fox bared his teeth. 'I should, and I would if I could, Queen of All Cats. Now begone before this bile I taste becomes poison.'

Patch had to maneuver carefully to avoid being cut by the shattered glass. The ground outside was a field of uneven concrete, dimly lit by a few human lights, surrounded by small mountains. The wind was cold and smelled of rust and chemicals without even a trace of trees or grass, but Patch drank it in like it was the wind of the highest sky. He had escaped the awful killing place, he stood once more beneath the moon. And the stars. For it was deepest night.

'We must find shelter,' one of the other freed squirrels said fearfully.

'Yes,' Patch said. 'Do you know this kingdom?'

'No.'

'We can't stay and talk! We must find shelter, now, it's night!' another squirrel exclaimed, and this one matched her actions to her words by turning tail and running. The other squirrels followed her example until only Patch and Zelina remained, and Patch was trembling nervously.

'What's wrong?' Zelina asked, puzzled. 'We've escaped!'

'It's night. We have to find shelter.'

'What's wrong with the night? I have often stood on the metal stairs outside my palace at night and watched the moon.'

'Owls!' Patch said.

It was more than owls. Squirrels fear the night for the blindness it brings, for its cold winds, and for the rats and raccoons that emerge and prowl through their native darkness. But above all they fear the owls, the deadly, relentless killers that cruise silently through the night sky, invisible and undetectable, able to see through darkness from far away the motion of mouse or squirrel or rat, and then swoop down and strike and kill and carry away, leaving nothing but darkness and silence in their wake. It was an article of faith among squirrels of the Center Kingdom that a nighttime expedition would lead to death by owl. And it was not so very far from the truth; for dozens of owls hovered every night between the city and the stars, circling slowly, seeking prey.

'We have to find shelter,' Patch repeated.

'There's a sky-road,' Zelina said, and indeed across the concrete plain there stood a severed trunk from which wires hung.

'No,' Patch said. 'We must stay out of open places, near the walls, in the shadows.'

'I think your fear is strange,' Zelina said, but she sounded nervous, and did not protest further.

Patch led the way along the mountain that had held them, sniffing the air, hoping to find some scent of trees. But there was nothing. Only human-smells.

'There has to be a tree somewhere,' Patch said desperately.

'We can take shelter on the ground,' Zelina suggested.

'On the ground the rats will find us. We must have a tree.'

'Metal stairs.'

'What?' Patch asked.

'Over there.' She indicated a kind of metal latticework that clung to the wall of a building across the concrete plain. 'See that tendril of the sky-road that connects just beside them? We can jump over. No rats will reach us there. And the metal will keep the owls away.'

'It's nothing like a drey,' Patch objected. 'It's open on all sides. And it's human. It's *metal*.'

'I shall spend my evening on the metal stairs, which I assure you are fit for a queen, even if some bedraggled squirrel does somehow consider them insufficient and unworthy,' Zelina said haughtily. 'As for you, I wish you luck in finding a tree before an owl finds you.'

Zelina ran toward the sky-road, keeping near walls and to shadows like Patch had suggested. After a moment Patch sighed and ran after her. Both ran on three legs, favoring their wounded limbs. Their journey was slow but they were not attacked. The metal stairs had a cold, slick, disagreeable feel, and although Patch had to admit that an owl was unlikely to try to swoop down through the lattice of bars that stood on either side of the zigzagging stairs, he still felt unsheltered. He was exhausted, but he slept poorly.

CITY OF CLANS

atch awoke with the sun. Leaving Zelina to sleep, he slowly climbed up to the top of the metal stairs, and onto the roof to which they opened. The roof was flat and white, and dotted with protruding metal things the size of humans. Patch leapt up to the short brick wall on the roof's perimeter and looked around.

His heart swelled. For he saw the enormous mountains that surrounded the Center Kingdom, so near that they blotted out a sizable arc of the western sky. He had feared that the humans had taken him far from his home; instead, they had brought him much closer. Patch compared what he saw to that long-ago sky-view from Karmerruk's claws, and thought he was only a day's journey distant from the river that ran down the eastern shore of the Center Kingdom's island. He didn't know how he would traverse that river, but having already crossed one bridge, he felt confident he would find a way.

The area around him was an amazing three-dimensional labyrinth of human chaos and construction. There were other buildings, wide and flat and low, like the one on which he stood. There were countless wire fences topped by barbed strands. There were scores of sleeping automobiles. There were highways and plots of pitted, cracked concrete, and in places the highways crossed atop one another, forming spans and tunnels of concrete. Even the walls of a narrow, muddy river in the middle distance were concrete. A huge metal bridge crossed that river. There were sky-roads of posts and wires, but they were sparse and disconnected, isolated spurs that ran between buildings or along highways for only some distance, rather than covering all the human territory like a vast spiderweb in the way of the sky-roads of the Ocean Kingdom.

In the distance, across the narrow river, the biggest machine Patch had ever seen passed by. It looked like a dozen solid-walled metal cages linked together, and it groaned and shrieked and howled as it moved, and lights as bright as the sun flickered from where its wheeled feet met the metal rails on which it rode.

'Moon in the heavens!' Zelina cried out from behind him. 'Your tail!'

Startled, Patch ran back to the metal stairs. Zelina was awake, and not alone. There was a strange squirrel on the metal stairs with her. Zelina had inadvertently cornered the squirrel, who she was examining carefully. Fully a third of the squirrel's tail was missing.

Patch had seen this before, of course. Squirrels are capable, when seized by a predator or perhaps trapped by a falling tree, of detaching part of their tails in order to escape. This is not done lightly; a squirrel's tail, aside from acting as rudder and sun-shade and blanket, is its crowning glory of beauty and vanity.

'Go away!' the squirrel said, frightened; Zelina was no larger than a squirrel, but she was still a predator.

'What have you done with Patch?' Zelina demanded.

'I'm right here,' Patch said from the top of the stairs, and then, to the squirrel, 'I'm sorry, don't worry, it's all right, she's a friend.'

The squirrel looked suspiciously at Zelina, and even more suspiciously at Patch, and demanded, 'Who are you?'

'I am Patch son of Silver, of the Seeker clan, of the Treetops tribe, of the Center Kingdom,' Patch said. 'Who are you that asks?'

'I am Wriggler son of Downclimber, of the Seeker clan, of the Hidden Kingdom.'

Patch looked at him quizzically. 'Of what tribe?'

'We have no tribes in the Hidden Kingdom. Only clans.'

'You say you are of the Seeker clan?'

'You say *you* are of the Seeker clan?'

The squirrels looked at one another, amazed. Squirrels inherit their clan from their father and their tribe from their mother, so there were members of the Seeker clan among all four of the Center Kingdom's tribes. But Patch had never imagined that he might have clan-brothers and clan-sisters outside of the Center Kingdom.

'Why do you have no tribes?' Patch asked.

'The Hidden Kingdom isn't like the Center Kingdom or the Hill Kingdom. We have no great forest. We are too scattered to have tribes.'

'If you have no forest, then where do you live?'

'We live here,' Wriggler said. 'We live in what you see.'

'But there are no trees! Where do you sleep? What do you eat?'

'Come and I will show you.'

Wriggler leapt up to the roof of the building, and along the wall that was its edge. Patch followed, intrigued, and Zelina followed him.

'Must the cat come along?' Wriggler asked.

Outraged, Zelina answered, 'I will have you know that I am the Queen of All Cats!'

Wriggler sighed but did not protest further. He led them along a tendril of sky-road to a row of connected buildings with sloping roofs. There were a few cherry trees that grew from the highway before these buildings, but they were like the trees in the mountains, scrawny and disconnected, with only a tiny square of dirt around their trunks. Still, they were beginning to blossom, and Patch's mouth watered; cherry blossoms weren't filling, but they were tasty.

'Can we stop and eat?' he asked.

'I'll bring you to real food,' Wriggler assured him. 'You see up at the top of this building? My drey is there.'

'Your drey is in a human building?' Patch asked, amazed.

'Come and see.'

The roof of the building was built of human-made tiles, and at its very peak, a few tiles had fallen away, revealing a wooden-walled hollow within. Wriggler's drey was lined with leaves and papers and looked very warm and comfortable.

'I have two clan-brothers on this street as well,' Wriggler said. 'We're all Seeker clan around here. I'll introduce you if I see them. Would you like to eat?'

'Oh, yes, please,' Patch said.

'Follow me.'

They took the sky-road across the highway to a big building with a flat roof. The air here was warm and smelled wonderfully of food. Wriggler and Patch downclimbed a sky-road pole to a narrow concrete strip between buildings. Zelina, as usual, had to find her own slow way down to the surface, with many teetering hops from building to sky-road to wire fence to a massive, foul-smelling rusted metal box on the ground between the buildings. She was still ungainly but Patch thought she was getting better at descents now, with practice.

'There's usually good food here,' Wriggler said. He led them to a heap of wrinkled, shining black seedpods, sniffed around, selected one, tore open a squirrel-sized hole with his sharp teeth, and disappeared inside. The seedpod writhed and shook as Wriggler squirmed into it, and then emerged.

'Moldy multigrain bagel!' he said happily. 'Delicious!'

Patch followed Wriggler into the seedpod, and while something else inside smelled terrible, the chunks of food he found were indeed wonderful. When he came out Wriggler was looking very suspiciously at Zelina and the dead sparrow she was eating.

'She only eats little birds and mice,' Patch assured him.

'My mother always told me, never trust a predator,' Wriggler said darkly.

'How did you lose your tail?'

Wriggler sighed. 'A dog in a park. I was burying a nut, it was stupid of me, we have enough food here without nuts even in winter, but I couldn't help myself. It was downwind, and there were so many human noises around ...'

Patch winced in sympathy.

'Some of the females don't care,' Wriggler said, looking sadly at his much-reduced tail. 'Or that's what they say. But when I chase them they don't let me catch them. I suppose you don't have any troubles with chasing.'

Patch didn't want to talk about chasing. 'I need to get home to the Center Kingdom. Do you know how we can cross the river into the mountains?'

Wriggler considered. 'There are bridges. But they're for humans. And falcons live on the bridge towers. I've never heard of a squirrel going across.'

Patch was not dissuaded by this news. Since leaving the Center Kingdom he had done many things nobody had ever heard of a squirrel doing. The prospect of one more did not particularly perturb him.

WATER'S EDGE

ut in each of the several days that followed, the wide river that separated Patch and Zelina from the island of the Center Kingdom seemed to loom larger and more impassable. Aided by Wriggler, who shared the enthusiasm Patch had once had for exploration, and by Wriggler's friends Quicknose and Backflip, they roved down the eastern shore of that river. They moved along sky-roads and rooftops and sometimes, greatly daring, across highways. They rested in the strips and squares of greenery and trees called *parks* that seemed randomly dispersed among the concrete highways and buildings of the human lands. They ate nuts and shoots from those trees; scraps left fallen beneath tables and benches behind those buildings full of foods where humans went to eat; food discarded along with other human rubble in the garbage bags Patch had once thought of as seedpods. They drank rainwater that puddled on ceilings and collected in rooftop gutters.

They met and spoke to other squirrels, some of them clanbrothers, most of other clans. Like Wriggler and his friends these lived in small groups and came together in larger numbers only for mating season. Dogs barked at Patch and Zelina frequently from windows and highways. They saw several cats from a distance, but Zelina was not eager to make contact with any of her subjects. She explained that since she had been betrayed, deposed, and exiled, she was disinclined to allow news of her return to spread before the opportune moment. Once, late at night, as they looked for a temporary drey large enough for them all, they passed very near several raccoons, and all of them froze with fear, but the raccoons merely leered at them and passed on without speaking.

As for birds, aside from the usual masses of pigeons, they saw amazing numbers of crows, in groups large enough that when they roosted on a tree there were often more birds than branches. Wriggler, Quicknose and Backflip were as surprised as Patch and Zelina; such congregations of crows were unheard of. Patch tried talking to several of them, but the crows were curt, hard-eyed, and unfriendly. Usually they simply flew away without a word; and if they did speak, it was never more than 'Be silent, groundling. Be away and stop pestering me.'

Patch had never seen or heard of crows in such numbers. But then there were lots of things going on he had never heard of before. War in the Center Kingdom, according to the Old One. Redeye working with rats, and maybe Sniffer too. He thought of the clever rat who had spoken of Lord Snout and rat armies, and of the rumors that Karmerruk had heard, rumors of strange and terrible things. He wondered if they might all be true, if the whole world was changing, and something awful was happening.

But no, he reassured himself; all these oddities and rumors were just coincidence and rat-chatter. Maybe there was a war in the Center Kingdom, it was hard to disbelieve anything the Old One had said, but surely it would soon be resolved; he could not imagine such a conflict lasting long. The tribes would soon find a way to settle their differences.

In the Hidden Kingdom there could be no such war, because there were no tribes; and yet Patch couldn't help feeling sorry for the squirrels of the Hidden Kingdom. It was good to have a tribe, to feel part of something larger. When he got home, Patch told himself, it would mean more to him to be of the Treetops. And when he got home he would find Silver there, and Twitch, and Tuft, and Brighteyes, and life would go back to the way it had always been, except he would no longer be so solitary, and he would make a point of belonging to his tribe.

But the more they traveled, the less any route across the river became apparent. No boats traveled from one side to the other. The river was wide, dark, and cold, it exuded a foul and oily odor, and it was clear from watching its flotsam that its currents were strong and treacherous. As for the bridges, there were several, but all were concrete monstrosities that extended for a very great distance, and were packed with automobiles and humans at all hours of day and night. Only one bridge, the farthest south and most magnificent, had a concrete trail devoid of automobiles. This trail was always busy with humans, and sometimes they had dogs, but they might have risked it all the same – if not for the fact that this was the same bridge on which several families of falcons nested.

In sum, after three days of close investigation the river seemed impassable and the Center Kingdom unreachable. Until Zelina conceived an extraordinary alternative.

PASSENGERS

ave you gone mad?' Patch spluttered.

'I think it is a perfectly elegant solution to our problem,' Zelina said. 'Look. There is the river we need to cross. There is the bridge we dare not run across. And there is the big automobile that will carry us.'

'You have gone mad. You want to get into an automobile, like a human, and –'

'Not in,' Zelina said. 'On. We shall ride on the roof.'

'How will we get to the roof?'

'From time to time the big automobiles stop right here.'

They perched on a thick sky-road wire near one of the many places where two highways met in a forest of metal branches and hanging lights. It was true that the big automobiles, the ones that looked like long metal boxes, or solid-walled cages, did stop directly beneath this wire. But –

'I am not jumping onto and riding an automobile,' Patch said flatly.

'They have flat roofs. They're as large as some of the buildings we've crossed.'

'Buildings don't move!'

'The entire appeal of automobiles is that they *do* move. They will carry us across the bridge and the river. One might carry us all the way to the Great Avenue for all we know.'

'And how would we get off? The sky-road is too high above us to jump up to.'

'I don't know,' Zelina admitted. 'But when we face that problem, we will be on the other side of the river, and so we will have successfully mastered the *current* problem. I believe in dealing with one obstacle at a time.'

'But … what if …'

Patch fell silent. He couldn't find the right way to argue. The problem with her plan was not that it didn't make sense. The problem was that it was insane. The idea of jumping onto a death machine and riding it along a strip of wasteland was the craziest he had ever heard. He looked down the sky-road to Wriggler, Quicknose and Backflip, but they were distracted some distance back by their own conversation.

A big death machine came to rest beneath them, emitting plumes of air that stank of oil and chemicals, wheezing and hissing so loudly that Patch could hardly hear anything else. It was so obviously something that should be avoided, rather than adopted, that Patch cried out with horror when Zelina leapt on top of it. 'Come on, Patch!' she shouted. 'Now is the time!'

No, Patch thought. *Absolutely not.* Under no circumstances would he follow the mad Queen of All Cats onto this stinking, eruptive death machine.

But then it began to pull away, and his legs crouched and leapt almost as if commanded by someone else, and he skidded across the metal roof of the big automobile, dangerously close to its edge, before he regained his balance and scampered next to Zelina – skated, really, his claws clicking against the cold and slippery roof.

The big automobile rumbled and hissed and shook beneath them. Patch could barely believe what he had just done. He turned to look toward Wriggler and Quicknose and Backflip, and saw them growing smaller. For a moment Patch felt motion in his gut; then, for a brief period, the big automobile seemed stationary, and it seemed like it was the world around them that was moving; then the vehicle came to a sudden, shuddering halt, and both Patch and Zelina lost their balance and went skidding forward across its roof; and then it started up again, and they went skidding backward. If not for the shallow corrugations that gave their claws something to hook onto, they would both have fallen and died.

'You crazy idiot!' Patch shouted furiously at Zelina.

Zelina did not dispute his words. She smelled of and trembled with terror. The big automobile rocked, banged, and rattled as it navigated its stop-start way along the clogged highway, and on its roof Patch and Zelina staggered and slid erratically about, keeping desperately away from the roof's unwalled edges. Their battle for life and balance was so fraught and demanding that Patch did not even realize they were on the bridge until they were more than halfway across. By then he was too frightened of falling to be worried about falcons.

They stopped for a relatively long period about three-quarters of the way across the bridge, and Patch and Zelina managed to catch their breath. Patch felt sick and dizzy from having been thrown about. The air was laced with the acrid fumes of automobiles, but the breeze from the great waters to the south kept it breathable. Loud honking noises and human shouts rose and reverberated all around them as they tried to cling to the middle of the automobile's roof.

'This is the worst idea any animal has ever had!' Patch shouted.

'I didn't make you jump,' Zelina pointed out. 'And we're almost there.'

The vehicle lurched forward again, and they went sprawling. But they had learned something from the first nightmarish maelstrom of motion, and by lying on their bellies and reaching out with the claws of all four limbs, they managed to limit how far they slid, and then crawled back to the center of the roof.

The view beneath them from either side slipped suddenly from water to concrete. They had crossed the river. Patch tried to open his memory book and calculate how far he was from the Center Kingdom proper, but his mind was whirling with too much fear and excitement to concentrate.

'Look for a place to jump off,' Zelina said.

Patch looked. He realized with growing horror that there was no sky-road at all around them, no system of posts and wires along which they could climb, and no trees. There was only concrete and metal, staggeringly high mountains that blotted out the very sun, concrete highways and walkways, metal posts and automobiles.

'I don't see anywhere,' Patch said.

'Neither do I.'

The big automobile roared and wheezed forward. When it turned corners, which it did several times, Patch and Zelina slid away from the turn and nearly off the side of the automobile. After the first such near-death experience they learned to move to the opposite side whenever they felt a turn beginning. Patch still had to focus entirely on remaining perched on the automobile rather than falling and being crushed between its wheeled rubber feet and the concrete. Cats, however, have better balance than squirrels, which is why Zelina was able to devote enough attention to the world around them to notice their salvation.

'Trees!' she cried. 'Look, Patch, trees!'

They were few in number, they were scrawny and bedraggled and seemed to be growing straight out of concrete, but there were indeed trees lining this latest highway onto which they had turned; and when the big automobile stopped next, there was a tree immediately beside it. Patch and Zelina did not hesitate to leap onto its branches. Shortly afterward the vehicle pulled away and disappeared down the highway, leaving Patch and Zelina in the safety of a tree, on the island of the Center Kingdom, temporarily triumphant.

IV. THE ISLAND
OF THE CENTER KINGDOM

DOGS

t last, after long days of dangerous travel, Patch had returned to the island of his birth. But the longer he stood atop the tree onto which they had dismounted, and tried to figure out how to travel through the mountains to the Center Kingdom, the more he realized that his problems had not diminished. If anything they had proliferated. He didn't know where on the island he was, but he knew he was still a very long way from home. There was no sky-road at all, and the island's highways and walkways were busier, louder, and more dangerously crowded than any Patch had ever seen before. The one small consolation was that there were very few dogs; but the smell of rat was pervasive.

They stayed on the tree for a long time. Zelina was reluctant to downclimb at all, for the tree's lowest branches were high above the earth, and Patch was reluctant to venture into the walkway teeming with humans from which the tree sprouted. It was not until the sun was hidden behind the mountains to the west, and the flood of humans had diminished to a trickle, that Patch ran down the slender tree trunk onto the walkway. Zelina tried to follow, and promptly fell – but landed gracefully on her feet, unhurt.

They immediately ran to the edge of the nearest mountain. The rat-smells were stronger there, but humans kept a little distance from the mountains. Some of the humans they passed stopped, turned to look at them, and spoke to one another. Patch and Zelina ignored them. He led her north; he knew, at least, that home was that way. When they reached the intersection of two highways, the large one they followed and a smaller one that intersected it, he crouched in the shadow of the corner mountain, and tried to measure the timing of the lights above him.

'Wait,' Zelina said.

Patch looked at her. He was quivering with tension. Running

around on human walkways, surrounded by death machines on highways, still felt profoundly unnatural, and the still-frequent passing
humans, some of whom stepped unseeingly within a tail-length of
Patch, were even more disturbing. But Zelina seemed considerably
more relaxed. 'What?'

'We should wait and travel by night.'

'We can't travel by night. There are owls –'

'There may be owls flying above the Center Kingdom, and above
the river, and perhaps even across the river,' Zelina said, 'but the sky
above us now, you will notice, is almost entirely occupied by mountains, leaving very little room for owls. The daytime is too busy, there
are too many dangers, something will crush us. But the city night is
quiet.'

'How do you know?'

'I used to watch the Great Avenue from the metal stairs outside
my palace. Believe me, Patch. We can't run along these highways to
your home while the sun is high. You'll never reach home alive. You
must trust in the moon.'

'So what are you saying?'

'Let's go down the smaller highway, find a tree or a rooftop, sleep
for a little, then travel by night.'

Patch considered. Travel by night was unnatural and unnerving.
But so was virtually everything else he had done to get home. 'All
right.'

As they proceeded down the smaller and less-trafficked highway,
they passed, across the highway, a large dog with patchy fur, leashed
very closely to one of the withered alder trees that grew amid the
mountains. Patch kept a very careful eye on it, in case the leash was
weak; but even though they were upwind of the dog, it did not howl
for their deaths.

'Hurts bad!' it whined piteously instead. 'Oh, hurts bad, hurts
bad, hurts so bad!'

Patch, surprised, looked more closely. The dog must have somehow circled repeatedly around the tree to which its leash was tied,
because its entire leash was wound around the trunk so tightly that
the dog's side was rubbing painfully against the rough bark. The
dog badly wanted to get away, but dogs were not known for their

thinking, and this one was unable to understand that it should go backward. Instead it kept trying to leap forward and break free of the leash, but each time it succeeded only in choking itself and further chafing its now-bloody side against the bark.

'Dogs are so stupid,' Zelina said contemptuously, as it launched itself forward again, was dragged back by its own collar, and nearly fell.

'Hurts,' it gasped, panting raggedly. 'Hurts bad, can't escape, oh, help me, help me, help me!'

Zelina started walking again. Patch did not. He remembered when he had been caught in the wire snare, and how his leg had burned with pain, and the awful despair he had felt, knowing that no one would come to help, feeling that he might dangle there forever. Looking at the trapped dog, he felt this a little bit again, just a twinge of half-remembered feeling, like the shadow of a real object. He hated and feared dogs, but he wished this dog wasn't trapped. Its patchy fur reminded Patch of the pale mark on his own forehead from which he had taken his name.

'Hurts,' the dog groaned, 'hurts so bad, so bad.' It threw itself forward again and made violent choking noises until it had to let itself fall back and breathe again.

'Stop it!' Patch shouted to the dog. 'Just go around the tree the other way!'

The dog ignored him. 'Hurts bad, hurts bad, so bad!'

Patch looked up and down the highway. No automobiles were coming. He sighed and raced across.

'Patch, what are you *doing*?' Zelina asked from behind him, astounded.

'Look,' Patch said to the dog, 'just go around the tree the other –'

'Kill you and eat you!' the dog howled, leaping to its feet and choking itself again in an attempt to leap at Patch. 'K-k-k … oh –' And it fell back to the ground. 'Oh, hurts so bad, so bad.'

Patch considered a moment. Then he moved around the dog, behind the tree, and shouted, 'This way!'

The dog leapt at him again. Patch began to run around the tree. As the dog pursued him, howling with hate and rage, its leash unwound, until it finally reopened all the way to the knot that bound it to the trunk, and the dog had regained enough freedom that Patch had to stay a considerable distance away from the tree.

'Kill you and eat you! Kill you and eat you!' the dog cried excitedly, straining to reach Patch with its slavering fangs, its previous pain and captivity apparently forgotten.

'How stupid,' Patch said, disgusted. 'I should never have helped you.'

He turned to walk away.

The dog said, confused, 'Help me?'

'Yes,' Patch said, turning back. 'And "kill you and eat you" is the thanks I get.'

'You help me,' the dog said, its eyes finally lighting up with comprehension. 'You help me. I don't hurt now. You help me.'

'Yes.'

'Oh, thank you, thank you, thank you! I don't hurt! I don't hurt! Oh, thank you, little squirrel! You help me! I will never kill you and eat you!'

'You're welcome,' Patch said, a little mollified.

'What is your name, little squirrel?'

Patch said reflexively, 'I am Patch son of Silver, of the Seeker clan, of the Treetops tribe, of the Center Kingdom. Who are you that asks?'

'I am Beeflover. Oh, thank you, thank you!'

'You're welcome,' Patch said. 'Good-bye.'

The dog barked endless thanks as Patch waited for a gap in a stream of death machines and then scampered casually across the highway; such crossings were by now becoming almost routine. The sun had almost entirely set and he and Zelina needed to find a tree – but she was nowhere to be seen. Patch followed her scent, thinking that she had left him, disgusted by his attempt to aid a dog, and gone ahead to find a tree.

Then, in the distance, he heard Zelina's scream of pain and rage, and he began to run.

elina stood on the walkway between a mountain and a tree, surrounded by four much larger male cats. She was bleeding from her face and her left flank. She whirled in quick circles, slashing at the air, trying to fend off all her assailants at once, but the other cats were closing in on her. They smelled feral and angry.

'Stop it!' Patch cried out.

The intercession of a squirrel was so unusual that the four large cats actually did stop and turn to look at Patch.

'This is none of your concern, squirrel,' one of them said. 'Go back to your tree. This is our territory, well-marked. She sent no emissaries. She sought no permission.'

Zelina huddled in terrified silence.

'Permission?' Patch asked, outraged. 'She needs no permission! She is the Queen of All Cats!'

For a moment the four cats were silent, taken aback.

'Don't speak nonsense,' one of them objected uncertainly.

'Tell us any more lies like that, squirrel, and we'll rip your guts from your belly too,' another warned.

'It's no lie,' Patch said. 'I've traveled with her for days. All the way from the Ocean Kingdom. She is the Queen of All Cats.'

'There is no Queen of All Cats,' said the largest male cat, who was pale, very strong, and covered in scars. 'The Queen of All Cats is a myth.'

He sounded angry. But he also sounded not entirely convinced of his own words.

The four cats turned to Zelina, whose small black form still huddled in the center of their circle.

'Is it true?' the largest cat asked. 'Do you claim to be the Queen of All Cats?'

For a moment there was no response, and Patch feared the worst.

Then Zelina rose and stared this largest cat in the face. Her fur bristled and her green eyes flashed like flames. She reeked of blood and rage.

'I am the doomed queen,' she said. 'I am the exiled queen. I am the queen who loves her subjects even as they try to murder her. I am the queen who must kill, and kill, and kill again, until the highways flow with blood. I am the queen who speaks with tigers. I am the queen who has escaped dogs and foxes and humans and rats, but who will never escape her destiny. I am the queen who does not fear the death you bring, who will never beg for her life, who will die as a queen even as I am torn apart. Do with me what you will, you vicious and ignorant brutes, I am and I shall remain, the Queen of All Cats!'

An awful silence seemed to hang over the whole island. Zelina deliberately turned her back on the cat she faced and walked slowly over to stand next to Patch. The four male cats did not try to prevent her.

'Come,' she said to Patch, 'let us be gone.'

Patch wanted to flee from the cats at top speed, but he followed Zelina's lead, and instead they marched slowly away.

'Wait!' one of the male cats cried out.

Patch hesitated, but Zelina's stately walk did not waver.

'Wait, please! Please, your majesty, we didn't know! Please, forgive us!'

Zelina stopped and turned back to them.

'Can you take us to the Great Avenue and the Center Kingdom?' she asked.

The male cats looked at one another uncertainly.

'It's a long way,' said the largest of them, 'very long.'

Zelina said, 'Show us.'

And soon a somewhat disbelieving Patch found himself and Zelina walking along still-busy highways, led and escorted by four large male cats. It was very strange moving through the night, half-blinded. Human lights winked and flickered all around them, in mountains, in death machines, hanging from metal trees. The darkness seemed to sharpen Patch's nose, accentuated the city's rich and rotting symphony of smells. Wherever he smelled rats, he smelled fear as well; no rat wanted to be anywhere near five cats.

They walked all through the night. When day came, they had reached a plain that was mostly concrete but had dribs and drabs of greenery, and a few trees. Patch slept up a small maple tree; Zelina and her companions stayed at its base. By the time Patch awoke, the sun had traversed most of the sky, and three more cats had joined Zelina's retinue. It was exceedingly strange to wake up so very late in the day. Patch's whole body felt queasy, and he hardly ate before descending to the base of the tree and beginning another journey through the night toward his home.

HUMANS

n the middle of the night the city's human walkways were largely, but not entirely, deserted. Some humans reeled past stinking of fermentation, their feet falling so randomly that they were dangerous to be near, and Patch marveled at their uncanny ability to walk on two legs. Some walked quietly, looking ahead of them, seemingly ignorant of all the world around them. Some – usually lone humans, or pairs – crouched to gawk at the spectacle of eight cats and a squirrel journeying through the night. Some slumped on the walkway, lying wrapped in woven covers like caterpillars in cocoons, or sat with their backs against mountain walls.

Late in the night they passed one of these sitting humans, a hairy-faced male dimly illuminated by a hanging globe of light. He smelled of filth. He seemed asleep, but, as they passed, this human's eyes opened, and fixed on Patch; and the human said, in bad and broken but comprehensible Mammal, 'Hello, squirrel.'

Patch froze, utterly amazed, and Zelina and her seven cats halted as well.

'Hello, squirrel,' the human repeated. The phrase required no pheromones, only noise, the dipping motion of a head, and a scrabbling motion of forelegs. The human's sounds and actions were imperfect but unmistakable.

'Hello, squirrel,' it said again.

'Hello,' Patch replied after a moment. He was ready to run.

'Hello, squirrel.'

'Hello, human.' Patch had not thought he would ever speak those words.

'Squirrel eat food?'

After a moment Patch said, 'I am a little hungry.'

The human seemed confused – and indeed he was, for *hunger* was a concept communicated with pheromones, and humans have long ago lost that part of animal speech.

'Squirrel eat food?' the human repeated.

Patch decided to answer in kind. 'Squirrel eat food.'

The human reached into its ragged coverings, and Patch tensed, but when the hand emerged it held a paper bag that smelled like heaven. The human dipped a hand into the bag and let fall a heap of little seeds onto the walkway.

'Be careful,' Zelina warned Patch. 'It could be a trap. It could be poison.'

'Good food,' the human assured Patch, and began to eat from the bag itself.

Patch stared incredulously at the human. Had the human actually understood Zelina's warning? And the way it was eating – why, this human was eating like a squirrel did, with rapid, twitching, repetitive motions, stopping between bites to look quickly back and forth. This human moved and even smelled a little like an animal, like a creature of instinct, not a creature of thought.

Patch began to eat the seeds. Then he began to devour them. He did not think he had ever tasted anything so wonderful in all his life.

'Try it! Eat!' he told Zelina.

She took a mouthful, crunched, and shrugged; to her it was nothing special. But to Patch it was the finest food he had ever encountered. When he had finished he looked hopefully up to the human, and the human let fall another handful of seeds, and Patch ate until his belly had no room for more.

'Good squirrel,' the human said. 'You stay, good squirrel? You stay?'

'No, I'm sorry,' Patch said, with genuine regret. 'I must go home.'

Home was a pheromone concept too.

The human's face wrinkled. 'Me no stay,' it said. 'Me always go. Me go, me go, me go again. Me always go. You come back, good squirrel. I see you more.'

'I see you more,' Patch agreed.

Almost immediately after they left the strange human behind,

Patch was barely able to believe that the encounter had really happened.

'I didn't think humans could speak to animals at all,' he said to Zelina.

Zelina said, 'I have lived with humans almost all my life, and I have never heard of it happening before.'

Patch thought of Siva the tiger and the 'human brother' Siva had spoken of. He reminded himself to find Daffa the pigeon when he returned to the Center Kingdom, and to find some way to deliver a ball of glass to Siva's human brother.

The sky above them began to slowly brighten, almost imperceptibly, with the first glimmerings of impending dawn. Patch realized how tired he was. Zelina and the largest cat, who was named Alabast, held a brief conference.

'Alabast says we will soon reach a square of trees and grass,' Zelina said to Patch. 'We can sleep there. If we go all through the night that follows, we can reach the Great Avenue before dawn, and your Center Kingdom is only a little beyond.'

Patch did not reply. Instead he sat back on his hindlegs, his eyes suddenly wide and alert, and sniffed the air.

'Patch?' Zelina asked. 'Patch, did you hear me?'

'He's here,' Patch said. 'By the full moon, he's here right now. I can smell him.' He ran a little way along the walkway, his nose to the ground, toward a set of tiled steps that descended into the underground. 'His scent is fresh, he went down there just now!'

'Who was here?' Zelina asked, bemused. 'Who are you talking about?'

Patch said, his voice quiet but passionate: 'Sniffer.'

Then he pursued his enemy's scent down the steps into the underworld.

he underworld was painfully bright. The stairs led down into a large chamber with tiled walls and concrete floors. The ceiling's fast-flickering lights reflected off the white tiles, giving Patch a headache. A line of widely spaced block-shaped metal things, from which spokes and bars protruded, stretched across one end of the chamber; beyond them, Patch saw another strip of concrete floor, and then darkness. A human sat in a tiny boxlike building at the end of the series of metal things. The air down here smelled old and strange and musty, and it was laced with Sniffer's scent.

There was plenty of room between the metal blocks. The area on the other side was a concrete strip that extended for a considerable distance to either side, but ended only a few dozen squirrel-paces beyond the blocks, at a cliff that dropped down into darkness. Another concrete platform was visible on the other side of the dark abyss that smelled of smoke and metal. Pillars were stationed at regular intervals all around this underground space, angular metal pillars that rose from the abyss and circular concrete ones along the platform. Patch didn't like having something solid between himself and the sky, not at all, but Sniffer's scent was fresh, and it led him to his left, along the platform, toward the tiled wall at which it ended. The abyss continued past the platform end, became a tunnel into darkness.

He was stopped suddenly by a horrible noise of grinding and screeching, the most awful thing Patch had ever heard. It grew louder, came closer, until his ears actually hurt. A great wind began to blow. Then lights flickered and a colossal machine emerged from the tunnel. Lightning flashed beneath its spinning metal feet, and its screams were deafening. It was made of a dozen huge, solid-walled, shining metal cages, all linked together in a long line, and through its many windows Patch caught glimpses of a few human shapes. The machine ran on one of four sets of metal rails along the base of the abyss. Patch was very glad that it shrieked past without stopping and soon disappeared into the other end of the tunnel.

He still smelled Sniffer. He also smelled rats: many, many rats.

Patch hesitated. Then he followed Sniffer's scent to the end of the platform. He walked to the edge of the abyss and peered around the corner of the wall, down into the tunnel, and at the farthest edge of his vision, he saw the silhouette of a squirrel surrounded by rats. He heard fragments of voices: 'Birds ... battle ... slaughter ... king ... Ramble.'

Then the squirrel stiffened, sniffed the air, and turned to look straight at Patch.

'By the moon in her stars,' Sniffer said, amazed. 'Patch son of Silver.'

Patch winced at his own stupidity. He should have known that Sniffer's extraordinary nose would soon discover his presence. He realized he had no idea what he was going to do now that he had found Sniffer. A concrete ramp led down into the tunnel, but he certainly didn't intend to charge at Sniffer, not with all those rats beside him, rats with whom Sniffer was obviously conspiring.

Patch heard scuttling sounds from above. He looked up. Something, no, many somethings were moving on the framework of metal girders that hung high above the platform and just below the ceiling. Girders which served as a sky-road for rats. Many, many rats.

Patch turned and ran – but from the other end of the platform, and from little holes in the platform wall to his right, rats were beginning to emerge, huge rats nearly as big as Patch, warping and contorting their bodies to squeeze through the small holes into which a squirrel could never fit. Patch heard rats moving about in the abyss to his left as well.

'Hold him!' a rat voice cried from behind Patch. A familiar rat voice. 'I would speak to this squirrel before he dies.'

A wall of rats formed up across the platform about two-thirds of the way back toward the metal blocks. Patch halted and looked around wildly, seeking some avenue of escape. None was apparent. A river of rats was streaming onto the platform behind him from the tunnel below, with Sniffer among them. There were rats above, rats below, rats on both sides. And he recognized the rat that strutted next to Sniffer, the largest rat he had ever seen. Other rats were squinting and looking away from the lights and tiled walls, but this rat seemed unfazed by their brightness.

'Patch son of Silver,' said Lord Snout. 'You're supposed to be hawkmeat. How is it that you're still alive?'

Patch ignored Snout and looked at Sniffer. 'You led them to Jumper, didn't you? You gave them the food we had all buried so we would starve. You told the hawk where to find me.'

Sniffer looked very uncomfortable.

'Didn't you?' Patch demanded. His voice was brittle with rage and terror. 'Tell me! Tell me, you traitor, murderer, brother to rats!'

'Patch,' Sniffer said, 'you must understand, everything I did was for the greater good. We couldn't go on the way we were. Certain sacrifices had to be made. And those sacrifices included lives. None of this was my idea, it was the eldest, he came to me, he showed me the necessity. Necessity is a cruel and terrible thing. But it cannot be avoided.'

They stared at each other in silence for a moment.

'Enough talk,' Snout said. 'I suppose it doesn't matter how you came to be down here. I promised you some time ago that I would eat your eyes from your skull. Now –'

Then Snout fell silent and took two sudden steps back. He was staring past Patch's shoulder.

Patch turned around just in time to see the charge of Zelina and her seven cats. The wall of rats between Patch and the cats broke almost immediately, and suddenly the platform was a screeching, squeaking, maelstrom of rats, running panicked from the cats, scurrying past and around Patch as if he were an inanimate obstacle. For a few moments Patch couldn't move, the rats were too thick around him.

'Hold!' Snout bellowed. 'In the name of the King Beneath, attack! Attack and kill them all!'

The rats began to re-form around Snout just as the cats reached Patch, their mouths and claws smeared with rat blood. They didn't have time to run. Snout countercharged, Sniffer beside him, and the rat army followed.

Patch gaped at the rat nearest him, the rat running straight toward him, fangs out and glistening. For a moment he was too frozen with fear to fight.

Then Alabast leapt into the oncoming wave of rats. The big

white cat raked his claws across the eyes of the rat coming at Patch, while biting another and knocking two more off their feet with his pale and massive body, and the battle turned into a yowling, screaming melee, a chaos of blood and fangs. Patch howled too, with growing fury as much as fear, and when another rat was thrust toward Patch by the current of rat-flesh behind him, Patch lunged forward and bit its throat. His mouth filled with sour blood, and Patch immediately let go and spit it out. The rat screeched with pain and fled.

Through the chaos Patch saw Sniffer not far away, and Patch felt his rage blossom within him like a flower, and expand into an awful and terrible thing like a burning sun in his heart. He charged through the sea of squalling rats toward the squirrel that had once been his friend. He was close, so close, he could see Sniffer's shocked and frightened eyes, and Patch opened his mouth to bite and charged faster –

Something white-hot burned into Patch's left hindleg. He screamed and turned to see Snout's yellow fangs sunk deep in his flesh. Then Alabast loomed above them, and Snout released Patch and fled from the big white cat. The rat army followed their leader and pulled back from the battle. But they soon re-formed a short distance away.

A dozen rat corpses lay on the floor, and a dozen more who still lived but could not move twitched in agony, and Patch and all the cats still stood. But there were teeming masses of rats on either side, and all the cats were bleeding, most from multiple wounds. It was apparent that Patch and the cats could never win this battle, nor fight their way back outside before being overrun.

HOME

In the blood and terror of the battle Patch had not noticed a faint change in the character of the light around them. Now he saw an intensifying glow in the tunnel's distant depths, like a fire that has found new fuel. A powerful wind began to blow from the tunnel, ruffling the fur on Patch's tail. A huge noise of clanking and clattering grew audible, and then louder, and then so loud neither squirrel nor rat nor cat could hear a thing as a chain of shining solid-walled cages the size of human houses shrieked out of the darkness, so close to the platform edge that this machine on rails was like a steel wall moving along the length of the platform. Light shone from the windows that lined the cages. The machine screeched and shuddered to a halt. Then dozens of human-sized doors slid open along the length of the platform, revealing the cages' painfully bright interior, lined with benches occupied by a few slumped humans.

'Hurry!' Zelina cried, and leapt into the nearest cage.

Despite being surrounded by an army of rats this option had not even occurred to Patch. But the other cats followed Zelina, and Patch scrambled in behind them. Snout and Sniffer approached the open doors uncertainly, followed by their army – but the several humans within leapt to their feet and began to cry out. The rats hesitated at the threshold.

A strange two-note chime sounded, and the doors hissed shut, leaving the rats outside.

The cage began to rattle forward, and they all staggered a little. Patch almost lost his balance, and had an awful memory of sliding about on top of the big automobile that had carried them to the island, but then the cage's motion stabilized; it shook violently, and made awful grinding noises, but was steady enough that he could remain standing. The humans in the cage approached Patch and the cats, speaking to one another excitedly, but did not come too near.

The cage slowed, and Patch and the cats skidded forward a little, and then it stopped, and the doors opened again – but this platform looked different, and there were no rats on it. Another human walked into the cage and stopped dead, staring at Patch and the cats. Then the two-note chime sounded again, and the doors hissed shut, and the cage rattled forward.

Patch's leg began to hurt again where Snout had bitten him. The excitement of battle had doused the pain for a time, but now it began to throb like fire, and it hurt even worse when he had to use the strength of his legs to stay upright as the cage once more decelerated and stopped at a different platform.

'We should get out!' Alabast cried to Zelina. His pale body was streaked with blood and his muscles were rigid with strain.

Zelina stepped toward an open door and sniffed the air delicately. Like all the cats she was bleeding from several places, but none of her wounds seemed serious. 'Not yet,' she said. 'I remember this. This is a *train*. This was how I traveled to the palace, when I was a kitten. I was so frightened. Not yet.'

Several stops later, when Patch – with his badly bitten leg – was beginning to wonder how long he could stand on the floor of this shaking, wobbling, accelerating and decelerating 'train', Zelina sniffed the air again, pricked up her ears, and said, 'Here!'

They emerged onto another platform, passed through another line of strange metal human-things, and climbed a long series of stairs. They passed two staring humans, but Patch was so tired and drained, and his leg hurt so much, that he barely noticed. All he could think about was how much he wanted to be under the sky again.

Finally there were no more stairs. Patch tottered wearily behind the cats, along yet another concrete walkway. His head hurt and he felt dizzy. He was only barely aware that above them the sky was streaked with dawn, and he nearly ran into Alabast before realizing that they had stopped at a particularly wide highway.

'By the moon,' Zelina said softly. 'The Great Avenue.'

Patch looked up from his pain and exhaustion, along the endless silhouettes of mountains that loomed over the Great Avenue. It did not seem so different from any other wide highway – except it was divided, down the middle, by long strips of earth in which flowers and bushes grew. This living spine of the road was interrupted wherever a smaller highway intersected the Great Avenue, but it was still a welcome sight.

Patch sniffed the air. He smelled cat-blood, and concrete, and mountains, and automobiles. He smelled the flowers that grew along the Great Avenue. But also, faintly, in the western breeze, Patch smelled a rich melange of earth, water, trees, and living scents. It was a smell he knew immediately, a scent he knew in his bones.

'The Center Kingdom!' Patch cried, his wounds and weariness momentarily forgotten. 'I can smell it! We are near!'

'My palace is just there, up the Great Avenue,' Zelina said. 'I can see it. I can see my palace, Patch. We are home. We are home!'

They stared at each other in amazement.

It was Alabast who broke the silence. 'What would you have us do, your majesty? We have brought you here, as you commanded. Shall we escort you now to your palace?'

Zelina looked at him and considered. 'No. You have served me well and bravely. I have no further need of you now. But I would have you stay near the Great Avenue for seven days, and return to this spot each morning, in case I need command you again. Until then, go and rest and heal, all of you. I must return to my palace alone.'

One at a time, the seven cats bowed their heads and loped away.

'Can't they help you fight the cats who exiled you?' Patch asked, perplexed.

Zelina looked at Patch silently for what felt like a long time.

Then she sighed and said, 'It was no cat who exiled me.'

'Then who –'

'It was my human attendant's male child,' Zelina said. 'One day when she was absent, he came to the palace, captured me, carried me away in an automobile, and took me to the wilderness where you found me. I don't know why. I cannot imagine why. Excepting the journey when I was a kitten, and the metal stairs outside the window, I had never been outside the palace before. I was so frightened when you found me, Patch. So frightened and in such despair. I knew there was no hope for me there. I knew I would die. I had heard many times the myth of the Queen of All Cats, and alone in that broken shell I took courage from telling myself I would die as she would die. I even told myself I *was* the Queen of All Cats.'

'But you are,' Patch said, confused.

'No, Patch. That was only a story I told myself. I even allowed myself to believe it, to ease my dying. And then you came. And you said you would find your way back here. And I allowed myself to hope it might be possible. And by the moon, beyond all hope, here we are.'

'You're not the Queen of All Cats?' Patch asked, still confused.

'There is no Queen of All Cats. The Queen of All Cats is a myth. A legend of a lonely cat who travels through the world, unknown and unloved, but who is truly the queen of us all, and who one day will return to lead us. She isn't real. She was never real. I was never a queen. It was just a story.'

'But the other cats think you're a queen. I thought you were a queen. You seem like a queen. If everyone acts like it's real, then it's not just a story.'

'There's a difference,' Zelina said.

'What difference?'

Zelina paused. At length she said, 'These are subtle questions, Patch. Day is coming, and soon the highways will be busy. We should both go home.'

'I guess you're right,' Patch agreed.

Despite his gladness at being almost home, Patch felt a painful twinge of sadness at the thought that he would no longer be traveling with Zelina.

'I owe you my life, Patch son of Silver,' Zelina said.

'I owe you mine too.'

They looked at each other.

'But I still think jumping onto the big death machine that crossed the bridge was the worst idea any animal has ever had,' Patch said, and both of them laughed. 'You should come visit me in the Center Kingdom. Ask any squirrel, they'll know how to find me.'

'I will,' Zelina said. 'Now that I have left my palace once I think I will leave it again. The world is not all frightening. Some of it is really quite wonderful.'

'Good. Then I'll see you soon.'

'I'll see you soon,' Zelina agreed, 'my friend.'

They looked at each other a moment longer, breathing in one another's scent. Then, at the very same moment, they turned and went their separate ways. Patch was excited to be going home to the Center Kingdom. But he wished Zelina was coming with him.

It wasn't far to the Center Kingdom. But by the time Patch saw it, the leg bitten by Snout was hurting terribly. He knew, as he stood with only a single highway between himself and his home, that he should feel gladdened with triumph and excitement; but his whole leg hurt very badly, and he felt dizzy and sick as well, and all he could think of was his need to rest. Although there were few automobiles on the highway he was limping so slowly that he was barely able to scamper across. Shortly afterwards he was walking once again on the grassy earth of his home.

There was an elm tree near the edge of the kingdom. Patch forced himself to climb its trunk. By the time he got to a flattish crook between two big branches, his head was pounding with pain, he was walking on only three legs, and he was so dizzy that the world wobbled around him with every step. And despite the rising sun he felt cold. But at least he was up a tree and safe.

Patch turned to the wound on his leg, planning to lick it clean. He was shocked by what he saw. His whole leg was red and swollen, and an awful black mucus was oozing from the wound.

This was no mere bite wound, Patch realized. Snout's bite had been poisonous.

Patch didn't know what to do. He wanted to run, to seek help, but he was too weak to move. Soon he was too weak even to stand. His headache grew steadily worse, and the world steadily colder and blurrier, until finally Patch collapsed into the crook of the elm tree.

He understood dimly that the poison was killing him; that he was home, but he was dying. The last thing he felt was the rough texture of elm bark against his face. He had a sudden vivid memory of the scent of his mother, Silver.

Then the world went dark.

PART TWO

V. JOURNEY TO THE NORTH

WHITE

atch howled with pain. Something was tearing at his left hindleg, his poisoned leg, the leg that already burned as if with fire. And there was nothing he could do about it. He was too weak to move, too powerless to do anything but suffer.

'I'm sorry,' a gentle voice said. 'I'm so sorry. I have to open it to let the poison drain. It's your only chance.'

Then teeth ripped at his flesh again, and Patch screamed again, until his mind could withstand the pain no longer, and he passed once again into darkness.

The next time he awoke there was food in front of him, a soft, moist maple bud so close that all he had to do was reach out a paw and sweep it into his mouth. But he couldn't move. His body would not follow any commands at all. He was paralyzed, frozen in place like a statue. His left hindleg was made of agony, and his breath was fast and shallow.

'You're awake,' the gentle voice said, and something hopped into the elm bark before him. Another squirrel. Patch tried to see who it was, but he could not even move or focus his eyes. All he could make out was the other squirrel's white paw as it gently nudged the maple bud into his mouth. Patch couldn't even chew, but the bud slowly dissolved in his mouth, as his mind dissolved into darkness.

The next time he awoke to teeth ripping and slashing at his left hindleg again, and it hurt even worse than before, but he could not even scream. This time the merciful darkness did not come. The pain seemed like it would never end.

'I'm sorry,' the gentle voice said. 'I'm so sorry.'

The next time he awoke he was shaking uncontrollably, and the other squirrel had to work patiently for some time before it was able to nudge the maple bud into Patch's mouth. But his leg hurt a little less.

The next time he awoke he was able to reach out feebly for the maple bud and flower petals before him and eat them himself as the gentle voice said, 'Good, good.'

The next time he awoke he ate a whole acorn that had been left beside him, and was able to rouse himself enough to look down at his wounded leg. It was still grossly swollen and painful, but it was no longer bleeding black ooze. The other squirrel was nowhere in sight, but he could smell her, his senses were returning too.

The next time he awoke he smelled her nearby, and he was ravenously hungry, he had to devour both the acorns beside him before he was able to think of anything else. After eating he thought that if he had to, he might be able to stand, although the effort would surely be ruinously painful.

'You're better,' said the gentle voice from above him. 'You're going to live.'

And a small female squirrel with pure white fur, pink eyes, and a half-severed tail descended a branch and stood next to him in the wide crook of the elm tree in which Patch had lain for days.

'Who are you?' Patch asked, amazed.

'I am White daughter of Streak, of the Runner clan. Who are you that asks?'

'I am Patch son of Silver, of the Seeker clan, of the Treetops tribe,' Patch said. 'What is your tribe?'

After an uncomfortable moment White said, 'I have none.'

'Oh,' Patch said. 'Of course. I'm sorry.'

In his fever he had asked a profoundly thoughtless question. Albino squirrels were believed tainted, cursed by the moon. They were cast out from their families and tribes as soon as they reached adulthood, and shunned for the rest of their lives. They were very rare. Patch had seen only one before in all his life, an older female, when exploring the territory of the Northern tribe, at the very edge of the Center Kingdom.

'What happened to your tail?' Patch asked, figuring he might as well get all of the awkward questions out of the way.

'I lost it in the war.'

'The war? What war?'

White looked at him as if he was crazy. 'I don't think you're well yet,' she said. 'You should rest. Sometimes the blackblood disease ruins your memories.'

'My memory is fine,' Patch objected.

'Do you remember being bitten?'

'Of course. By Lord Snout. In the underworld beneath the mountains. Then the cats saved me, and we escaped in the train.'

'You poor thing. You're delirious. You need to sleep.'

'I am not delirious! But I should have remembered the war. The turtle, the Old One, he told me there was war. He said Redeye is lord of the Meadow, and calls himself king. Is that true?'

'That is true,' White admitted.

'And the war is not over?'

She hesitated. 'I don't know. I haven't heard of any fighting since the Battle of the Meadow. King Thorn has retreated to the Ramble, and Redeye has stayed in the Meadow. They say both armies are readying for another battle, and both kings look to see what the Northern tribe will do.'

'The Battle of the Meadow? What happened there? How were you in it?'

White sighed. 'Both answers are sad and stupid … I heard that King Thorn was calling all squirrels to him. Even outcasts like me. I thought this was my one chance to be accepted, so I joined his army. The other squirrels pushed me, and bit me, and called me awful things, but I stayed. I thought if I proved myself in battle they would be my friends. It's so strange, when I think of it now. The more they tormented me, the more I wanted their friendship. When we went to the Meadow and found ourselves fighting an army of rats as well as squirrels, many of Thorn's army fled. But I stayed and fought. I killed three rats and a Meadow squirrel, and I escaped to the Ramble. Many didn't. Some who did had the blackblood disease, like you. I learned how to help them. But the squirrels in my war-clan, especially the ones who had been cowards, they said I was the coward who had run away. They said it was my fault that half the war-clan died. They said I was a traitor and a spy for Redeye. They attacked me, I lost my tail, I barely escaped with my life. I wanted to go back to the North, but the journey is too dangerous. I came here, where neither the Meadow nor the Ramble tribe come. And when I found you dying, Patch son of Silver, I considered a long time before deciding to try to save you, because no other squirrel has ever done anything for me.'

'I'm sorry,' Patch said.

'So am I.'

'What of my tribe? What of the Treetops?'

White looked at him sadly. 'I came too late, didn't I? Your memories and mind have been ravaged.'

'My memories and mind are fine,' Patch said. 'I've just been away from the Center Kingdom for some time now.'

'Away? No one goes *away* from the Center Kingdom. Where were you?'

'Everywhere,' Patch said with feeling.

'How did you get there?'

'I was carried away by –' Patch stopped, realizing that the story of Karmerruk the hawk might not be a particularly good one with which to convince White of his sound mind. 'It doesn't matter. When I left, it was still winter, and there was no war. What has happened to the Treetops?'

After a moment, White said, in a voice scarcely more than a whisper, 'If what you say is true, Patch son of Silver, if you truly did not know, then I am sorry to be the one who tells you. The Treetops are no more. So many were sworn to the Meadow in the winter, and so many who did not swear were killed, that only a handful of survivors remain, too few to be called a tribe.'

Patch stared at her. 'No more? That's crazy. That can't be right. Where did you hear this? Some chipmunk told you? No. I don't believe it.'

'I'm sorry,' White said.

'My whole tribe can't be gone,' Patch said. He suddenly felt gravely tired, and very heavy, like he was made of stone. 'You must be wrong.'

'Sleep,' White said. 'Things will seem better when you're stronger.'

But they both knew that wasn't true.

hen Patch awoke he could stand and walk on three legs. He could not yet put weight on his left hindleg without provoking a wave of pain, but the leg's swelling was much reduced. And he was ravenous. White had left him a small heap of moist flower bulbs and ginkgo nuts, and he devoured them greedily, but they barely took the edge off his hunger.

As he finished, he heard a flutter of wings behind him, and an amazed, familiar voice said in Bird: 'Patch? Is that you?'

Patch turned to see his bluejay friend, Toro.

'Patch!' Toro exclaimed. 'It's been so long, I thought you were dead!'

'I nearly was,' Patch said, delighted. 'Many times. Toro, you don't know how good it is to see you.'

'I'm glad to see you too. What happened to you?'

'Do you know a hawk named Karmerruk?' Patch asked.

Toro shivered. 'Yes. He's what bluejays talk about when we want to scare one another.'

'He caught me, but he didn't kill me, because ... well, it's complicated. The point is, he took me far away, and it's taken me since then to come back. And now, my people are at war, my tribe is gone, I don't know what's happened to everyone.'

'I have noticed squirrels behaving strangely,' Toro said thoughtfully. 'I've seen squirrels fighting, mostly in little groups, but there was a huge battle some days ago in the Great Meadow. There must have been hundreds and hundreds of squirrels fighting each other. It looked like the ground had fur. And there were rats fighting too, in the middle of the day! Nobody's ever seen anything like it. And now half the kingdom is empty of squirrels.'

'I suppose it's good for you.'

'It was. There was so much food out there, some bluejays were getting so fat they were having trouble taking off. But not anymore. There are crows all over the Kingdom now, masses of them, invading our trees and eating our food. Nobody's ever heard of that happening before either.'

'Did they come from the east?' Patch asked, thinking of the trees full of crows he had seen in the Hidden Kingdom.

'They did. And they –'

'Go away from him!' a no-longer-gentle voice screeched in clumsy Bird, and a furry white blur launched itself up the elm tree and at Toro. The bluejay took to the air just in time to avoid White's charge.

'No, don't!' Patch cried out. 'He's a friend!'

'A friend? He – Patch, you're not well. He's a bluejay! He was going to eat your food!'

'No, he wasn't. He really is a friend.' Patch looked up to Toro, perched on a high branch, and switched to Bird. 'It's okay, Toro, you can come back down.'

After a moment Toro fluttered down and landed on a nearer branch, keeping his distance from White, who for her part remained equally suspicious of the bluejay.

'Who is she?' Toro asked.

'She's taking care of me. A rat bit me and I was poisoned. I'm not well yet. I owe her my life.'

'I thought you looked weak and skinny. You should eat more. Want me to bring you some acorns?'

'That,' Patch said, 'would be wonderful.'

'Coming right up.' Toro flapped his wings and flew away.

White stared at Patch with amazement. 'You speak Bird?'

'I do.'

'You're friends with a bluejay?'

'I am.'

After a moment she said, 'Yesterday you said that you were in the underworld beneath the mountains when Lord Snout himself bit you, and you were saved by cats.'

'That's exactly what happened.'

'You don't *smell* mad. Or delirious.'

'I'm not,' Patch said. 'I've just had rather a lot of things happen to me lately.'

'I see. Including blackblood disease. Well, you won't have to go through that again. If you have it once, and you're one of the few that survives, you become immune.'

'I'm glad to hear it,' Patch said with feeling.

White smiled at him wistfully. Then she looked down to the ground below and asked, 'Well, now you're home, what do you think you'll do?'

'I don't know. You say my tribe is gone … I don't know what to do.'

'You can stay here as long as you want, if you like. My drey is a little higher up. There's plenty of space in it. I mean, just until you figure things out.'

'That's very kind of you,' Patch said. 'But I do have my own drey. If no one else has taken it. And I need to find out what happened to my friends and family.'

'Oh. Yes. Of course. I'm sorry to – I didn't mean – I know you don't want to share a drey with an albino half-tail, I didn't mean to offend you, I'm so stupid, I don't know what I was –'

'Offend me?' Patch asked, bemused. 'White, I owe you my life. And after the things I've seen and done on my way home, believe me, I don't care about your fur or your tail. I'm an outcast too. I mean, if you're right, I don't even have a tribe to be outcast *from*. I'd like to stay. But I have to try to find my family and friends.'

'Oh,' White said, sounding relieved. She paused. 'I understand. Well, not really. I've never had family. Or friends. But I can imagine.'

Patch said, 'You have a friend now.'

She looked at him and smiled.

There was a fluttering of wings and Toro landed, keeping Patch between himself and White. He released the meaty acorn he held in his claws. Patch caught it before it rolled off the elm tree and devoured it greedily. There was no conversation while he ate.

When Patch looked up, his belly now half-satisfied, he saw Toro staring silently at the sky, as still as a statue. Perplexed, Patch turned to look at White. She too was staring silently upward; she too had gone still; and deep terror was etched on her face.

Patch lifted his head to see what they were looking at.

A red-tailed hawk perched on the branch directly above them.

'Patch son of Silver,' Karmerruk said. 'We meet again.'

ave you come to break your oath?' Patch asked.

'No. Nor will I prey on either of your friends.'

Toro relaxed slightly.

'It's all right,' Patch said to White. 'This is Karmerruk. He's ... an acquaintance.'

White's pink eyes were very wide as she stared at Patch, and then at the hawk, and back at Patch again.

'Then what do you want?' Patch asked, switching back to Bird. 'Have you come to carry me to the Ocean Kingdom again?'

'No, Patch son of Silver. On the contrary, I was very glad when I looked down at this elm and saw you had returned to the Center Kingdom. I never thought you would be able to return over so great a distance. I salute your strength and courage. As I said before, you have the heart of a hawk. But that is not why I have come. I have come to ask you a favor.'

'A favor?' Patch asked, bewildered. 'What can I possibly do for you?'

'You are a mammal who speaks Bird better than some birds I know. A rare talent, Patch, and a valuable one. I wish to communicate with your king.'

'Which king?'

'The true king. King Thorn.'

'But you work –' Patch stopped himself, remembering their last conversation. 'But you are associated with Snout.'

'No longer. On the contrary. I swear to you by the blood of my nestlings that I seek the death of that rat lord. I have, ever since I began to learn some worrisome truths and terrible rumors. Ever since I saved your life.'

Patch thought *saved your life* was an extremely skewed description of their previous encounter, but supposed there was no gain to be had from arguing. 'What truths?'

'The truths I would communicate to your king.'

'You may as well tell them to me. You're going to have to anyway.'

Karmerruk paused. 'I suppose that's true. I'm sure you know

already that the rats have conspired with the rebel squirrels against King Thorn. What you may not know is that the rats are also killing any mice they find, and chipmunks too. Not for food. Killing them and leaving their carcasses to rot.'

'Why would they do that?' Patch asked, surprised.

'I don't know. But I *do* know that I do not like having my food slaughtered by anyone but me. I know I do not like the terrible rumors I have begun to hear in the wind, that the King Beneath is real, and the Queen of All Cats has arisen.' Patch twitched. 'I know I do not like the monstrous flock of crows that has occupied so much of this kingdom. I do not yet know what lies at the heart of all this, but I know that I would speak with your King Thorn. I need you to be my translator.'

'Can't you find someone else?'

'Someone else?' Karmerruk was offended. 'I give you the opportunity to be a voice that speaks for hawks and royalty, and you ask me to find someone else? There is no one else, Patch. I have looked.'

Patch sighed. 'All right.'

'Excellent. Then I shall take you to the Ramble –'

'No!' Patch exclaimed. 'I'm sick. I've been poisoned. I won't have you carrying me around like a mouse you're about to eat. I'll walk to the Ramble when I'm ready.'

'When you're ready? And when will that be?'

Patch considered. 'Maybe tomorrow. Maybe the next day.'

'Maybe tomorrow? The decisive battle could come today! We dare not wait!'

'Then go find someone else.'

'I told you,' Karmerruk said darkly, 'there is no one else. I will not have your stubborn selfishness stand in my way!'

'If you take me there now I'll be no use. I nearly died of the black-blood disease. I have no strength.'

Karmerruk looked at him. At length he said, 'One day, Patch son of Silver. I will give you one day. You will go tomorrow or I will carry you there myself.'

Patch sighed. 'All right.'

Karmerruk frowned. Then he beat his great wings and soared into the air. The backwash knocked Toro off the elm tree, and the bluejay had to dive down, circle around, and fly back up to the branch.

'What happened?' White asked.

Patch translated.

'Oh, no,' White said. 'You can't. You see what King Thorn's soldiers did to me. They're awful, awful! And besides, you're much too weak to travel!'

'I'm much better,' Patch said, but although what he said was true – he had gotten stronger even since waking up – he had to admit that he was still weak enough that the prospect of traveling all the way to the Ramble was quite daunting.

TOWARD THE RAMBLE

arly the next morning, six days after he had collapsed on the very edge of death, Patch descended slowly back to earth while White watched anxiously from above. When he finally reached the ground he waved good-bye with his tail and set out across the grass toward the wild Ramble in the heart of the Center Kingdom. He walked with only a slight limp, but he knew climbing would be painful and running impossible.

The morning was bright and beautiful. Despite Patch's many worries, despite the terrible news of Redeye's victory in the Battle of the Meadow and the destruction of the entire Treetops tribe, despite his fears for the fates of Twitch and Tuft and Brighteyes and above all his mother, Silver, it was wonderful to be home again, breathing the rich spring air, walking across the green fields and beneath the majestic trees of the Center kingdom. Patch felt almost like he had never left, as if his perilous journey across half the world had been nothing but a terrible nightmare.

There were no other animals around. This corner of the kingdom was always quiet. The Dungeon was nearby; and animals stayed away from the Dungeon as if its steel walls might reach out and swallow them if they came too near. Even Patch, who had spent much of his life roving around the kingdom in restless exploration, had been here only a few times before, and had not remained long.

He walked northward, toward the Ramble, until he caught a whiff of the unforgettable smell of the Dungeon: the mingled scents of dozens of alien creatures, all stinking of madness and despair. Uneasy, Patch detoured west rather than come any nearer. His wounded leg was aching like a bad cramp by the time he reached the stately procession of massive elm trees that led to the Ramble. These elm trees formed Patch's favorite sky-road in all the Center Kingdom – but he was earthbound by his wounded leg, reduced to trudging on the grass beneath.

The colonnade of elms ended at a concrete plaza adorned by various manmade constructions. On the other side was one of the great automobile highways that ran right across the Center Kingdom. It was one of those days when humans had invaded the Center Kingdom in droves, and he had to plan his route carefully. Humans no longer held any great fear for him, but some of them had dogs. Patch went around the plaza, staying on grass. There were no automobiles, but he still had to wait before crossing the highway. A huge horse was passing, moving steadily despite the burden it dragged, a huge wooden box on wheels. Three humans rode atop the box.

Patch stared up at the huge animal as it clopped past. He was always awed by horses' enormous size. Most said they were the largest animals in the Center Kingdom – though Patch had heard whispers that within the Dungeon were pale and gargantuan predators from the uttermost North, bigger than any horse, imprisoned by walls the size of tall trees. Once Patch had dismissed those rumors, but since his encounter with Siva the tiger, he was no longer so certain in his disbelief.

Karmerruk had spoken of another rumor: that the King Beneath was real. *The king in whose name you and all your kind will die and be devoured,* Lord Snout had said, on the day that Patch had been unlucky enough to meet him. Was it the King Beneath who had sent the rat army and fomented this war among squirrels? Was he responsible for the crows, too?

It was wonderful to be home: but if what White had said was true, if his tribe was gone, and if he failed to find his family and friends – could a place without any of those things really be his home?

Patch told himself to stop gnawing on such thoughts. The King Beneath was a myth. White was wrong about the Treetops. He would find Silver, and Twitch, and Brighteyes, and Tuft. He would go to King Thorn and help Karmerruk to kill Redeye and Snout and Sniffer, and then the war would be over, and peace would return.

Past the highway he continued up a wide and grassy hill dotted with cherry trees and pockmarked with huge granite outcroppings. The bright sun was approaching its zenith by the time Patch crested the summit and looked across the Narrow Sea to the raw and wild Ramble, the sprawling heart of the Center Kingdom. He frowned when he saw that the trees of the Ramble were thick with crows. Crows were harmless, as far as he knew, but it didn't seem right that they had occupied King Thorn's territory.

He began to move northwest, intending to circumnavigate the sea and approach the Ramble from the west; but he had not gone far when he encountered a cold northeasterly wind that blew directly to him from across the Narrow Sea. This wind stopped Patch in mid-step for a long moment, as if he had turned to stone. It carried a stench of blood and death so overpowering that his eyes watered and his ears seemed to ring with dissonant noise.

Something was wrong in the Ramble, terribly wrong.

THE RAMBLE

atch's instinct, strangely, was not to flee in terror from the stench of slaughter; rather, he felt compelled to rush immediately into the Ramble, as if he were desperately needed. Instead of continuing the long way, around the water, he changed his course and trotted straight for the bridge that spanned the Narrow Sea.

A mere moon-cycle earlier, no squirrel in all the Center Kingdom would have dared that bridge no matter what the provocation. It was a human pathway. But in that time, Patch had traveled along human highways, escaped a locked steel cage, slept on a metal staircase, perched on a moving automobile, and ridden with humans through underground tunnels. He saw no dogs nearby; and while the gross corpulence of humans still unnerved him, this was overwhelmed by his powerful urge to *hurry*. He crossed the wooden bridge as fast as he could on his pain-streaked leg, heedless of the dozen humans who stared, amazed, as Patch wove his way between them.

Once across he left the human trails and followed a dry watercourse up a hill, heading for the huge willow tree that housed the court of King Thorn. The thick reek of blood and battle was so intense that he had to breathe through his mouth, but he sensed no other signs of violence. The silence was absolute but for the skittering crows and a few clumsy humans, and the Ramble's dense tangle of close-grown trees, granite mounds, steep ravines, high grasses and thick underbrush was like being surrounded by opaque walls.

Then Patch saw a group of crows squatting on a rock, clustered so close together that they looked like a single squirming knot of black feathers. Trickling bloodstains were visible beneath their skeletal feet. The grass and bushes beyond them shuddered with spasmodic motion; there were animals moving within.

Patch plunged into the grassy undergrowth, fighting his way through dense brush and fallen branches. He soon came upon five crows arrayed in a tight circle, eating something. A dead squirrel. Beyond them, another three crows pecked at the corpse of a rat. The ground was damp with blood. The crows interrupted their feeding just long enough to glance up at Patch with black and shining eyes, and then returned to their carrion feast. Patch hesitated a moment, not knowing what to say or do, then pushed his way around and past the feeding crows, deeper into the thick grass, moving fast and blindly. He could hardly see more than a tail-length in any direction, but he passed a dozen squirrels and rats en route to the willow tree. All were dead and covered with crows.

Once at the willow, he climbed desperately, hardly noticing the stabbing pains in his poisoned leg. His heartbeats felt like thunderclaps, and his head buzzed with panic. When he climbed out onto the pale bark of the first branch, he looked down onto a field of carnage. Shifting clots of crows were visible as far as he could see, feeding on scores – no, hundreds – of corpses. More crows lined the branches of the Ramble's trees, waiting their turn, while their kin below gorged themselves on the dead until they could eat no further.

123

There was a crow perched only a tail-length away from Patch. It was even blacker than those Patch had seen in the Hidden Kingdom, so dark that it seemed more a bird-shaped piece of the night than a real animal.

'What happened here?' Patch asked in Bird. 'When?'

It turned its head toward Patch, fixed him with its blank and glossy eyes, smiled, and said nothing.

Patch took a step toward it. 'Tell me what happened!'

The crow's dry cackle sounded like the splintering of dead bones. It spread its wings, stepped off the branch, and flew away.

'Help,' a soft voice gasped from above, a squirrel's voice. 'Oh, light of the moon, help me, they will eat me alive.'

TAILDANCER

atch looked up and saw faltering motion in the branches above, obscured by the long green curtains of the willow tree's leaves. He took a deep breath, gritted his teeth against the agony in his leg, and climbed up the willow's trunk. In the crook where a big branch met the trunk, two crows were pecking at an animal that lay twitching and gasping. It was so covered in blood, its face and fur were so badly torn, that it took Patch a moment to recognize it as a squirrel.

'Get away from there!' he shouted in Bird, and charged at the crows. His bad leg buckled beneath him, and he almost fell, but the ferocity of his cry drove away the black birds; they leapt away from the willow and glided off to find other prey.

'Help me,' the squirrel groaned. She was young, barely adult. 'Oh, please, help.'

Patch knew at a glance that her wounds were mortal. He saw bones and organs through the many rents in her fur.

'I'm sorry,' he said.

'I don't want to die. This can't be my time. I'm too young.'

Patch didn't say anything.

'Who are you?' she asked.

'I am Patch son of Silver, of the Seeker clan, of the Treetops tribe.

Who are you that asks?'

'I am Taildancer daughter of Shine, of the Runner clan, of the Meadow tribe.'

'The *Meadow* tribe? But this is the Ramble – what happened here? When?'

'War,' Taildancer said. 'Last night. There was a battle. It was awful. We attacked the Ramble. I didn't want to. None of us wanted to. But they made us.'

'Who?'

'King Redeye, and Sniffer, and the rats. We had to obey. They only give food to squirrels who fight. So many of the Meadow have starved.'

Patch blinked with confusion. 'Starved? But it's spring! There's food everywhere!'

'No,' she said. 'They take it all. We have to give whatever we find to the rats and the Gobblers, and they guard it, we're only allowed to eat what they give us. They kill squirrels who keep food, or who bury nuts, or sometimes just for going somewhere alone. Sometimes for no reason at all. It isn't just the rats. Other squirrels, Redeye's clan, the Gobblers, they spy on the rest of us, they tell the rats everything.'

Patch stared at her in silent horror.

'We didn't mean for this to happen. We just thought a Meadow squirrel should be king. We thought the Treetops didn't have any food because they were lazy and wasteful, so they should join the Meadow. Redeye said we were the greatest tribe, and we believed him. We thought we would bring every squirrel together and end all the rivalries. We thought it would make things better for everyone. Where did it go so wrong? How did everything become so awful?'

Patch had no answer.

'They made us attack last night, in the dark,' Taildancer said. Her voice was growing weaker. 'There were owls. We surprised them, they were sleeping. We beat them, they ran away to the North. We thought the battle was over. We'd taken their trees. But then the rats came after every squirrel who was left. Meadow, Ramble, they didn't care. There were so many of them. I killed three but there were so many. All I could hear was screaming, everywhere below, I thought it would drive me mad. Then it was quiet for a little while. Then the sun rose, and the crows came, and the screaming started again. It's quiet now, though, isn't it, Patch son of Silver? It's peaceful.'

'Yes,' Patch whispered. 'It's peaceful.'

'I'm glad you found me. This is my time, isn't it? I'm glad I'm not alone.'

Taildancer's one remaining eye closed and did not reopen. Patch stayed next to her for a long time, watching her motionless form. Then, wincing with the pain in his leg, he climbed to the very top of the mighty willow.

Standing on a branch so slender it threatened to break beneath his weight, he looked around at the crow-laden trees of the Ramble, at the green Center Kingdom. He was high above the stink of blood and war, and the treetop air was clear and clean. He could smell the Great Sea to the north. He even caught the scent of King Thorn himself. That was not surprising; the King had, after all, lived in this tree. What amazed Patch, what so surprised him that he nearly fell, was the faintest whiff, the thinnest hint, of another squirrel as well.

Patch sniffed the air again and again. He wondered if perhaps his mind was betraying his senses, mixing hope and reality into delusion. But in the end he could not deny what his nose was telling him. Either he had gone mad – or his mother, Silver, had stood on this very branch, not so long ago.

The sun was halfway toward the horizon by the time Patch climbed painfully back down the great willow and began to make his way northeast through the blood-soaked hills of the Ramble. If King Thorn and Silver were still alive, they would be in the North. There was no other safe place left in all the Center Kingdom.

Patch limped numbly onwards, trying not to think about what he had just seen and smelled and heard, as the shadows lengthened around him. He wished he had stayed with White. He was so dazed, his mind so distant from the world, that he did not realize he was surrounded until it was too late.

here were four of them, big squirrels, well-fed. Their faces and fur were slashed and scarred and darkly stained with blood, they wore expressions of contorted rage and hate, and they had caught Patch between two cedar trees on the slope of a hill above a human highway. He felt a sick, sinking feeling in his gut. This was trouble, bad trouble, he knew it already. And there was no way out. He looked up to the sky, hoping; but neither Toro nor Karmerruk was there to help.

'Who are you?' the largest of them demanded, a squirrel almost as big and strong as Patch's friend Twitch.

'I'm just walking,' Patch said, avoiding the question. 'Is something wrong?'

'Who are you?' the big squirrel repeated angrily. 'Are you of the Ramble or the Meadow?'

'Rat bite,' growled another of the squirrels, a relatively small one with a bloody socket where her left eye should have been. 'I know my bites, that's no squirrel bite, that's a rat bite on his leg, he's of the Ramble, he's one of them!'

The four squirrels closed in on Patch, murder in their eyes.

Patch said, slowly and distinctly, 'I swear by the moon I am not of the Ramble.'

An odd shivery feeling came from inside him and spread right to the edge of his skin, as it had the last and only other time he had ever sworn by the moon. For a moment he felt weak and sick, and the world around him blurred, all its shapes ran together into a single streaked mass of colors. When the world came back, the four squirrels had drawn away from him, a little awed.

'Then who are you?' the biggest squirrel asked, quietly this time.

'I am' – Patch hesitated a moment, 'Pale son of Shiny, of the Seeker clan, of the Meadow tribe.'

'The Meadow, eh? What are you doing all alone?'

'I ...' – Patch improvised, 'I was in the battle last night, I was pushed off a tree by one of the Ramble, I must have lost my senses, I just woke up. I'm coming back to the army. Which way is it?'

'He's lying,' said the one-eyed female. 'He's a spy. He's Northern tribe.'

'I am not!' Patch said weakly. He hoped he wouldn't have to swear it by the moon. The aftereffects of that last oath had not been pleasant.

'Northern squirrels are red,' another of them objected.

Patch realized none of them seemed to suspect he might be Treetops. That was lucky, in a way – but it was also awful confirmation that White's terrible tale had been true, that his whole tribe had been extinguished. He felt cold, as if he had dived into winter-frozen water. Cold and suddenly angry.

'Who are you?' he demanded. 'Why should I answer to you?'

The squirrels looked at one another, a bit taken aback by Patch's temerity, until the largest said in a surprised voice, 'Who do you think we are? We're Gobblers. We're here to find deserters.'

'I'm no deserter.'

'We'll see about that,' the fourth squirrel said. 'What is the name of your rat?'

Patch just looked at him. He didn't even understand the question.

Then the one-eyed female squawked, 'Humans!'

And indeed a small family of humans, two large and two small, were advancing toward where the five squirrels stood. The Gobblers immediately scattered – but Patch, thinking fast, remained where he was. The humans left him unmolested and continued to the nearby highway.

Patch followed, staying as close as he could. He glanced over his shoulder, and saw to his dismay that the Gobblers were pursuing, fangs bared. He hurried to keep up, but even the little humans were moving too quickly for him, and every step seared his leg with agony.

The humans grew distant, and then the Gobblers broke into a run. They were upon him in heartbeats.

Patch turned to face them, ready to die fighting – and the Gobblers looked past Patch, blanched, spun in place so quickly that the one-eyed female actually fell in her haste to put her head where her tail had been, and fled. All of them dashed to and then up the nearest cedar tree, sprinting as if pursued by death itself.

Patch's heart convulsed. As he turned toward the highway, part of him already knew what he would see. It was every squirrel's most terrifying nightmare. A big dog had pulled free from its human masters and was charging straight at him, its eyes alight with the vicious thrill of the hunt.

Patch tried to run, and his leg gave way beneath him, and he fell. Then the dog was standing above him. Fangs glistened in its stinking, slavering mouth. Its leash dangled limply to the ground. There were no humans anywhere near. Patch closed his eyes. This was the end. He hoped it wouldn't hurt too much.

The dog roared so loudly that it took Patch a moment to decipher its words:

'Oh, thank you, thank you, little squirrel! Oh, you saved me, you saved me!'

After a long and bewildered moment Patch dared to open his eyes, just as the dog licked him with its huge, oozing tongue. Patch recoiled, revolted, and disgust gave him strength enough to drag himself to his feet. He looked past the dog's huge toothy maw to its face, and his mouth fell open with amazed recognition.

'Beeflover!' he cried.

'Little squirrel!'

In the distance Patch saw humans racing toward him. Beeflover's humans, pursuing their dog.

He felt dizzy with surprise. There was too much going on. He felt almost as if blackblood poison was beginning to surge through his system once again. But he knew he had to think, and think quickly. Once the humans arrived and took Beeflover away, the Gobblers would return; and Patch had no strength left with which to run.

'Beeflover,' he said, 'can you carry me across the highway?'

Beeflover's eyes lit up. 'The highway! Oh boy! Of course! Oh, that will be fun, little squirrel, let's go, let's go!'

Patch shut his eyes with terror as the dog's fangs dipped toward him, and then closed, clamping onto his body with surprising delicacy. Then Patch was rising through the air, cradled between Beeflover's open jaws. Patch opened his eyes, saw the world roiling and tumbling around him, realized a dog was running while holding him in its mouth, and shut them again as tightly as possible. He tried not to breathe through his nose. Beeflover's breath was even worse than the outgassing of a death machine.

Then Patch felt a violent yank, and he was falling. He tumbled to the ground, yowled with pain as his wounded leg made contact, and staggered back to his feet. Beeflover looked down at Patch, grinning hugely. Two humans stood above Beeflover, holding his leash and chastising him loudly.

'That was fun!' Beeflover shouted, before his humans dragged him away.

Patch looked around. He was very near the highway, where a horse was *clop-clop-clopping* toward him, shackled to a wooden box. He could barely walk, and Beeflover was gone, and the Gobblers were already back on the ground and resuming their pursuit. There was no way he could outrun them. He had only one hope.

Patch waited motionless as the Gobblers came closer. Their faces shone with malevolent triumph.

But as the horse passed, dragging the huge box on wheels behind, Patch used what felt like all the remaining strength in his three good legs to leap up to the flat stick of wood that ran between the box's enormous wheels. For a long and dizzying moment he scrabbled on the edge of this ledge; then, just as he thought he was about to slide off, his claws caught a knot, and he climbed all the way on.

The horse *clopped* steadily onwards along the highway, quickly widening the distance between himself and the gaping Gobblers. And as they dwindled and disappeared into the distance, despite the terrors and horrors of the day gone by, and even though he lay drained and near collapse, Patch allowed himself a small triumphant smile.

THE ANCIENT

 atch hoped the horse might carry him all the way to the North, but it turned around just past the Turtle Sea. He managed to scramble back onto the ground without incident, and limped slowly away from the concrete trail, seeking food and some kind of shelter for the night. The sun was now hidden behind the mountains to the west.

He found and ate a few fallen ginkgo nuts. They seemed only to intensify his hunger, but he was too weak and tired to find a proper dinner. Instead he staggered uphill to a nearby bush and curled up on the dirt beneath its dense branches. It wasn't much of a drey, but it would have to do. He hoped his leg would be better tomorrow. It hardly hurt anymore; it seemed distant from him, like it was no longer really part of his body. He knew dimly that this was even more worrying than pain.

Everything was wrong. He had worked so hard and braved so many dangers to return to the Center Kingdom, and now he was in straits as desperate as any he had faced on his journey home. The Ramble was a sea of blood and mangled flesh and carrion crows, and King Thorn had fled to the North. He had failed Karmerruk, he was crippled by a poisoned leg that felt like it would never heal, and he was so hungry. Feeling not just exhausted but actually empty, hollow like a dead tree, Patch lay down and closed his eyes.

Then, what felt like only a heartbeat later, he opened them again.

For a breath Patch lay very still. Then he sniffed the air carefully. There was a strange and electric smell in the air, a rich, feral scent he had encountered before, Patch was sure of it, though he did not know where or when. The mere presence of this scent seemed to restore a little of his strength and curiosity. He fought his way back to his feet, waddled over to the edge of the bush, and peeked his head out between the branches.

From the very middle of a concrete clearing, a colossal stone spire jutted into the sky like a single sharp tooth, human-carved on all sides with strange and spidery shapes. It looked as old as the earth itself. A confused series of images flooded Patch's mind as he looked at the spire, images that seemed to hang in the air before him: a golden-eyed creature with a tiger's body and the head of a man; an endless expanse of wrinkled sand littered with thousands of human skeletons; a full moon rising over a vast triangular edifice surrounded by a baying herd of dog-things. For a moment Patch thought he heard voices whispering in some hissing, incomprehensible language, and all his fur stood up on end.

The images dimmed and cleared, and Patch saw something like a dog standing at the foot of the stone spire, watching him with a leery grin full of sharp teeth. For a moment he thought it was Beeflover. But this dog – if it was a dog – was smaller, and its eyes were golden, and it was lean and wiry with muscle.

'Patch son of Silver,' it said, in a low, amused voice. 'We meet again.'

Patch twitched with surprise. 'Who are you? How do you know my name?'

'Oh, I know a lot of useless things,' the dog-thing said airily. 'You can call me *Coyote*.'

Patch shivered when he heard that name, though he did not know why.

'Isn't it beautiful?' Coyote asked, indicating the huge stone spire. 'The stories it could tell, if stones could speak. It knows tales of ancient blood and sacrifice, of whole armies slaughtered so that a single human could try to cheat death. You should bring Zelina here. She would see some interesting things.'

'You know Zelina? How is she? Where can I find her?'

'Oh, don't worry, she's fine. She'll find you when the time comes. But I didn't bring you here to gossip, Patch son of Silver.'

'Bring me here?'

'Look at that,' Coyote said. He motioned to the highway visible beyond the spire, where automobiles moved slowly, like beetles crawling on a branch. 'They're so clever, those humans. Always making some new machine. Soulless hunks of metal. I don't like machines, Patch son of Silver. Sometimes I like to throw things into their gears. Like a stone, or a stream. Or a squirrel.'

'I don't understand,' Patch said nervously.

'Don't worry, I mean it metaphorically. But you know what I do like? I do like the Center Kingdom. Birds come here from so far away, do you know that? You must, you speak Bird so well, such a rare ability in a little furball like yourself. They come here from the four corners of the world, and to that little forest where the Old One lives, and they mingle, and after a season they return to their homes. The world is a terribly big place, little squirrel. Much bigger and much more terrible than you will ever understand.'

'The Old One?' Patch asked, by now thoroughly bewildered.

'Never mind. Come with me, Patch. I want to show you something. Let's stir things up a little. Let's play a little trick on the King Beneath and see how nimbly he can dance when there's a little breath of chaos in the air, shall we? Follow me.'

Patch hesitated. 'Where?'

'Not far. We'll get there by nightfall. I can promise you that. I know everything there is to know about nightfall.'

'I can't. I'm sorry. My leg, I can't walk.' Patch was relieved to have this excuse. He didn't want to spend any more time around Coyote than absolutely necessary. He seemed friendly, his amused smile never wavered, but there was something terrifying about him, something old and pitiless.

'Your leg, yes, your poor poisoned leg. Let's take a little look.'

Coyote loped over toward the bush that sheltered Patch. Patch stiffened, but there was clearly no point in trying to run away.

Up close, Coyote's wild scent was intoxicating, like breathing in someone else's dreams. Coyote lowered his head to Patch's wounded hindleg, and licked it once with his red and rasping tongue. It felt dry, like a stone dragged over Patch's skin. The leg immediately began to tingle with warmth.

'No more excuses,' Coyote said. 'Follow me.'

He turned and walked toward the northwest. Patch took a tentative step forward. To his amazement his poisoned leg felt strong again, and painless. Confused, nervous, but also grateful, Patch followed the mysterious golden-eyed Coyote into the light of the setting sun.

THE GATE BENEATH

urry,' Coyote said, in a scolding voice. 'We must reach the gateway before nightfall, or you'll be ratmeat sure as sunrise. Run, Patch. *Run!*'

Coyote broke into a loping gallop, and it was all Patch could do to keep up. They ran north, toward the Great Sea; first across green fields, then down toward a steep stone-walled canyon along which a human highway ran. This was Meadow territory, and Patch was nervous to cross it, but he saw no other squirrels. Indeed while he was with Coyote he saw no other creatures at all, not a bird or even a beetle.

'Here,' Coyote said, halting on a steep and overgrown slope that led up from the lip of that canyon. 'Look carefully.'

Patch frowned. The air here stank of rat, and the patches of sand on the grassy slope were lacy with recent rat tracks. The slope was thickly covered by a creeping plant that was something between a vine and a bush. The wall above was made of crumbling brick. In a dark hollow at the very base of that wall, almost entirely hidden by the shining leaves of the creeper plant, a few shattered bricks lay loose in a small pile. A damp and sickly wind sighed out of the small dark hole uncovered there; a wind like a dying breath, a wind that smelled of rats, and darkness, and water, and a hundred years of decay – and something else, something Patch did not recognize, something that made him think of slithering monstrosities. He shivered and backed away slowly from the dark hole in the broken wall.

'Of course there are countless roads to the Kingdom Beneath,' Coyote said. 'Every sewer, every gutter, every broken basement wall. But this gate is special. This passage is very old, little Patch, older than almost all the human mountains. If you would seek the King Beneath, you would do well to begin your journey here.'

'I'm not looking for the King Beneath,' Patch said, alarmed. 'I'm looking for King Thorn.'

'Of course you are. And you know where he is. He's in the North.'

'Then I'm going to the North.'

'Of course you are.' Coyote's smile widened. 'And I suggest you hurry. It will be night soon. And come nightfall, this is not a healthy place to be, not for the furry likes of you. Lord Snout is coming, and he is not alone. I suggest you put distance between yourself and this gateway before it grows dark, Patch son of Silver. All the distance you can manage.'

Patch looked at Coyote for a moment. Coyote leered back. His teeth seemed somehow sharper now, and his golden eyes were no longer full of laughter; they were glittering predator's eyes. Patch backed slowly away.

'Run, Patch,' Coyote whispered. 'Run for your life, and for your soul.'

With those words terror rose like a tide in Patch's mind, drowning out all the rest of his thoughts. He whirled and ran as fast as he could. When he reached the Great Sea he was only barely aware of it; he kept on, to the North. Despite the threat of owls he ran until it was too dark to see, and when he climbed a tree for the night, he went as deep into its interwoven branches as possible. There he huddled gasping with fear, as if surrounded by deadly enemies.

It took him a long time to find sleep that night, and all his dreams were nightmares.

THE NORTH

 atch woke to the sight of dawn glistening on the Great Sea. Long-legged birds stood in neat lines in the water, hunting for unwary fish. Unthreatened humans ran as if pursued by tigers along their pathway that surrounded the sea. Patch stood on a maple tree midway between the sea and the mountains. Neither territory was more than a tall tree's length away. The Great Sea sprawled across almost the entire breadth of the Center Kingdom; the lands north and south were connected only by a narrow lane on the western edge of the kingdom, and this even narrower strip on the east. Once it had seemed vast beyond all comprehension. But compared to the great waters Patch had seen in the Ocean Kingdom, it was little more than a pond.

Patch filled his belly with sweet maple buds and began to race north, keeping to the sky-road when he could. This too was Meadow territory. It occurred to him that this was the first time he had traveled along the Center Kingdom's sky-roads since Karmerruk had plucked him out of a cherry tree so many days ago, and he reveled in the journey. He felt young and strong and full of life. Yesterday's nightmares were forgotten, shriveled by his full belly, melted like a thin mist by the bright sun.

He might not have believed that last night's encounter had actually happened, were it not for the whiff of that feral smell that still clung to his fur. Coyote was clearly no normal animal. He wondered if it was Coyote of whom the Old One had spoken: *My oldest friend, my most ancient adversary.* He couldn't understand why Coyote had shown him a gateway to the Kingdom Beneath, a kingdom that Patch did not intend to ever visit.

But his leg was fully healed, and he felt grateful for that, and he was almost at the border of the North, where he might find King Thorn, and Silver, and other squirrels who would not treat him as an enemy. It was hard to believe that not long ago at all he would have laughed at the notion of an enemy squirrel. Now friends seemed as rare as albinos, his entire tribe was endangered, and the idyllic peace of the Center Kingdom, which had seemed as changeless as stone, had melted away as suddenly as ice exposed to the summer sun.

The Great Sea was just beginning to disappear behind him, replaced by folded hills and massive granite ridges, when Patch was interrupted by a startled voice that shouted: 'Halt!'

Patch stopped and looked up. Two small red squirrels stood on the branches at the very top of an ash tree, their tails erect, as if ready for a fight. Patch knew by their fur that they were of the Northern tribe.

'Sorry,' Patch said. 'Is this your tree? I don't mean to trespass.'

'This tree is the territory of King Thorn,' the larger squirrel said sternly, 'as is every other tree in the Center Kingdom.'

Patch wondered how Karmerruk and Toro would feel about that claim, but decided not to argue. 'I'm looking for King Thorn. Where is he?'

The red squirrels looked at each other. Their fur was really not so different from that of other squirrels, more a dull reddish-gray than the red of a berry, but it was different enough that all other tribes referred to squirrels of the North as red.

The smaller one asked, 'Who are you?'

'I am Patch son of Silver, of the Seeker clan, of the Treetops tribe. Who are you that asks?'

The two squirrels conferred briefly. Then the large one said, 'We are of the North. Are you alone, Patch of the Treetops?'

'Yes.'

The two squirrels peered suspiciously southward, as if Patch might be at the head of some vast army. Then the second squirrel sighed and said, 'Follow me.'

Patch hesitated. 'Follow you where?'

'To King Thorn. I am going there now, to report. But whatever your plea, I doubt he will see you. He is busy preparing for battle. The rats and the Meadow are already on the march. War is coming to the North.'

VI. THE WAR
FOR THE CENTER KINGDOM

THE KING'S GUARD

he little red squirrel led Patch up and down steep ridges and muddy hills, past the mind-warping Labyrinth, along the expanse of the Northern Sea, then across a human highway and down into the Ravine. This circuitous course took almost the entire rest of the day, but the direct route passed through grassy fields that were Meadow territory.

The Ravine was the central part of the Northern River, which began as a long pond surrounded by willow trees on the western edge of the Center Kingdom, and flowed to the Northern Sea in the kingdom's northeast corner. Beyond the river, in the triangle demarcated by its waters and the kingdom's northern and western edges, lay the territories of the North; steep and densely wooded hills almost as wild as the Ramble.

By the time they arrived, the sun was well on its way to setting. The trees of the Ravine were busy with squirrels, their fur mostly Southern gray not Northern red. Patch and his guide approached a mighty oak tree, its trunk encircled by a dozen watchful squirrels. Other guards, high above, watched the sky-roads.

'The court guard,' the red squirrel explained. 'They watch the king's tree day and night so the Meadow won't ambush us again. Stay here.'

'Here? Why?'

The red squirrel slowed her pace and eyed Patch suspiciously. 'The password is secret. We don't know you're not a spy. Stay here.'

Patch halted just beneath the king's tree's branches and watched the little red squirrel trot up to the court guard. Some of them were red, some gray. All were very large and strong. And one of them looked very familiar –

'Twitch!' Patch shouted, and sprinted past the little red squirrel, ignoring her outraged cries. 'Twitch, you're alive!'

Twitch stared as if Patch had grown a second head. 'Who are you?' he asked wonderingly. 'You look just like Patch. You sound just like him too.'

'I am Patch! Twitch, it's me!'

Twitch shook his head sternly. 'Oh, no. You can't be Patch. Patch is dead. A hawk took him away. I saw it.'

'A hawk took me away,' Patch agreed, 'but I'm not dead. It's me, Twitch. It's really me.'

The other guards watched in rapt silence.

'If you're Patch,' Twitch said, his voice hopeful but suspicious, 'if you're my best friend, then, then – then what's my favorite food?'

Patch burst out laughing.

'What?' Twitch demanded. 'What's so funny?'

'Twitch, that's the worst question ever. Everyone who's ever known you for more than a few heartbeats knows your favorite food is tulip bulbs.'

Twitch's eyes widened, and then he charged forward, so excited that his attempt to sniff Patch closely instead turned into a head-butt that knocked Patch half-senseless to the ground. Patch had almost forgotten just how big and strong Twitch was.

'Patch!' Twitch bellowed, as Patch rolled groggily to his feet. 'It's you, it's really you, you're not dead, you're alive!'

'A few more head-butts like that and I might not be,' Patch said, dazed but laughing. 'I thought *you* were dead, Twitch. I heard almost all the Treetops died in the war, or swore to the Meadow.'

Twitch's smile faltered, and dimmed into a grim expression Patch had never before seen on his friend's face; and Patch realized he was not the only squirrel who had changed since their last meeting.

'It's true,' Twitch said quietly. 'Almost all of them are gone. Killed in battle or moon-sworn.'

Patch swallowed, and forced himself to ask. 'What about Silver?'

'Silver?' Twitch's ebullience returned with that one name. 'Oh, she's wonderful! When there was no food, after you went away, I was so hungry, she came and brought me acorns!'

'Then she's alive?' Patch asked, hope bursting in his heart.

'Oh, yes! I mean, I think so. I mean, nobody told me she isn't. I think somebody would have told me, Patch, I really do.'

'Silver was here two days ago,' another guard squirrel said. His fur was streaked with white, but he moved with easy grace as he came over to Patch and sniffed him closely, as if inspecting him for some kind of taint.

'Where is she now?'

The old warrior looked suspicious. 'I understand you're a friend of Twitch's, but why do you care about Silver?'

Patch said, outraged, 'She's my mother!'

'Your *mother?*' The old squirrel took two steps back and looked at Patch carefully. 'You're saying you're her son? The son who was taken away by a hawk?'

'That's what I just said!' Twitch said. 'Didn't I say it, Patch? Didn't I just say you were taken away by a hawk? Sometimes I don't think anyone really listens to me.'

Patch said to the old squirrel, 'Who are you?'

'I am Sharpclaw son of Throatbiter, duke of the Strong clan, soldier of the Ramble tribe, commander of the King's Guard.'

'Fine. Where's my mother?'

Sharpclaw regarded Patch carefully. 'Your mother, if that is what she truly is to you, is away on a mission. Beyond that I cannot speak further. But if all goes well she will return soon enough.'

'Return from where?'

'I said I cannot say,' Sharpclaw said sharply. 'We're at war, young squirrel. I don't have time to bandy gossip. Why are you here? What is your business with King Thorn?'

Patch hesitated. He hadn't really had any purpose beyond finding out what had happened to his friends and family. It was true Karmerruk had asked him to translate, but he didn't think this was a good time to claim he had been sent here by a hawk.

'Do you support the true king?' Sharpclaw asked.

'I guess.'

'Then you will serve in his army.'

'His army? But –'

'We're at war, boy,' the old squirrel said angrily. 'If you don't intend to fight, then begone from here now, for none of us will have any time for you, not even Twitch, no matter how old a friend you are. We have no time for friendship. The final battle could be tomorrow. Join us or begone.'

Patch looked around. He sighed. Then he said, 'I don't want to go.'

Sharpclaw smiled thinly. 'Then I welcome you to the army of King Thorn. I think I know just the place for a wanderer like you. You can stay the night in that beech barracks over there. We'll get you to your post first thing in the morning.'

WAR-CLAN

ighteye frowned. 'So you're the new recruit. Patch son of Silver.'

Patch nodded.

'You know it's dangerous here. Death stalks us every night.'

Patch looked around, wondering where exactly death stalked. They stood high on a cypress tree just south of the Ravine. The squirrels who lived in the grassy fields farther south were distant from their tribal brethren across the Great Sea, but they were still gray squirrels of the Meadow tribe; and from what Sharpclaw had said, Redeye and his army were on the march. But no Meadow squirrels were visible from the cypress. The only animals in sight were a few distant pigeons, a dozen humans chasing a ball across the fields, and the half-dozen other Ramble squirrels under Nighteye's command, scattered on the branches of the cypress.

'Did you fight in the Battle of the Meadow?' Nighteye asked. Nighteye was like a younger version of Sharpclaw, a big, strong squirrel with magnificent fur and a casual air of command.

'No,' Patch said, 'I wasn't –'

'Did you fight in the Battle of the Ramble?'

'No. I got there the next day.'

'The next day,' Nighteye repeated. 'Too late to help. Too late to fight.'

'I was hardly able to –'

'Because you were carried away by a hawk,' Nighteye said, disbelief dripping from every word, 'and you had to journey across half the world back to the Center Kingdom, and you just happened to get back just in time to miss the battles.'

Patch said, 'That's what happened.'

'And you just convinced this hawk to let you go.'

'I speak Bird.'

'You must speak it very well indeed to talk your way out of a hawk's claws.'

Patch didn't know what to say.

'Your mother is a brave and daring squirrel,' Nighteye said, 'and for her sake I will take you into my war-clan. Perhaps we can make a squirrel out of you yet.'

'Twitch says he's all right,' another of Nighteye's squirrels said hesitantly. Patch had been introduced but had already forgotten their names. All were of the Ramble.

'Twitch. Yes. Twitch is your friend, isn't he?' Nighteye asked. Patch nodded. 'Twitch is very strong and very brave. But he is not good at choosing his friends. Sniffer was Twitch's friend too, wasn't he? And your friend as well.'

'What are you saying?' Patch demanded, angry now.

'I'm saying you were with Sniffer when you disappeared, and now you come back on the eve of a great battle and claim you want to join the army. If you weren't your mother's son, Patch, I would send you back to the South.'

'I didn't even want to join the army!' Patch protested. 'Sharpclaw said I had to!'

'Ah, so you say you're not a spy, just a coward.'

'I am not! I – you wouldn't believe how many times I almost died coming back to the Center Kingdom!'

'No, I wouldn't.' Nighteye frowned. 'Well, we'll see soon enough if you have any of your mother's blood. This is a scout squad, Patch. Our job is to find danger before it finds King Thorn. And we work both day and night. How do you feel about that? How do you feel about darkness and rats and owls?'

Patch stared Nighteye straight in the eye. 'I've seen worse.'

Nighteye glared back, his face stony with disgust and disbelief. Patch's gaze did not waver. A momentary flicker of doubt crossed Nighteye's face; but then his expression hardened, and he said, with contempt, 'Fine bold words. We'll soon see if you have the heart to match them.'

Despite Nighteye's ominous words, Patch did not find the first afternoon of scout duty to be particularly desperate or dangerous. The war-clan left the cypress and went south, moving fast, traveling as far as the edge of the Great Sea, spreading out and seeking traces of rats, or Redeye's army, or any squirrels. They found nothing but day-old scents and a few abandoned dreys. The Meadow squirrels who occupied these grassy plains seemed to have retreated farther south.

They returned before nightfall, divided into pairs, and spread themselves out along the nearby trees of the ravine, close enough to hear one another's calls. One member of each pair had to be awake all night, listening for suspicious noises. If he heard anything, the whole war-clan would investigate. At the Battle of the Ramble, the Meadow squirrels had attacked by surprise, climbing trees in the dead of night and killing Ramble squirrels while they slept in their dreys. The battle was over almost before the Ramble knew it had begun. The job of the scout squads was to prevent that from happening again.

Patch soon decided that the worst thing about being a scout was not danger but tedium. It was so hard to stay awake when the sky was dark, the Center Kingdom was silent, and his whole body was crying for him to crawl into a drey and fall asleep. It helped that his night partner, Longtail, had suffered a broken nose in the Battle of the Meadow and now snored loudly, but Patch still caught himself nodding off on several occasions that first night. Fortunately, he was awake every time Nighteye came by to inspect his post. As far as Patch could tell, Nighteye didn't sleep at all.

In the morning they went back out to the Great Sea on another scouting run. Patch tried to be friendly to Longtail and the other members of the war-clan, but all of them treated him with silent disdain. When they spoke, it was invariably reminiscences of the Ramble, and of the two great battles, and Patch had nothing to add to that. He soon gave up. It didn't matter. What mattered was that his mother was alive, and he would see her soon. Things would be different when Silver came back.

awk!' Nighteye cried, and all the war-clan fled into a big bush on the periphery of the Great Sea. Most hid in the bush's dense heart, but Patch stayed at the edge, looking up through the branches, trying to see if it was Karmerruk gliding through the cloud-patterned sky above. After a moment he decided this hawk was too small, and retreated deeper into safety.

'What's the matter?' one of the other squirrels sneered. 'I thought you liked hawks. Why don't you go out there and talk to it? Why don't you ask it to find Redeye and Sniffer?'

'I don't know that hawk,' Patch muttered.

The other squirrels laughed harshly.

'You better find the hawk you do know,' Longtail said. 'You better ask it to carry you away before the next battle comes. We're not going to let you run away from this one. If you try to run, you lying coward, I'll hamstring you myself and leave you for the rats.'

The other squirrels grunted with general approval. Patch turned toward Longtail, hurt and betrayed; hadn't they shared a post last night, and hadn't Patch done his duty?

'I'm not a liar,' he said quietly, knowing no one would believe him. 'I'm not a coward. I've fought rats before. I fought Lord Snout myself.'

At this the other squirrels began to shout with outraged disbelief.

'Lord Snout!' Longtail sputtered. 'Next you'll be saying you killed the King Beneath all by your lonesome. You shut your mouth. You think if you make your lies bigger we'll start to believe you? We know what you really did. You found the biggest tree you could and you hid there while Redeye and the rats were killing us and killing your whole tribe. Now you're running to your mother because nowhere else is safe.'

'Maybe it wasn't a tree,' another scout, named Quickjaw, said venomously. 'Maybe it was a deep dark hole. Maybe you met something down that hole. Maybe you made an *agreement*.'

Patch didn't know what to say. He suddenly felt like he was surrounded by enemies, not by Ramble squirrels who were supposed to be on the same side. He had come so far and endured so many hardships to get here, hoping to find his friends, and a tribe to truly belong to at last; and instead he was being treated like a traitor, scarcely better than a rat.

'Easy,' Nighteye rumbled. 'He's Silver's son, he's Twitch's friend. He may be a liar and a coward, but I don't think he's a spy.'

'I am not –' Patch began, his voice hollow, already knowing it was useless.

'Quiet,' Nighteye said. 'We've had enough lies from you for one day.'

'He even *smells* like a rat,' Quickjaw said.

Longtail laughed. 'He does! Smell him!'

Patch sniffed, almost involuntarily. Then he stood straight up and sniffed the air again, warily and carefully. There was barely the hint of a smell – but Patch had grown familiar enough with the scent of rat to be certain of its presence, however faint.

He said, quietly, 'There are rats near.'

'More stories –' Longtail began.

'No,' Nighteye said in a forceful whisper. 'No, look.'

From their vantage point they could see, beneath the bush's lowest branches, a thin arc of the ground around them. Something was moving to the south. A group of somethings, gray and furry, with shining wormlike tails; more than a dozen rats, venturing north from the direction of the Great Sea.

'Redeye's army,' Longtail whispered. 'We have to send word. I'm the fastest.'

Nighteye shook his tail no. The movement was barely visible in the darkness. 'That's no army. Look, there's nothing behind them. It's just one group. A scout squad, like us. They're upwind. They don't know we're here.' He paused. 'But they'll find out soon enough. Everybody ready. We're going to charge.'

'We have to warn the king!' Longtail said, his voice quiet but shrill.

'No,' Nighteye said calmly. 'What you have to do is follow my orders. And I order you all to charge when I say. Ready.'

Patch swallowed. He suddenly felt a little sick. His heart thumped faster and faster as he squatted down to the dirt. Around him the others were doing the same. Patch could feel the hot blood pulsing through his body. His muscles felt loose and quivery. He wondered if he would have the strength to charge, if maybe the other squirrels were right, maybe he was a coward after all –

'Now!' Nighteye commanded.

And Patch leapt forward like a dog breaking free of its leash.

SKIRMISH

 nless their advantage is overwhelming, or they are commanded by a strong leader, rats' first instinct is always to flee. Most of them scattered like a cloud of flies when Patch and the Ramble squirrels erupted unexpectedly from beneath the bush. A few were too surprised to move, and Patch charged right into one of those stunned rats, bowling it over, tangling his own forelegs with its tail. His nose was pressed right up against its sour-smelling neck. For a moment he didn't know what to do.

The rat bit at him. Patch dodged instinctively, just in time; then, while the rat's head was extended in attack, he bit back. His sharp teeth passed through and met in the rat's fleshy neck, and his mouth filled with the sour, iron taste of blood. Gagging, Patch let go, and blood spurted onto his face. Both he and the rat backed away from one another, but the rat's motions were twitching and spastic. As blood poured from its neck, it fell over, convulsed sluggishly, and died.

Patch looked around. He had been so focused on his private battle that he had forgotten the rest of the world. All around him other squirrels were finishing off the rats who had been too surprised to run. Longtail hung back by the edge of the bush, looking uncertain, while Nighteye and three others pursued the escaping rats. Patch paused and then chased after his commander.

The rats fled across the concrete trail that hugged the very edge of the Great Sea like skin on bone. The squirrels pursued them onto a little finger of land that extended into the water. From here a big metal pipe descended into the Great Sea, and another, smaller pipe ran directly underground, into the Kingdom Beneath. The fastest rat began to squeeze itself into that pipe, folding and twisting its body grotesquely, seeming to physically shrink into that opening hardly bigger than Patch's paw. But it took time to contort itself into that narrow space, and the half-dozen other rats had nowhere left to run. Rats can swim, but squirrels can swim faster.

Cornered, left with no other choice, the rats turned and fought; and when they did, they were strong and fast and vicious. One moment Nighteye was chasing them like a hawk chasing sparrows, and the next they were all over him like burrs, clawing and biting.

Patch didn't hesitate. He leapt straight into the melee, knocking two rats off Nighteye, including the largest and filthiest in the group. He didn't really remember what happened next. The world turned into a tangle of mud and fangs and claws and rat tails. Claws raked his back, and sharp teeth gashed his side; and he bit back, and his mouth filled with blood again; and then suddenly all three of them were in the water, and Patch was half-stuck in thick mud as he clawed and bit desperately at a rat that seemed to be everywhere at once. The rat was on top of him, biting him, and then he was on top of the rat, ripping at its belly with his teeth, and then it was gone, leaving a feathered blood-trail in the water as it tried to swim away. It didn't get far before it went limp and floated belly-up.

The other rat, the one that had bitten Patch, a big rat with darkly mottled fur and blood-streaked eyes, lay on the edge of the Great Sea with its throat torn out. Patch dimly realized that he had done that. He looked up to Nighteye and the other squirrels. They too were surrounded by dead rats. The battle was over. Patch thrust his head all the way into the water, opened his mouth, and tried to let the Great Sea wash away the taste of rat-blood. It didn't work. He didn't know it yet, but that taste wouldn't go away for days. Eventually he gave up, emerged from the water, and rejoined Nighteye.

The war-clan commander looked at Patch thoughtfully. 'You killed two.'

'Three. There's another back there.'

'I think they would have had me if you hadn't rushed them like that.'

Patch shrugged.

'You would have been bit, that's for sure,' Quickjaw agreed. 'Bit by – oh, no!' He ran over to Patch and sniffed his side closely. 'Patch, you're bit!'

'It's nothing,' Patch said. 'Just a scratch.'

'Was it that one there?' Quickjaw indicated the big and odd-looking rat with his tail. 'Did that one bite you?'

'I think so.'

'Oh, sun and moon and stars,' Quickjaw swore. He turned to Nighteye. 'Did it bite *you*?'

Nighteye looked grim. 'No. Patch got to it first.'

'We have to get you back to the court right now,' Quickjaw said to Patch.

'Why?'

'That rat, see its fur, its eyes, the way it smells like it's been dead for days already? It carries the blackblood disease. You've been bit. We don't get you help, you'll be gone before the day is out. Even if we do ...' Quickjaw hesitated. 'We have to get you back to the court, that's all there is to it. Some squirrels there know how to cure it. Sometimes. If you're strong and lucky. Some squirrels survive.'

The other squirrels watched Patch with wide and silent eyes, as if he were already a ghost.

Patch said, 'It's all right. I don't need a cure.'

'You don't understand, you'll die, you'll fall asleep for a week and then you won't ever wake up –'

'No. I've had it before. I'm immune.'

That stunned all the other squirrels into silence.

'You survived the blackblood disease?' Nighteye asked, awed.

Patch nodded.

'Patch, if this is one of your stories –'

'I don't tell stories,' Patch said hotly. 'I'm not a liar.'

Nighteye looked at him. 'You expect us to believe you were really carried away by a hawk? You really fought Lord Snout?'

'It was Snout who gave me the blackblood disease.'

After a moment Nighteye said, 'You know, I could almost believe you. Whatever you are, you're no coward.'

Patch gave him an angry look. 'Do you think I care what you believe?'

Nighteye opened his mouth, then closed it again.

'We have to go back to tell the king,' Longtail said.

Patch didn't know when he had joined the other squirrels; but he knew Longtail hadn't been there for the battle.

Nighteye nodded. 'You and Patch go now, tell them. And Patch, you stay at court for the night. Just in case.'

Patch nodded. Without another word he began to run northeast, toward King Thorn's oak tree. He didn't bother looking back to see if Longtail followed.

KING THORN

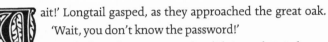ait!' Longtail gasped, as they approached the great oak. 'Wait, you don't know the password!'

Patch slowed. It was true, he didn't, and Twitch was no longer on duty. He allowed Longtail to match his pace, but he didn't look at the other squirrel.

'Those things I said, I was just joking,' Longtail said, between deep breaths. His boast of being the fastest runner had clearly not been true. 'We're partners, right, Patch? We're scout partners, we have to look out for one another.'

Patch halted in front of the curious guards. 'Just say the password,' he said curtly.

Longtail said, 'Jumper.'

The guards nodded and stood aside to let them climb. As he ascended, Patch wondered who had chosen as password the name of Jumper, last lord of the Treetops, who Patch had seen devoured by rats and Redeye what felt like so very long ago.

The oak tree was crawling with scores of squirrels, some watching and guarding, others huddled on branches in little groups. The trunk was a highway of fur as squirrels raced up and down, carrying messages to and from King Thorn's court. This oak tree was, in a way, the center of the Center Kingdom. Patch had never smelled such a melange of squirrel-scents in one place before. But even amid this thick cloud of many scents, one stood out like a green leaf on a dead tree. The scent of Silver. His mother was here, now, on this oak.

Patch sprinted straight upward, to the very top, shouldering past other squirrels who tried to bar his way, ignoring the shouts from all around, until he was at the very crown of the tree, where a half-dozen branches joined together to form a kind of platform; and there stood Silver, speaking to a big red squirrel and a little squirrel with a pinched face, while a dozen others watched from the surrounding branches.

Silver stopped in mid-sentence and turned toward Patch. She stood very still for a moment, staring at her son. Her fur shone in the sunlight. She looked as if she were dreaming, or had just awakened from a dream.

'It's true,' she said wonderingly. 'You're really alive. Oh, Patch, oh, my son, you're alive!'

She rushed to him and they nuzzled closely, rubbing their necks and tails together, tasting one another's scent, until their reunion was interrupted by a dry cough.

'I hate to interrupt this touching encounter,' said the little squirrel with a pinched face, 'and I am delighted your son has somehow survived this war, but we still must attend to important matters of state.'

Annoyed, Patch looked at this little squirrel and demanded, 'Who are you?'

An awed hush fell over all the other squirrels in sight. Longtail, who had just made it up to the crown, emitted a horrified little whimper.

The little squirrel looked too shocked to answer. It was the big red squirrel next to him who spoke. He sounded amused. 'You didn't ask me, Patch son of Silver, but for your information, I am Stardancer son of Swimmer, baron of the Seeker clan, lord of the Northern tribe; and this is Thorn son of Shaker, baron of the Strong clan, lord of the Ramble tribe, true King of the Center Kingdom.'

Patch's mouth fell open. Surely this Stardancer was joking. This little squirrel with the fussy mannerisms and the expression of someone who had just eaten a bad grub couldn't really be King Thorn.

The little squirrel looked coldly at Patch. 'This is a council of war, Patch son of Silver, and your presence is neither requested nor desired.'

'Patch, I'm sorry, the king is right,' Silver said. 'We have business here. Redeye and the rats are coming. Go down two levels and wait for me there.'

'I know,' Patch said. 'They're coming from the west. I'm in Nighteye's war-clan, we just fought a group of rats northwest of the Great Sea, that's why I came here to the oak. They were out in daylight, they must have been scouting for their army.'

'We will take that under advisement,' Thorn said haughtily. 'Now descend.'

Patch hesitated and looked at Silver.

Thorn said, his disapproval now verging on anger, 'I am your king, Patch son of Silver, and I have heard the news you bear and given you an order. Not many are favored with my personal attention. Now begone!'

Silver nodded.

'All right, all right, I'm begone,' Patch said, feeling somehow betrayed and disappointed. He pushed his way past Longtail and went back down to where he had seen a pile of acorns; but the squirrel there said the acorns were for the court guards and the lords, and others had to forage for themselves.

Despite the burgeoning spring, food was in short supply near King Thorn's court, and it was late afternoon by the time Patch finally returned to the oak tree with a full belly. His foul mood vanished almost immediately. Silver was waiting for him on the ground beneath its branches.

'I'm sorry, Patch,' she said. 'You don't know how happy I was to hear you were alive. And that was nothing compared to how happy I was to see you. I wanted to run away and spend all day talking to you, but I couldn't, there's a war on, I had to stay with the council.'

'I understand.' Patch wasn't at all upset with her; he was angry with King Thorn for not being the wise, mighty, magnificent and magnanimous squirrel that Patch had always envisioned.

'But we have time now. Come and tell me, where have you been? What happened to you?'

Patch curled up with his mother and began to tell her the story of all his many adventures. At first she listened with full attention, gasping when he told her of Jumper's death. Once his story left the Center Kingdom, though, he soon sensed that she was listening to him with only one ear; so he raced ahead, telling her the things that seemed important, rather than the full story he longed to recount.

'I've been thinking,' he said, once his story was fully summarized. 'The things I've seen, my friends, we could help King Thorn. Karmerruk said he wanted to help, if we could find him. And I bet Zelina would help too. She doesn't like rats, and she's the Queen of All Cats, I mean, sort of. Also, I was thinking Toro could find Redeye's army, and then King Thorn's army could go outside the Center Kingdom to sneak up on them, there's a little strip around the edge of the kingdom where humans go but not death machines.'

Silver smiled faintly. 'You've been very brave, Patch. It's amazing what you've been through. I'm so proud you've survived.'

'I didn't just survive. I think I could really help. If we can find Karmerruk, that's a start – imagine if there was a hawk on our side!'

'Patch –'

'He wants to kill Lord Snout. If Snout shows his face aboveground, Karmerruk can just pick him up from the air, no matter how many rats are around him! And Redeye and Sniffer too!'

Silver sighed. 'Patch, please. A hawk fighting on our side? We can't afford to waste our time on daydreams. We're at war. You've spent your whole life dreaming and wandering. And I love that about you, I've always admired it, but now you have to stop. It isn't safe to dream and wander anymore. Longtail told me how brave you were this morning, how you killed three rats, I'm so proud of you. And you've always been so smart. But you have to be serious now, you have to stop chasing dreams. I'm sorry to talk to you like this, but we're fighting for survival here, all of us. If Redeye wins, the rats will kill us all. All of us, you understand? Redeye and the Meadow too. Every squirrel in the Center Kingdom. You have to be serious.'

'But you don't understand,' Patch said, 'you didn't see Alabast fight, the cats fought a whole rat army and survived –'

'Patch. No. You can't go into the mountains looking for your friend the cat who thinks she's a queen. You certainly can't go looking for a hawk. As for going around the edge of the kingdom, you'll never convince Thorn or Sharpclaw to do that, it's unheard of, it's wasteland, there are dogs and death machines. I should know. I just came back from the mountains.'

'You did?' Patch asked, astonished. 'What were you doing there? I didn't think anyone else had ever gone to the mountains.'

'I have been to the mountains twice now,' Silver said. 'The first time was near the end of winter, before the hawk took you. I must have just missed you. You see, I was looking for Lord Jumper –'

SILVER'S TALE

I remember I spent that whole winter day digging in snow and frozen dirt, looking for food for Tuft and Brighteyes. Their babies were hungry, and babies have to eat every day, Patch, or they weaken and die so fast, so terribly fast. But there wasn't any food. It was that day I realized this wasn't just a bad winter, it was much worse, it was famine, disaster. You were away somewhere, as usual. I meant to go find Jumper, but there was no need. He was waiting for me when I came back to my drey to warm up. He and a little squirrel called Redeye.

How could we have known? We couldn't even imagine that we'd been betrayed by our own kind, that Redeye and Sniffer had been working with the rats all winter, stealing a little of our food every night so all our buried nuts were gone before spring. There are still some squirrels who don't believe it. But most are dead now. Brighteyes is dead, Patch. I saw her die in the Battle of the Meadow. I'm sorry. I don't know about Tuft or the babies. They're sworn to the Meadow now, but I still hope they're alive. I still hope.

Jumper said Redeye knew where there was food; he had come from the Meadow to help. Redeye wanted me to come with them. I would have died like Jumper. But something didn't smell right about Redeye. His eyes, he wouldn't look at us. And Jumper had waited outside my drey, but Redeye had gone right in without any invitation. Jumper was desperate, he was lord of a tribe suffering a deadly famine, he was ready to believe any offer of help. But my gut told me that Redeye would make things worse. I should have argued with Jumper. No: I should have killed Redeye then and there. But how could I have known? I just told them I couldn't go, I had to stay with my grandbabies.

Jumper was supposed to come back that night with food, but he didn't. I spent that night with Tuft and Brighteyes. It was so cold, you remember their drey wasn't a cave, it was twigs and bark. We were all so cold and hungry, her babies were crying all night, oh, Patch, I feel sick to my heart when I think of that night. When morning came and Jumper hadn't returned I followed his trail. It wasn't hard. Redeye had that strange smell. I followed them to the edge of the kingdom, and then their scent disappeared into a little hole under a tree root. It was just big enough for a squirrel. If I hadn't been so hungry, if it hadn't been for Brighteyes, I would never have gone into the underworld. But I did.

I don't know how to tell you what happened next. It was awful. There wasn't just one tunnel, there were so many of them, all of them stinking of rat. The smell was awful. I'm not like Sniffer, it was hard for me to follow Jumper and Redeye's trail. At first I could guess at it, because most of the tunnels were too small for a squirrel. Then we went into a metal thing, a human thing like a hollow trunk, it was full of water that smelled like sickness, I could hardly breathe. Other hollow metal things connected to it, smaller, like branches. Sometimes the water was so deep I had to swim in it, even though it was half-mud, and full of dead things. There were insects everywhere, cockroaches, beetles, things hissing at me. I would have gone on but I lost their scent, I didn't know where I was or how I could get back. Oh, Patch, I thought I would die. I don't know how long I wandered. I think a whole day and night. I heard things moving down there, rats and other things, I don't know what. The air made me choke. I couldn't find a way out. It was like living in a nightmare.

Then I found Jumper's scent again, his scent and that of squirrel blood. I followed it for a time, I lost it again, and then I smelled fresh air. I had thought I would never smell it again. When I saw daylight it was so bright it hurt my eyes. I almost ran out into the light, and if I had I would have died, because this metal branch ended high up a great cliff wall, the edge of a hole in the side of a mountain. Like someone had taken a bite out of the mountain. I smelled rats, and Redeye, and Jumper, and I heard voices far below. But by the time I could see again it was too late. Jumper was dead, they were eating him. Yes, Patch, I was there. I must have been too far above for you to scent me – or maybe by then I smelled more of the underworld than of myself.

Eventually I managed to climb out, across the cliff, and into the wastelands between the mountains. I almost died on the crossing back to the Center Kingdom, a death machine ran right over me, but I threw myself to the ground and survived. When I returned, Tuft and Brighteyes were gone, and I heard that you and Twitch and Sniffer had gone to King Thorn. I ran to chase you, but I never found you. After the hawk took you, Sniffer convinced Twitch to go back home. I don't know why he let Twitch live. It was Twitch who told us later that he'd seen Sniffer that winter, digging up nuts and talking to rats in the night; of course the big silly squirrel thought it was nothing at the time. But how could he have known? How could any of us have known?

I went to King Thorn and told him what I had seen. If I hadn't, Redeye would have come to King Thorn too, lured him away from the Ramble, and betrayed him to the rats, as he did with Jumper. Thorn sent squirrels to capture Redeye. Redeye killed them and proclaimed himself king. You know what happened after that. Our tribe is fewer now in number than the branches on this tree. Redeye and the rats are killing the Meadow squirrels even as they rule them. Those two awful battles, in the Meadow and the Ramble, so many dead on both sides. You've seen how many crows have come, the way they watch us, only waiting for us to die and be devoured.

Three days ago King Thorn sent me out into the mountains again. To the squirrels of the Western Kingdom, by the waters. Their land is not far, but the mountains between are terrible, Patch, terrible, I don't know how you made your way back through them. I hope I never have to travel through them again. The Western Kingdom is still rich and peaceful. There are many squirrels there, they received me politely, but they know us only from legend. I do not think they will aid us. I do not think they believed me when I told them the rats would destroy them next, though I am sure it is true. I think they will leave us to our fate. I think my mission failed. I think –

Sharpclaw? What is it, what's wrong – is it Redeye, have they found his army? Oh, no. Oh, bloody moon and darkened sun. Yes, I will come, I will come right away. You were right, Patch. By the Great

Sea, just where you fought the rats. That isn't far. They'll reach us tomorrow, if they don't attack tonight.

The crows, Patch. Look, to the west, to the setting sun, look into the light. The crows are coming.

UNDERSTANDING

atch spent that night on a low branch of King Thorn's court. There were so many squirrels on the oak tree that its branches sagged and creaked. The court was alive with furtive whispers and scurryings – until there was any noise in the distance, or any unexpected windblown scent; then every squirrel fell into grim silence, fearing that attack was imminent, that the third and final battle of this war had begun. Patch's heart pounded as if he were running for his life, rather than sitting motionless on a branch. His insides felt like they had been tied tightly together and squeezed. That night seemed endless, as if the sun had stopped its eternal dance around the world, and only the pale moon and sullen stars remained in the heavens.

He must have fallen asleep, because dawn seemed to come abruptly, as if the dark vault of the night had fallen suddenly to reveal an eastern sky streaked with sunrise. The court guard had already descended to the earth to scout the nearby territory. Patch saw Twitch among them. Other squirrels upon the oak murmured with surprise and relief. Redeye's armies of rats and rebel squirrels had not attacked. They might still invade at any moment; but that prospect was easier to face with a bright warm sun crawling into the sky.

Patch shook himself to some semblance of wakefulness, and began to look for Silver. He found Nighteye instead.

'Follow me,' his commander said. 'We have work to do.'

Patch blinked. 'But – what work?'

'You're a soldier. You do whatever work I tell you.' Nighteye hesitated a moment and then said, in a less belligerent tone, 'The king is sending out all the scout squads to find and report on the enemy. Go over under that maple, there's food there. Hurry. We leave soon.'

Indeed there were piles of food under the maple, acorns and

nuts and bulbs and buds, collected by those too old, young, or crippled to fight in Thorn's army. Longtail was there, and greeted Patch like an old friend. Patch reluctantly nodded an acknowledgment but did not speak.

Nighteye led his war-clan southeast, across the Ravine, and to a hilltop above the grassy fields between the Great Sea and the Northern River. From that vantage point they saw those fields alive with motion, full to bursting with hundreds of scurrying squirrels. Patch guessed that Redeye's Meadow army, strengthened by so many moon-sworn Treetops squirrels, was roughly as numerous as the combined forces of the Northern tribe and those Ramble squirrels who had survived the war's first two battles, plus the scattered remains of the Treetops ... but the rats were on the enemy's side, and they were far more numerous than either squirrel army.

'They're coming,' Longtail breathed, frightened, as Redeye's army began to advance, moving in long clustered chains of war-clans. From the treetop it looked almost as if they were giant furry ants rather than squirrels.

Nighteye shook his head. 'No. They're not coming toward us. They're going northeast. Why? Why not attack?'

All of Nighteye's war-clan looked at the chain of hills that led northeast to the Northern Sea, and at the dark carpet of crows that covered them. A few crows had come to King Thorn's court – and had quickly been driven away by angry squirrels – but the vast majority of the sun-darkening flock had settled on the territories that Redeye was now inexplicably invading. Why was Redeye turning his back on Thorn and marching to the Northern Sea? Why was he not engaging the true king in a third and final battle?

Patch contemplated this question while his war-clan returned to King Thorn's court. As the oak tree came into sight once more, it occurred to him that it wasn't Redeye who truly commanded the enemy army, but rather Lord Snout; he remembered what a clever rat had told him once, when he was trapped in a wall of cages in the Hidden Kingdom – and he gasped, as an answer struck him like a fallen tree.

Snout didn't want Redeye to be King of the Squirrels. All he wanted was death and desolation. He wanted Redeye's army to ravage every part of the Center Kingdom, before finally closing in on King Thorn's court like a leash choking a dog; and then, after the final battle, his rats would kill whatever squirrels remained, as they had done after the Battle of the Ramble. Snout was not fighting to control the Center Kingdom through his puppet-king Redeye. He was fighting to destroy the very idea of the Center Kingdom, to slaughter every squirrel within its bounds. He was not yet ready for the final battle, because this was not a war. This was a slow and methodical extermination.

BESIEGED

Sometimes in the desperate days that followed it seemed to Patch that time itself had shattered like glass, splintered into sharp and disconnected fragments. On the rare occasions he had the opportunity to sleep, he woke as if propelled into a strange new world, unsure for long moments whether he had escaped his dreams or fallen deeper into their senseless, dizzying currents. That vicious skirmish fresh in his mind, their battle against Meadow squirrels on a tangled sky-road across the Ravine, Longtail's dying screams, their desperate escape across the river – had those things happened before or after he slept? Had he really stood beside Nighteye atop that tall cypress, spying on Redeye's army as they passed below, knowing that the slightest sound or motion would mean their deaths – and if so, had he really seen his moonsworn brother, Tuft, among them? Had he just now been awoken by the distant screams of pain and cries of battle, or only by the dim echoes of such memories?

By day, King Thorn sent out his squirrels, trying to push the enemy back; by night, rats scrabbled at the edges of the king's territory, looking for unguarded shadows, sleeping sentries, any chance to skulk past the armies of the true king and prey on the weak and defenseless. Patch and his war-clan fought skirmishes every day and night. The enemy, although usually superior in number, rarely stayed long enough to kill or be killed. Instead of fighting a pitched battle they gnawed slowly and grimly away at King Thorn's armies and territories, killing a squirrel here and a squirrel there, occasionally surrounding and slaughtering an entire war-clan, and driving back Thorn's hungry and exhausted defenders one tree at a time.

In the first two days of the war for the North, Patch was sent with Nighteye's war-clan across the Northern River, to carry the fight to the enemy. On the second night, they were withdrawn back to Thorn's court, in order to protect both it and themselves. On the third day, they crossed the river, and fought a running sky-road battle against two dozen Meadow squirrels, in which Longtail died bravely. From that night on they did not venture across the river. Instead they were sent to help wherever Redeye was attacking. Sometimes he seemed to be attacking everywhere at once. King Thorn's territories grew smaller daily, and his armies fewer in number. Their food grew scant, and their nights sleepless.

One night, as Patch stood watch high on an oak tree, eyeing the dark forest as if death lurked in every shadow, rigidly aware of each rustling leaf and hint of a new scent, knowing that if he failed in his duty then his whole war-clan might be killed, and King Thorn's territories overrun – on that night, it occurred to Patch that for the first time in his life he felt like a member of a greater community, something nobler than himself and far more important. Finally he understood the sacrifice required to truly belong; the acceptance of his tribe as greater than himself. He had made that great and terrible leap only to find himself part of a tribe slowly being consumed by a relentless foe, slaughtered one by one, reduced bit by bit to nothingness.

On the next day the crows came to roost in King Thorn's territories, and in his trees; his subjects had grown too hungry and exhausted to drive them off. Soon even the king's oak-tree court was occupied by drooping, black-winged crows, watching with blank eyes, waiting for their inevitable spoils of war. Even humans began to notice that something strange was happening in this corner of the Center Kingdom. Not many came through these regions, but those who did often stopped and stared at the crows massed on the trees, and the dead bodies of rats and squirrels, and sometimes they stood and watched two howling, writhing squads of the enemy armies tear at one another with fang and claw.

When Patch had any excuse, he returned to the king's court and sought out Twitch and Silver. When they met, they sat together without words. There were no words left worth speaking. Everyone knew that there was no escape, and no apparent hope. The annihilation of the Center Kingdom was only a matter of time.

And then, early one desperate morning, Patch was awakened from a rare moment of sleep by a sharp pain at the tip of his tail.

ENEMY OF MY ENEMY

atch leapt snarling from his interrupted slumber, ready to kill whatever had attacked. A huge dark shape stood on the branch beside him. Patch launched himself at it, fangs bared – and then something hit him, it was like being struck by a branch, and he fell thudding to the ground below. Fortunately he had slept on a low branch. He came to his feet bruised and angry but not seriously harmed, his tail erect with rage and fear.

Then he stopped, looked around, and decided this time he really was dreaming, he had to be. Because he had slept on the oak tree that was King Thorn's court, and it and all the trees around it were covered with Ramble and Northern and Treetops squirrels; and all of those squirrels, including Sharpclaw and Twitch and the court guard, were frozen in place like carved statues, horrified expressions on their motionless faces; and the crows on the branches were staring in the same frozen manner; and all eyes were fixed on a point just behind Patch.

He heard a fluttering sound. Slowly he turned around.

'You have been exceedingly remiss in your mission, Patch son of Silver,' Karmerruk said dryly. 'I imagined you eaten by crows. Why did you not send me word?'

Patch recovered enough from his surprise to say, 'How?'

'Your little bluejay friend.'

'I haven't seen him.'

Karmerruk nodded. 'I suppose he too thought you dead in the Ramble. Well, better late-hatched than fallen. Which of these ragged balls of fur is your King Thorn?'

Patch looked up the oak tree. 'He'll be at the top.'

'Is that so.' Karmerruk leapt into the air – then swooped down on Patch, seized him in his cruel talons, and carried him to the top of King Thorn's court with wingbeats so powerful the oak's branches shivered as if whipped by the winds of a storm. Patch moaned as Karmerruk deposited him on the crown of the oak tree, in the midst of the King's war council, which included Silver and Stardancer. All of them stared speechless at Patch and his avian companion.

'Let that journey be a reminder to you that I do not take kindly to delays,' Karmerruk said sharply to Patch. 'Now introduce me to your king and tell him I seek the death of his enemy.'

Patch took a moment to collect himself, then turned and said, 'King Thorn, this is Karmerruk, Prince of the Air. He would like to propose an alliance.'

Their situation was desperate, they were all frantic with anxiety and exhaustion, and fresh blood was seeping from Patch's fresh talon-wounds; but he still took a certain satisfaction from the stunned expressions of King Thorn and his council of war.

'It's too late,' said Stardancer, the red-furred lord of the Northern tribe. 'One hawk, however dangerous, can't save us.'

'Yes, he can,' Silver said. 'He can kill Redeye and Sniffer and Snout, if he can find them. Without them the Meadow army will fall back. Without them they may even recognize the true king. They don't want to fight us. They're being forced.'

Thorn looked to Patch. 'Is that possible?'

Patch translated.

Karmerruk clucked with dissatisfaction. 'I would have devoured Snout a long time ago if he ever showed himself, but he must know he is hunted, he stays in the night and the underworld. As for squirrels, how am I to tell one of you from another? Perhaps if you can point them out to me. But what I hoped is that you might lure Snout into the open.'

'How?' Patch asked.

Karmerruk shrugged imperiously. 'I don't pretend to understand the thoughts of crawling groundlings. That's why I have come to you.'

Patch translated for the war council.

'Just tell him yes,' Silver said, before Thorn could respond. 'Tell him we'll do anything he wants. They'll come for us soon, for the last battle. Redeye and Sniffer will be there, at least. If he can get them – any hope is better than no hope. With him at least we have a chance, however small.'

Thorn gave her an annoyed look, and opened his mouth as if to object, but Patch was already relaying her acceptance to Karmerruk.

Karmerruk nodded as if the conclusion had been obvious. 'Then I shall wait, rather than reveal myself too soon. When the final battle is joined, I shall come and find you, Patch son of Silver, and you shall point your enemies out to me. Remember that if you fail, your king and all his tribes will be utterly destroyed.'

He stretched his colossal wings, ready to fly away.

'Wait!' Patch said.

Karmerruk sighed and refurled his wings. 'What is it?'

'Last time I saw you, you said something about the Queen of All Cats.'

The hawk twitched. 'What of her?'

'Do you know where she is?'

Karmerruk paused before responding, and when he did speak, his voice sounded strange and whistling; and Patch found himself wondering if the Prince of the Air might actually be nervous.

'Even if I do, what is it to you?' Karmerruk demanded.

Patch chose his words carefully before speaking. 'I know she is an enemy of Lord Snout, and she knows the night and the underworld. She might be able to find him and drive him into your claws.'

Karmerruk frowned and considered for what felt like a very long time, as the squirrels of King Thorn's war council listened silently. None spoke any Bird, but it seemed almost as if they knew that this question and its answer were of the greatest importance.

'The enemy of my enemy,' Karmerruk muttered. 'Yes, I know where she is. I have seen her standing on the steel branches of her palace, undefended, looking down on the Great Avenue. I could have – but the prophecy – nothing that walks or flies or swims ...'

'Where is she?' Patch asked.

'She has left the mountains,' Karmerruk said. 'She is in the Center Kingdom as we speak, with her guards. I saw them in the Ramble earlier today. What are they doing here, Patch son of Silver? What do you know of her?'

Patch's heart leapt. 'She's in the Ramble?'

'Why would she and her entourage leave the mountains?' Karmerruk demanded. 'Do you know?'

Patch said, slowly and wonderingly, 'She might be looking for me.'

Karmerruk glared down at him. 'Very funny, little squirrel. I shall be back for the final battle. I shall expect you to treat my questions more seriously then.'

He leapt from the oak tree and soared into the air. The squirrels of King Thorn's war council stared at Patch. He considered telling them about Zelina; but they probably wouldn't believe him, and even if they did, there was no sense in giving them hope that might prove false.

'He'll come for the final battle,' Patch said.

Stardancer said, grimly, 'He won't have to wait long.'

AN ARMY OF THE NIGHT

ater that day, Patch and Twitch lay half-collapsed and half-asleep on the ground beneath King Thorn's oak tree.

'There isn't any food left,' Twitch said dolefully.

Patch nodded.

'Maybe if I go back to the maple there'll be food there. Maybe someone found some acorns!'

Patch sighed. 'I don't think so. But we can dig for more worms.' The ground around them was pockmarked by holes and little piles of earth where squirrels had done just that.

Twitch groaned. 'I don't want to ever eat another worm again. I don't think they're really food, Patch. I want acorns. Or tulip bulbs. Oh, tulips. Maybe there are tulips in the Labyrinth!'

The Labyrinth, a walled garden where humans tortured plants and flowers into growing in straight lines and sharp corners so unnatural that it hurt the mind to see, was east of Thorn's court, on the very edge of the Center Kingdom.

'We can't go to the Labyrinth, Twitch. We're surrounded.'

'Maybe we can sneak through. It's quiet. They're not attacking.'

Twitch was right about that much. There hadn't been any enemy incursions all day. Patch wondered if the enemy was massing for the final battle. If so, win or lose, this would likely be the last day alive for most of the squirrels around them, and for Patch and Twitch as well.

'Patch!' a voice shouted, and Nighteye pelted out of the bushes and toward them. 'Patch, you are needed!'

Patch came to his feet, his every muscle taut with tension. 'What is it?'

Nighteye looked at him for a long moment. It took Patch some time to recognize his commander's strange expression as awed deference. 'It was all true, wasn't it? Everything you said.'

'Yes. Why?'

'She's asking for you.'

'Who is?'

Nighteye said, in a hushed voice, 'The Queen of All Cats.'

A broad smile began to spread across Patch's face.

Twitch asked, 'Who's that?'

'A friend of mine,' Patch said. 'Where is she?'

Nighteye led him through what was left of King Thorn's territory, a few tree-lined ridges teeming with exhausted squirrels and watchful crows. From the crest of the final hill Patch looked down a gentle slope, across the Ravine, toward the trees where Redeye's army waited. He could see them moving in the branches and the shadows, and he could smell them in the wind. He smelled uncertainty among the enemy squirrels.

But most of all he saw and scented old friends. Standing on a concrete human bridge that spanned the Ravine were Zelina and seven other cats, all of them sleek and strong; and one of them, sleekest and strongest of all, his pale fur scored with countless battle-scars, was Alabast. Patch laughed with sheer delight and sprinted out across no-squirrel's-land to the bridge.

'Patch, oh, thank the moon!' Zelina cried. 'What's going on here? Those squirrels didn't want to let us past, and they stink of rat.'

'They're commanded by rats,' Patch said. 'Their king is moon-sworn to Lord Snout. We're fighting a war here. It's ...' He tried to find the words to explain how awful and final their situation was, how every squirrel of the true Center Kingdom was doomed to imminent death.

'Oh, how dreadful. But it's so good to see you. You look ...' She peered at him closely. 'Oh, dear. Frankly, you look even worse than the first time I saw you. Is that blood on your face? Patch, really, can't you keep yourself clean?'

'I haven't had – Zelina, there's a war on! Snout wants to kill every squirrel in the Center Kingdom!'

'Yes, I heard.' Zelina frowned as if he had reminded her of an inconvenient detail. And then she said, in a voice Patch had never heard from her before, a voice as smooth and cold as water-washed ice, 'And I am *most* displeased.'

Patch blinked.

'Did he think I wouldn't hear of this? Did he think I wouldn't intervene? My personal friendship with you aside, I can't allow the rats to rule this kingdom. Or does he dare imagine his sniveling armies of rats and moon-sworn traitors can stand against me? If he actually tries to fight, I'll gut him myself.'

Patch stared at Zelina, wondering if she had fallen back into the same delusional state in which he had met her.

'Milady,' Alabast said, his voice very serious, 'if these squirrels behind us are truly commanded by Lord Snout, then we are now surrounded by one of his armies. When he learns that you are here –'

'You said the messengers have been dispatched,' Zelina interrupted.

'They have. But as your warlord and chief bodyguard, I must advise you to escape now, before Snout learns of your presence and battle is joined.'

'We're not leaving,' Zelina said fiercely.

Alabast smiled grimly. 'So be it.'

The big white cat turned to face the squirrels of the Meadow, who watched from the distant branches with wide and worried eyes. And Patch blinked with amazement; for Alabast's motion revealed another white-furred creature, small and wide-eyed, huddled in the midst of Zelina's cats.

'White!' Patch cried. 'Sun and moon and stars! What are you doing here?'

'She brought us,' Zelina said. 'I wanted to see you, Patch, so we came to the Center Kingdom, and found your scent at her tree. She told us of the war, and where we would find you now if you were still alive, and very kindly offered to lead us here.'

'I thought maybe it would help,' White said quietly.

'It does,' Patch said.

But in his silent heart he didn't think it would help enough. Zelina and seven warlike cats would be deadly in battle, could probably kill dozens of squirrels and scores of rats; but that wasn't near enough. King Thorn's forces were outnumbered by hundreds and hundreds. Maybe the cats could delay defeat long enough for Karmerruk to kill Redeye and Sniffer and Snout before all was lost – but even that hope seemed faint and desperate. Their enemy was too shrewd and too numerous.

'Alabast is right,' he said to Zelina. 'You should go while you can.'

'Patch,' Zelina said, 'I do not shrink from blood and battle. I am the Queen of All Cats.'

Patch hesitated, then asked, very quietly, 'Are you really?'

Zelina smiled slightly and answered, in a similar near-whisper, 'It seems so.'

'Take us to your king,' Alabast suggested. 'We're exposed out here. And I'm sure Snout will attack the moment he learns of our arrival.'

'When do you think that will be?' Patch asked.

Alabast glanced up at the high sun, and said, casually, 'He'll come tonight. With every rat and squirrel he can muster. One way or another this will all be over by dawn.'

s Zelina, Alabast, Thorn, Stardancer, Silver and Sharpclaw made battle plans high on the great oak, Patch rested beside Twitch on the ground below, and tried to ready himself for death. Many other squirrels around them were watching Patch with sidelong, hopeful, expectant expressions, as if because a few cats had come for him he might somehow singlehandedly save the Center Kingdom.

He could not look at them. As far as Patch could tell, there was no way to win. His one hope had been that he might somehow spot Redeye and Sniffer in the enemy army, and point them out to Karmerruk, who could kill them like a lightning bolt with wings. But that hope had been extinguished by the prospect of fighting at night. It was true the moon would be full, and perhaps its pale light would be enough for the hawk to see by, but it would not be enough for Patch. There was nothing left but to fight to the end, to the death, to the last squirrel.

'Did your friends bring any food?' Twitch asked hopefully.

Patch shook his head miserably.

Twitch sighed. 'Well, I guess there'll be food tomorrow. I mean, if I'm still alive. I hope I am. I always hoped that when my time came, I wouldn't be hungry.'

'If you get the chance, Twitch, you should get away.'

'Get away?'

Patch looked sternly at his friend. 'Yes. You're strong enough, no one will choose to fight you if they don't have to, maybe you can escape the battle. Go across the mountains to the Western Kingdom. It's better than dying here.'

'Escape? Patch, I can't do that. I'd be the last one of my tribe! The last Treetops ever! I wouldn't have any friends, or anything! I'd rather it was my time.'

Patch sighed and nodded sadly.

Twitch said, 'I just wish I wasn't hungry.'

Patch heard hisses and gasps from above, and looked up to see White padding slowly down the oak trunk. Other squirrels drew away from her as if she carried the blackblood disease.

Patch bared his teeth angrily, and called out, 'White! Down here!'

Her eyes lit up and she trotted down to the ground and joined Patch and Twitch. Squirrels all around broke into a low hubbub of discussion – how was it that Patch, their one hope of victory, friend to cats and hawks, could consort with this half-tail albino?

'This is Twitch, my oldest friend, the strongest and bravest squirrel in the Center Kingdom,' Patch said. And then, to Twitch, 'This is White. She saved my life.'

'Oh, good. I'd hate it if Patch was dead. Did you bring any food?'

White said, 'No, I'm sorry.'

'I've never met a white squirrel before,' Twitch said, interested. 'Is it true you're cursed by the moon?'

Patch froze, worried that White would be horribly offended, but she actually laughed, if incredulously. 'Do you know, Twitch, you're the first squirrel to ever ask me that? Most others think they already know everything there is to know about me.'

'Oh, not me,' Twitch said, very seriously. 'I hardly know anything at all.'

'I think that makes you very wise. The answer is, I don't know, Twitch. I know I cannot stand direct sunlight, and have to spend the noon in shade. I know other squirrels think my presence is a curse to them. But I don't feel cursed by the moon. When I watch her in the sky, I feel like I'm seeing my true mother.'

Twitch stared at her, stunned. 'No one ever called me wise before.'

Patch said, 'Twitch, if you're bitten by a blackblood rat tomorrow, go to White before it's too late.' Not that he thought either would survive; but it was better to pretend that he expected victory.

'When is too late?' Twitch asked.

'Before the day is out.'

'Not necessarily,' White said. 'The blackblood-bitten sleep for days before they slip into death.' She hesitated. 'But few of them die in that way.'

Patch looked at her.

'There's something I learned, Patch. The day after you left, I decided – I didn't want to be alone. I followed your trail. I went to the

169

Ramble. There were crows there, eating the dead, but they didn't touch any of the blackblood squirrels. They left those squirrels for the rats.'

'And the rats ate them?'

'No. They *took* them. They dragged them away.'

Patch blinked. 'Took them where?'

'I don't know exactly. The underworld. The Kingdom Beneath.'

'Why?'

'I heard two rats talking. They said … they said the blackblood squirrels were food for the King Beneath. They said they made him stronger.'

After a moment Patch said, breathlessly, 'The King Beneath is a myth.'

'Are you sure?'

Patch thought of the terrifying, alien scent that had seeped out of the black hole Coyote had shown him, and said nothing.

'I wish you'd stop talking about food,' Twitch complained. 'It just makes me hungrier.'

Patch forced a chuckle. 'What would you like to talk about?'

'I don't know.' Twitch cast a longing eye toward the maple where the foodstores had been kept, when there had been food. 'I just wish we could finish with all this waiting.'

Patch said, 'It won't be long now.' The sun seemed to be falling unnaturally fast. It was already halfway toward the horizon.

'Look,' Twitch said. 'Here comes Silver.'

Patch's mother joined them. Her expression was grim.

'What is it?' Patch asked.

'They're coming,' she said. 'I don't think they'll actually attack until night, but we can't take chances. White, you stay with me. Twitch, Patch, join your war-clans, to your positions. This is it. Battle is coming.'

Twitch leapt eagerly to his feet. Patch stood up and stared at his mother. She approached him, and they nuzzled and drank in one another's scent, knowing it might well be the last time.

'You've been the kind of son that every mother dreams of, when she learns she is with child,' Silver whispered. 'So brave, so strong, so wise. Such wonderful friends. Our only hope comes from your friends. I hope we can sit down someday, Patch, and you can tell me all your adventures, every friend and every detail. I hope we find that time.'

Patch's throat was too full for him to speak, and his eyes were full of tears, the world seemed to be shivering uncontrollably.

'May the moon shine on us all,' Silver said; and then she was gone.

THE BATTLE OF THE NORTH

he Battle of the North began just after the sun had set, beneath a sky still filled with light, a sky in which only a few stars glittered. It began with the sudden charge of Redeye's entire army of Meadow squirrels. They were not divided into war-clans, as is customary with squirrel armies; rather, it was an all-out frontal attack across the length of the Ravine, as if the Meadow army was a single creature with hundreds of fangs and claws, seeking to overrun all of King Thorn's forces with a massed and overwhelming assault that very nearly succeeded.

Patch's war-clan was stationed atop the tallest tree on the battle-front, and had been told to remain there, to give Patch the best possible chance of spotting Redeye and Sniffer. Patch saw immediately that there was no hope of success. In the fading darkness all the squirming hundreds of squirrels below looked identical.

'Down!' he shouted to Nighteye. 'We have to go help!'

Nighteye hesitated. 'We were ordered to stay with you until –'

'Then stay with me,' Patch interrupted, and raced down the huge maple and into the fray.

Without realizing it he leapt from the trunk into a knot of snarling Meadow squirrels – and would have died a few breaths later, if his war-clan had not followed him and fought with breathtaking ferocity. The subsequent melee of fangs and claws and blood and shrieking fury seemed endless while it was happening. When it was over, when seven Meadow squirrels lay dead beneath the darkening sky along with Nighteye and two other of Patch's companions, it seemed to have lasted no more than a heartbeat.

For most, this first wave of battle was less devastating, but the general outcome was the same: Thorn's army repelled the Meadow charge, but at great cost to both sides. As the Meadow retreated, they left the air behind them filled with the screams and panic-smells of wounded and dying squirrels. Patch heard the agonized hissing of at least one cat as well, and hoped it was not Zelina.

The wounded squirrels who could limped back to Thorn's court. Others were dragged there by their friends. Others died where they lay. Those still able-bodied waited, peering into the distant night, now lit only by the pale disk of the moon.

Her silver light shone on a sudden explosion of motion, and a great cry of dismay and rage erupted from Thorn's army as a new force of Meadow squirrels charged. This time they were accompanied by what seemed like all the rats in the world, so many that it looked as if the ground itself were moving toward them.

'Fall back!' Patch heard Sharpclaw's voice. 'Fall back, or we are overrun!'

Patch, Quickjaw, and the other two war-clan survivors backed away from the oncoming wave of flesh, almost to Thorn's oak. Then battle was joined, and Patch lost all sense of place. There was nothing in the world but an unbroken sea of churning fur and flesh, an endless orgy of gouging and tearing and ripping with teeth. Quickjaw fell beneath two Meadow squirrels, and Patch came to his aid too late; he clawed the eyes from one, and bit the throat from the other, but his friend lay dead in a widening pool of blood.

Then there were more rats and more squirrels, and Patch didn't even know if the latter were friend or foe, and the ground was so thick with blood it was like wading in mud. Patch fell, and rats ran over him as if he were one of the dead. He barely managed to pull himself free from the blood-thickened muck. There was a tree nearby, he could see it against the darkness, and he leapt for its trunk and managed to climb halfway up, and tried to take stock of the situation while the battle swirled and raged below.

He sniffed the air instinctively, and froze. Sniffer was near.

Patch looked around, but all he could see was dim and frantic motion, squirrels and rats, rats and squirrels – wait. There, just *there*, behind the battlefront, at the edge of his moonlit vision, the largest rat he had ever seen stood with two squirrels: Lord Snout, Sniffer and

Redeye. They chatted complacently, as if victory were already assured, as the battle line raged past the tree on which Patch stood, ever closer to King Thorn's oak.

Patch dropped to the ground and charged. He was doomed; everything he knew would die tonight, friends, family, war-clan, tribe, kingdom, but maybe he could kill the worst of his enemies before he died. He knocked over the first two rats who got in his way, but then a thick cluster of rats first barred his path and then surrounded him. Patch fought in a whirling frenzy, biting and clawing like he was rabid, trying to make his way to Snout, Sniffer, and Redeye; but they were too many. A half-dozen rats leapt onto Patch and sank their teeth into his flesh. They dragged him down to the ground, turned his head to expose his throat to a killing bite –

And then another squirrel entered the fray, crashing into the rats, sending most of them tumbling away from Patch. It was Silver. But as Patch's mother tore apart the rats about to kill her son, Snout himself leapt on top of her, dug his claws into her sides, and bit her in the back of the neck. Silver fell heavily to her belly. She bucked and writhed, trying to free herself, but Snout was too big, too strong.

Patch, dazed and bleeding, tried to come to her aid, but he was surrounded by more rats, a river of rats had streamed onto the battlefield from somewhere, they were all around him, there was no way out.

Then he shrieked, as new agony laced into his back. He gasped, as the ground fell suddenly away from him, and a great wind beat at his fur. No, not wind. Wingbeats. He was rising above the battlefield, caught in Karmerruk's claws.

'No,' he panted, 'save Silver! Kill Snout! The big rat right next to me, you should have taken him! And Sniffer was there too, and Redeye!'

'Bloody moon and darkened sun!' Karmerruk cursed, wheeling around in a dizzyingly tight turn, and then swooping into a howling dive.

'Put me down, go back and get them!' Patch said.

Instead of putting Patch down Karmerruk simply dropped him onto a tall tree. Patch tumbled through its leaves, struck his head hard against a big branch, barely managed to catch hold of a smaller one, and dangled from it for a dizzying moment before he pulled himself to safety.

That effort and the blow to the head were too much for him. The world swam gray around him, and then went dark.

When he came to, the screams and snarls of battle still continued below. Patch tottered to his paws. It took him a moment to realize he stood on the maple that King Thorn had used to store food. He looked down, ready to charge back into the fray; but no hope remained. The war was all but over.

Beneath him the final battle raged around the base of Thorn's oak tree, where Zelina and her cats fought desperately, their backs to its trunk. The king's territories had diminished to that single tree, and the rats were everywhere, and worst of all, they were growing in number, in the dim moonlight Patch could see more reinforcements streaking in from all directions. He groaned with despair.

Then Patch blinked and squinted at the ground. Something about the scene beneath him seemed wrong. Those reinforcements.

He tried to focus his straining eyes on the creatures racing into the battle from all around. Were they rats? No, they couldn't be: rats were not so large, and did not move with such speed and liquid grace –

Patch gasped. Those weren't rat reinforcements. They were *cats*. Dozens of them, scores, more than a hundred, an entire host of cats racing into the battle, coming in ones and twos from north and south and east and west, leaping into the fray, tearing into Snout's rat army from behind, and shredding it like dry leaves.

Patch watched amazed as Snout's army came apart in the face of this deadly and unexpected foe. First it unraveled slowly from the outside; then the whorls and eddies of chaos spun inwards to the front, where the rats were on the verge of overrunning what was left of King Thorn's army; and then, sudden as a lightning bolt, the rat army dissipated all at once, scattered in all directions like a dandelion in a hurricane, and fled to the four corners of the Center Kingdom.

It took Patch some time to realize that the Battle of the North was over.

atch was dizzy and bleeding from a dozen wounds, but none seemed vital. He downstumbled to the ground and into a moonlit chaos of milling cats and squirrels. The ground was wet with blood, littered with corpses of rats and squirrels and cats; the sighs and groans of the wounded accumulated into a near-roar; and he had to breathe through his mouth to avoid being overcome by the stabbing intensity of the blood and death and desperation that permeated the air. He raced to where he had last seen Silver, and began to frantically search through the dead and wounded. But his mother was nowhere.

'Patch,' a drained voice called, and Twitch limped over to join him. Twitch's right foreleg could barely support his weight, and a huge, bloody flap of fur hung loosely from his back, along the length of his spine. 'We won.'

It sounded more an epitaph than a cry of triumph.

'Have you seen Silver?' Patch demanded. 'She was fighting Snout, I saw her.'

Twitch shook his head.

A huge flapping shadow settled to the ground before Patch.

'Snout escaped,' Karmerruk said in a grating voice.

He opened his claws and the ruined corpse of a small squirrel fell to the ground. Patch hesitated, squinted, and his eyes widened with recognition.

'Redeye,' he said. 'The false king.'

Karmerruk shrugged as if all squirrels were the same to him.

'My mother, with the silver fur, Snout was fighting her, did you see her?' Patch asked.

'No.' Karmerruk considered. 'I saw rats dragging away dead squirrels, and perhaps one seemed to shine in the light, but none of those rats were Snout.'

The hawk spread his wings and ascended. Patch stared after him, watched him disappear into the night sky, thinking furiously. He didn't want to think it, much less admit it – but in his heart he knew Silver was almost certainly dead, and the rats had taken her corpse. But why?

A new and feline voice interrupted his reverie. Alabast. The big white cat was scored with many fresh wounds, but still looked ready for battle. He said, 'Patch, the queen would speak with you.'

Patch followed Alabast back to the oak. Twitch staggered along behind. Around them, clouds of crows had already begun to descend and feed on the dead. Most of the living were too tired or hurt to drive them away. Zelina stood in the midst of a reverent crowd of dozens of cats beneath the great oak. There was blood on her whiskers. Stardancer and Sharpclaw stood outside the feline mob, and Patch paused briefly to speak with them.

'Have you seen Silver?' he asked.

Stardancer shook his head sadly.

'Redeye is dead.'

'So is King Thorn.'

Patch grunted. 'I suppose that makes you king.'

'Me ... King? But – the Center Kingdom has never had a Northern king –'

Patch shrugged carelessly and followed Alabast through the feline mob. Most of the cats looked at him suspiciously until they saw the way Zelina smiled at him.

'I dispatched envoys before I joined you here,' she said. 'There are many cats on this island, Patch son of Silver. Most live fat with their human attendants, but they were still born ready for battle, and I am still their queen. When roused we are the mightiest army on all this island, save perhaps for the humans themselves.'

'I'm very glad.'

'Is your mother –'

'She's gone,' Patch said, in a voice that was nearly a howl, 'she's gone, she's dead and they took her away.'

'Oh, Patch, oh, no,' Zelina breathed. 'Oh, I'm so sorry.'

Patch collapsed trembling to the ground, and Zelina came over to comfort him, and the cats all around sighed with surprise to see the sorrow and tenderness with which she touched him.

'Sleep,' she whispered. 'I won't tell you things will be better when you wake, dear Patch, but sleep. Day will come. You will heal. It was her time.'

Then a new voice said, 'Wait.'

Patch looked up forlornly at White, who had somehow slipped into the crowd of cats.

'They took her away?' the albino squirrel asked.

'Yes, I couldn't find her, Karmerruk said he saw rats dragging dead squirrels away, they must have taken her –'

'No.'

'No what?'

'Not dead. They don't take the dead. They take the blackblood-bitten. They take them to be eaten alive by the King Beneath.'

Patch came suddenly to his feet. 'Then Silver's alive!'

Zelina shook her head. 'By now she's gone, Patch. There are passages to the underworld all through this island. She's gone into the Kingdom Beneath.'

Patch thought of the dog-thing with golden eyes that called itself Coyote.

'I know,' he said. 'I know where they're taking her.'

TO THE GATE

his is madness,' Zelina said, 'you're hurt, Patch, you're exhausted, you have a head wound, you can't think right, you need to sleep! At least wait until dawn.'

'I can't. By dawn it will be too late.'

'No, Patch, don't do this. This is dark-mooned madness. You can't save her.'

'Maybe not,' he said, 'but I'm going to try.'

'How? Where are you going to go?'

'A place I know.'

'Even if you find her, even if you singlehandedly kill all the rats in the Kingdom Beneath, and Lord Snout and the King Beneath too, she has the blackblood disease, how can you save her? You'll never be able to bring her out to the surface to be healed.'

Patch shook his head. He knew Zelina only wanted to protect him, but she didn't understand. This wasn't a time for sensible questions and answers; this was a time for desperate action.

'There is a way,' White said.

All eyes turned to her.

'If you find her, there is a way to save her.'

'How?'

White took a deep breath. 'I will show you. I will come with you.'

A silence fell over the watching cats and squirrels.

'You know I can't come with you,' Zelina said quietly to Patch. 'I am a queen. I have my duties to my people. I cannot abandon them to join you in your madness.'

He nodded.

'Are you truly set on this?'

He nodded. After a moment White did too.

'Very well.' Zelina sighed, and then said in a ringing voice, 'Alabast, go with them as far as the underworld. Keep them safe as long as the moon smiles on them.'

Alabast nodded shortly, then turned to Patch and said, simply, 'Which way?'

Patch said, 'South.'

He hesitated before he left, then turned to Zelina.

'In case I don't come back,' he said, 'go to the stone spire. I think you'll see something there.'

Then Patch turned and began to run to the south, toward the Great Sea, moving at a staggering run, and White and Alabast followed.

They ran through the night. Weariness descended on Patch like a heavy cloud, and he soon felt as if his very bones had gone weak. He had to rest for longer and longer periods to recover his strength; but all through that night, he refused to stop and sleep.

'Something is following us,' Alabast said softly, as the three of them rested in the narrow forested passageway east of the Great Sea.

Patch blinked. 'What?'

'I don't know. It's downwind, and far away. It's bigger than a rat. And it must have cat's eyes or a dog's nose to be tracking us from so far away.'

Patch thought of Sniffer, the arch-traitor and architect of all this ruinous war.

'Maybe the queen sent another cat to watch over us?' White asked hopefully.

Alabast shook his head. 'That's not her way.' He looked to Patch. 'I can try to run it down.'

'No,' Patch said. Another possibility had occurred to him. Maybe it was Coyote.

They continued. Even after the moon sank beneath the horizon, and the night's darkness was pure and absolute, they followed Alabast's night-eyes around the Great Sea, alongside the human highway that spanned the Center Kingdom, and to the slope walled on one side by old bricks. Once there Patch did not need to look for the hole. Its scent of festering alien decay was unmistakable even amid the enveloping stench of rat.

'What is that smell?' Alabast whispered, and for the first time, Patch heard fear in the big white cat's voice, and his fur began to bristle like pine needles.

White said, 'The Kingdom Beneath.'

Alabast stared at the gateway as if the darkness itself might leap out and attack. A few heartbeats of silence passed. In them Patch heard a scuttling sound.

'There's something moving in there,' White whispered.

'It's guarded!' Alabast said. 'Back away, now!'

But he was too late. As he spoke, a score of rats poured out of the utter darkness of the gateway, and charged at the two squirrels and one cat. There was just enough time before battle was joined for Patch to realize that despite Alabast's strength and ferocity, the rats were far too many.

Then something big and sleek and fast leapt down from the top of the ditch into the heart of the rats. Patch, too consumed by immediate peril to wonder what it was, tried to dodge a charging rat, but moved too slowly. He stumbled and fell, and there were two rats on top of him; but then both were swept away by the long, sharp claws of a slashing paw.

Patch struggled to his feet and stared flabbergasted as Alabast and his unexpected savior fought the guardian rats until a dozen were dead and the remainder had fled.

'Talis!' he gasped.

And indeed it was the same fox he had met in the Hidden Kingdom. Yet Talis looked very different now. He was gaunt and scarred, and he stared at Patch with eyes that were wild and on the edge of madness.

'Patch son of Silver,' he rasped. 'Oh, how I long for your death.'

Alabast quickly interposed himself between the fox and the squirrel.

Talis smiled grimly. 'You're brave enough, cat. You wouldn't last more than a few breaths, if I could fight you. Don't waste your life on his.'

'You shall not pass,' Alabast said softly.

'Oh, please, don't be so melodramatic. It doesn't matter. I long for his death, but I cannot act against either you or him. I am moon-sworn to protect him, and to never again attack cat or squirrel.' He turned his staring gaze on Patch. 'You can't imagine what it's like. I have been searching for you for a whole moon-cycle now, and through every day and night, every breath and heartbeat, that oath has burned inside me like I swallowed a living flame. And when you are in danger it worsens. Last night I felt like the sun itself burned in me. I prayed for your death as I ran to find you and save you. But the moon laughs at me. I arrived too late and yet somehow you survived. You don't know what I've been through, what sacrifices I have made for the sake of this sun-cursed oath. I hate you with all my soul, Patch son of Silver. Before I met you I lived a life of song and poetry, I supped every day on sweet warm blood. Now my life is nothing but ashes and gnawed bones. Now all that I am is madness.'

Patch didn't know what to say.

'I swore to protect both you and that cat. How I hate you both, my twin torturers. How can I fulfill both oaths when you are no longer together? It's pulling me apart. I can't even sleep without dreaming of you both. You have made of me a mad and starveling thing. You are cruel, Patch son of Silver, you are a cruel and evil creature.'

'I am not!' Patch protested. 'I didn't know! I'm sorry! I only made you swear because otherwise you would have eaten me!'

'Better you had killed me. I would have ended my own life long ago, but that too would break the oath.'

'You should not have sworn,' Alabast said unexpectedly. 'An oath by the moon is nothing to trifle with.'

'Don't you think I know that?' Talis snarled. 'Don't you think I have brooded and will brood on nothing else for all my days until the last forgetting?'

'I'm sorry,' Patch said. 'I thank you for saving us. And I wish I knew some way to release you. But I have to go.'

'Go where?'

'The Kingdom Beneath.'

Talis arched his back and hissed. 'I could stop you. I could grab you and take you to a safe place and keep you there forever, you and that vicious cat-queen both. That would protect you, wouldn't it? I could keep you both safe and caged until you die. That would fulfil my oath.'

Patch tried to walk to the gate; but Talis leapt to intercept him, and stood between him and the sighing darkness. Alabast tensed, ready to pounce.

'No,' Patch said. He turned to Talis. 'You wouldn't be able to do it. Not without harming us. That would break your oath.'

'I'm a fox. I'm clever. I'll think of some way. I won't let you go from me, Patch. You can't understand. Even the thought is like swallowing poison.'

'If I die, the oath dies,' Patch said.

Talis hesitated. 'True.'

'I'm going into the Kingdom Beneath. And that hole is too small for you to possibly follow.'

'The Kingdom Beneath,' Talis said, and his burning eyes turned thoughtful for a moment. 'Why?'

'That's my business,' Patch said.

'Am I correct in surmising that you have virtually no chance of survival?'

Patch sighed. 'I'm afraid so.'

Talis considered. Then he stepped aside. 'It seems I am permitted some interpretation of the oath's execution … Go, Patch son of Silver. Go, and know that I burn and pray through every breath and heartbeat for your death.'

Patch looked at White. She was shivering, but she nodded. He looked up to Alabast.

'I can't fit in there either,' the big white cat said. 'And I'd rather fight a thousand rats than whatever is beyond that gate. Don't do it, Patch. Don't go. You'll never return.'

'Say good-bye to Zelina for me,' Patch said.

Then he marched through the gateway, and into the Kingdom Beneath; and White followed.

VII. THE KINGDOM BENEATH

DESCENT

atch and White passed through the little hole in the ancient brick wall, skidded down a steep dirt tunnel so narrow it scraped against Patch's back and sides, and emerged into empty and absolute darkness. Only the hollow echo of dripping water indicated that they were in some kind of vast cave.

After a few steps forward Patch came to a despairing halt. He hadn't understood that this was what the underworld was like. His eyes were useless, and his nose scarcely less so: the ground on which they stood was damp with rotting sludge, and the reek of decay was overwhelming. For a moment he thought his mission hopeless. He would never be able to find anything down in this opaque blackness. He was already lost, he was so exhausted he was stumbling, and his dozen battle-wounds were hurting more and more.

Patch shook his head, breathed deeply, took a few more breaths to steady himself and adjust to the darkness. He slowly came to realize there was more to this dark air than stagnant warmth. He felt and smelled a cool and sighing breeze, faint but unmistakable, a sickly zephyr imbued with a strange and bitter scent that made him shudder. It wasn't much of a trail, but it was something.

He turned to his left and began to walk blindly into that breath of alien air. White followed. He could hear her quick and nervous breaths. His instincts told him to turn back, run, escape. He ignored them.

'Are you sure this will take us to Silver?' White asked, and her voice was trembling.

Patch didn't reply.

'Because this feels like absolute madness!'

'You don't have to come. It's okay if you want to leave. I'll find a way.'

A long time seemed to pass before White answered, 'No. I'll stay.'

Patch hesitated, asked, 'Why?'

At first he didn't think she was going to answer. Then she said, quietly, 'My whole life, other squirrels have kept away from me like I was a rat. You don't know what that's like. When you left my tree, that whole day, I kept thinking, this will never happen again, I'll never find another squirrel who will talk to me, my whole life. You're my only friend. If I go back I'll never have a friend again. You don't know what that's like. It's better to die.'

They walked on in silence. Their paws squished against the mire on the ground, and Patch guessed from the resulting echoes that this tunnel was remarkably spacious, big enough for a large dog. He had the feeling they were descending. They encountered and detoured around collapsed bricks, rotting coils of fallen tree-roots, piled rat skeletons, rusting hulks of twisted metal. It was soon eerily easy to believe he and White had been stumbling blindly through this tunnel forever, that all his other memories were nothing more than soon-forgotten dreams.

The only good news was that everything here smelled old and long untouched. The rat guardians at the entrance must have come from outside. This ancient tunnel was entirely abandoned, not used as a highway by rats or anything else.

Had Coyote somehow known what would happen, when he had shown Patch this tunnel? Or – had Coyote *arranged* for it to happen? That strange and terrifying animal had helped Patch, had healed his leg, but to what end? Patch thought of what Sniffer had said: 'This wasn't my idea. It was the eldest, he came to me, he showed me the necessity.' Patch wondered what that meant, and who *the eldest* was. He didn't know. But he knew he didn't trust Coyote.

Most of all, though, more than anything, he had to try to rescue his mother.

'It smells different here,' White said eventually.

She was right. The wind they followed was unchanged, the wind that curled up through the tunnel like a cold and rasping breath, but the stagnant air through which the wind moved had grown thick with moisture, and the muck beneath Patch's paws became damp and then wet. He began to skid as much as walk. Then the tunnel floor ended abruptly, and Patch's forepaw broke through a thick layer of congealed slime and into a pool of water as warm as blood.

It wasn't a puddle. It was a pit. White and Patch walked back and forth across the width of the tunnel – which could have fit a half-dozen squirrels nose to tail – and found no bridge across the stagnant water.

'We'll have to swim,' Patch said.

White moaned softly. He couldn't blame her. The layer of sickening and malodorous scum that lay across the water was as thick as tree bark. But there was no other way forward. Patch took a deep breath and eased himself into the warm and stinking sludge. His battle-wounds burned with pain as the muck soaked into them, and he groaned and shuddered, but he swam resolutely across, carving a path through the scum that White followed.

At least the pit wasn't wide. Patch crawled out of it covered with filth, onto a damp brick floor that continued gently downward. White squelched behind him, murmuring miserably. The air here was different again. Patch smelled metal, and sensed a few very faint drafts from the sides of the tunnel. A little later he nearly fell into a hole in the ground.

This hole wasn't the source of the wind they were following, but he examined it carefully nonetheless. It was almost perfectly circular, and smelled strongly of rusted metal. He thought of what Silver had told him of her underworld journey, of metal tunnels like hollow branches. He had a sudden image of the Kingdom Beneath as a gigantic tree with this tunnel as the trunk, surrounded by a vast and interconnected tangle of hollow roots and branches that reached out to every corner of the island of the Center Kingdom. The notion that they were inside a kind of tree made him feel a little better.

They continued in silence for a time.

'What's that?' White whispered sharply.

'What?'

'That scent.'

Patch stopped and sniffed. The air was a roiling mixture of strange and repulsive smells. White was right, there was something new here, something that made Patch shiver with instinctive revulsion: not just a smell but a scent, an animal scent, slimy and slippery and cold as winter ice, unlike any Patch had encountered before.

He wanted to turn and run. Instead he forced himself to forge onwards.

They walked deeper and deeper into the clinging darkness for what felt like a very long time.

Then Patch became aware of something like an itch in his eyes, and a soft faraway roar. It took him several heartbeats to realize that the itch was the faintest of distant lights, and the roar that of rushing water. Soon afterward the tunnel opened out into a cavernous chamber.

UNDERWEST

he light was very faint and Patch could just make out the outlines of this new space. The tunnel led onto a slender platform that ran above and along the edge of what seemed to be a long, narrow pond, beneath a high arched ceiling made of cracked concrete. A seemingly endless torrent of rainwater kept pouring in from a gaping hole at one end of the chamber, but the pond's water level remained constant. Patch supposed water was also flowing out of it somewhere.

They prowled up and down the curving concrete walls of this chamber. Although the walls were cracked, there was no exit anywhere.

'No way out,' White said.

'Wait,' Patch said. 'We can see. Where's the light coming from?'

'The waterfall. It's coming in with the water.'

Patch considered. 'Water can carry light?'

'How else is it getting in?'

'Let's swim over and look behind it.'

It wasn't easy. Water fell from the misshapen hole in a mighty torrent, and a powerful current then sucked it along the pool and downward. When Patch jumped in, the waterfall shoved him away immediately, and then it was like something in the water was grabbing and pulling him, he had to swim hard just to get back to the edge of the pond and out.

'Careful,' White said.

'I'm fine,' Patch said, panting. 'I have an idea.'

He recovered his breath. Then he backed up along the little ledge that ran by the long side of the pond, and said, 'Get behind me.'

White warily did so. Patch took a deep breath. Then he ran forward toward the waterfall at the pond's narrow end, and jumped as hard as he could *through* the falling water. It slammed him downward like a falling tree, as he passed through – but he did pass through, and the water behind was remarkably calm.

There was a hole in the very corner of the room, behind the waterfall, where water-worn concrete had cracked and crumbled away; a hole from which a little bit of light seeped. The entrance to a tunnel, steep and narrow and uneven, but navigable.

Patch climbed into that hole and bellowed as loudly as he could: 'Come!'

A moment later, a drenched ball of white fur flew through the waterfall like a diving hawk, and White scrambled up next to him. They climbed excitedly, accompanied by a faint but constant wind. The light grew as they ascended. Finally they stepped out into a space so vast that for a moment Patch actually thought they were outside.

It was like a ravine as high as a tall tree and as wide as a human highway – but this ravine was covered by a stone roof. The pale light of dawn glowed through square openings as big as automobiles spaced regularly along the length of the ceiling. Metal grids were inset in these squares, standing between the ravine and the open air, and the light through these grids illuminated the ravine as the full moon shines on the night.

On the ground before Patch and White, a dozen metal rails ran down the middle of the ravine, shining girders that continued unbroken as far as the eye could see in both directions. These rails were set in wooden planks that lay crosswise beneath them, which in turn lay on a wide and dense field of pebbles that occupied all the ravine except for the narrow strips of dirt on either side. The steep walls were made of heaped stone and crumbling dirt, but something about them, their straightness and regularity, implied they were the work of human hands.

The air smelled of rain, and rats, and humans; but its dominating feature was the scent of scorched metal. After a moment Patch understood why. He had seen rails like these before, the other time he had ventured into the underworld, when Snout had bitten him.

These were train rails. And that little light in that great distance – that growing, oncoming light – that was probably a train.

'Careful!' he shouted to White. 'It's coming! Get back in the tunnel!'

She twitched and scampered back to the dark hole. He joined her.

'You didn't have to shout,' she said reprovingly, 'it's very far away –'

Patch didn't hear what she said after that. The noise of the train suddenly swelled and became deafening, and the earth itself began to tremble and quake; and then it was thundering past them, an iron colossus of unthinkable ferocity, its blurred carapace only a few tail-lengths away. The slipstream tugged at their fur like a wind from a terrible storm, raised clouds of dirt, and sent smaller pebbles hurtling through the air. The sound was immense, painful, as if the air itself were being torn in two.

'Light of the moon,' White whispered, wide-eyed, when it was gone. 'That makes death machines seem like mice.'

Patch peeked out into the ravine. No trains were visible in either direction. He walked out onto the pebbled field, avoiding the still-hot rails, and looked around. Should they follow the ravine, or investigate the caves and passages that pockmarked its sides? Was there really any chance that Silver was still alive? It didn't seem likely. But it was possible.

'I can't leave her,' he said to White. 'Not while there's a chance.'

'I know.'

He looked up at the metal meshes that stood between them and the daylit sky. He wished desperately that they could be on the other side. There were trees there, and a bird, standing on the mesh. He squinted. A robin?

'Hello!' Patch cried out in Bird.

The robin leapt up and fluttered away – but it circled around, settled back to the metal grid, peered suspiciously down, and said, 'Hello? Who's there?'

'I am Patch son of Silver, of the Seeker clan, of the Treetops tribe, of the Center Kingdom,' Patch said. 'Who are you that asks?'

'My name is Fila.'

'Where are you?'

'I'm standing on a metal grate,' the robin said, perplexed by the question.

'No, I mean, what kingdom are you in?'

'Kingdom? I'm a robin. Kingdoms are for groundlings.'

'But the groundlings around you, what kingdom are they in?'

The robin paused to think. 'I'm not completely sure. But I think I heard once that they call this the Western Kingdom.'

It flew away. Patch considered. That wasn't so bad. He remembered seeing the Western Kingdom when he had hung in Karmerruk's claws; a narrow green strip along the western edge of the island.

'We have to find food,' White said. 'I'm hungry.'

'I'm *starving.*' Neither of them had eaten since before the Battle of the North.

'If we dig maybe we can find worms.'

Patch frowned. He shared Twitch's opinion of worms: they weren't really food. 'I smell humans. There's usually good food somewhere around them.'

'But they're dangerous!'

'You mean compared to everything else down here?'

White considered. 'Good point.'

Patch led the way across the ravine and up the other side, toward the most pungent human-smells. They followed human footprints up to where the dirt became concrete, and into a human-sized passageway. The air here smelled fresh and clean, other than the powerful human-smells that made it obvious this was a human drey, and a lingering smell of rat. That last scent made Patch uneasy, but he supposed it was pervasive throughout the Kingdom Beneath, and maybe this was a path to the surface. He kept going.

They picked their way past inexplicable piles of human debris, none of it edible, until the passage suddenly ended. Vertical metal pipes crosshatched by flat bars ran a long way up one of the concrete walls until they reached a disk of solid metal set in the ceiling. A tiny arc of daylight was visible at the edge of that disk, like the thinnest of moons, and Patch eyed the vertical rails – but he couldn't climb them, no squirrel could. The crossbars were too far apart, the metal too smooth and slippery.

'I thought you said there'd be food,' White said, disappointed.

'There should be.'

Patch looked around. There were several bags of pale wrinkled plastic, like white versions of the garbage bags where he and Wriggler had fed in the Hidden Kingdom. He approached one, clawed it open, thrust his nose inside, and sniffed. But there were no food-smells, nothing inside but strange human fabrics. He withdrew, started toward another bag, and froze. He heard scuffing noises. Something big was coming up the passage toward them. A human.

'Get ready to run,' he said softly to White. 'Don't worry, they're big but they're slow, they'll never catch us.'

He looked up. The human was looming in the passageway. He tensed, ready to dash between or around its meaty legs when it came nearer.

But it did not come nearer. The human, a male, squatted down like a squirrel, and looked at Patch and White with oddly bright and inquisitive eyes for a few breaths. Then it said to them, in heavily accented but understandable Mammal: 'Eat food?'

White gasped with amazement. Patch only twitched with surprise; he had after all met an animal-speaking human before. He wondered for a moment if this was the same one, but no. It was just as filthy as the other, but its smell was noticeably different, and it was younger.

'Eat food?' the human repeated, very gently.

'Eat food,' Patch tentatively agreed.

The human reached into the strange fabrics it wore in place of fur, pulled out a heaping handful of brown oblong pebblelike things, and dropped them on the ground. Patch hesitated: he wanted food, but he wasn't willing to come that close to the human. As if reading his mind, the human stood and slowly backed away until it was almost entirely concealed by the shadows.

'I don't like this,' White said.

'I think it's safe. I met another human like this once before.' Patch took a breath. 'Watch me, and shout if something happens.'

He approached slowly, and began to nibble at a pebble-thing. The outer skin was like bark, but there was a nut inside. Patch tested it, then gobbled it down eagerly. It was hard and crunchy but incredibly tasty.

'It's good!' he exclaimed. 'Come on!'

White joined him, and they ate, at first keeping one eye on the human, then dispensing with caution and devoting all their attention to ripping open the shells and devouring the delicious nuts within. Patch ate until he felt his stomach bulging out against his skin.

When they had eaten their fill the human approached them again, slowly. Patch and White stood their ground, watching it carefully, still mistrustful but no longer fearful. It squatted to the ground close enough that it could have reached out and touched them, but it seemed to know that they would flee if it tried. It simply watched them, its head cocked inquisitively, like a squirrel trying to match its surroundings against a page from its memory book.

'Good food?' it asked.

Patch replied, 'Good food.'

The human bared its fangs, and Patch and White took a few steps back.

'No hurt!' the human assured them, closing its mouth. 'No hurt, no hurt!'

The squirrels looked at one another.

'I think it's harmless,' White said. 'It smells harmless.'

Patch nodded. He wondered if maybe the human could help find Silver. But no, probably not: even if they could communicate their quest, which he doubted, the human was much too big and clumsy to travel through most of the underworld tunnels.

'Patch, look!' White cried. 'Behind it! Rats!'

Patch looked, and leapt to his feet. She was right. Rats were coming down the passage from the ravine, half a dozen of them. They looked strong and moved fast. He looked around quickly. There were a few tiny holes in one of the concrete walls that looked big enough for rats to squeeze through, but there was no way out for a squirrel, not without going through the rats. The human had tricked them, they were boxed in. He tensed for battle.

ello,' the lead rat said cheerfully. 'Who are you? How did you get here?'

Patch and White twitched with surprise.

'We've killed rats before!' White cried. 'Lots of them! We'll kill you too!'

'Goodness me!' the lead rat gasped, and all of them scurried quickly away and clustered around the human's feet, leaving fear-smells in their wake.

The two squirrels looked at one another. This was not exactly the vicious attack they had expected. It had to be some kind of trick. Rats were famously cunning. They were stalling for time, waiting for reinforcements to arrive.

'Let's get out of here,' he said to White in a low voice.

She nodded. They began to sidle back toward the ravine, staying close to the wall free of ratholes, keeping maximum distance from the human and the rats.

'No go,' the human said. 'No go! Happy together. Happy together!'

'Shut up,' one of the rats hissed, 'let them go away, they're murderers, savage, vicious! They smell of blood, rat blood, they'll kill us all!'

Patch sniffed himself, a little taken aback, and had to admit he did still smell faintly of rat blood, despite his repeated immersions in water since the Battle of the North.

'Stay out of our way and we won't kill you,' White said.

The rats backed farther away, until they were lined up against the opposite wall, ready to escape through its ratholes. They smelled of fear. Patch was by now thoroughly perplexed. Rats simply did not behave like this.

'No happy together,' the human said sadly, as it watched the squirrels move away.

'They're rats!' Patch expostulated under his breath, feeling somehow guilty at having eaten the human's food and then made it sad. 'They'll kill us and eat us if they get the chance! They want to kill every squirrel in the world!'

'We do not!' the rat leader objected.

'You do so! Don't you try and trick me.'

'We're not tricking you. We're not like other rats. We don't serve the King Beneath.'

This notion was so astonishing that Patch stopped in his tracks. 'Of course you do. You're rats.'

'Does every squirrel follow the same king?'

'Well, no – but – then what king do you serve?'

'We serve no king at all. We serve ourselves,' the rat leader said. 'We try to help other rats. We don't kill anything. We don't have to, our human brings us food. You call us killers? How many rats have you murdered, squirrel? How many of us?'

'Er,' Patch said, suddenly feeling very awkward. 'It was ... I don't know ... but all of them were trying to kill me, it was never my idea.' He thought of the rats he had pursued rather than allowed to escape. 'I mean, not really. I mean, almost all of them. I mean, I thought all of you served the King Beneath. All the ones I ever fought did.'

'A likely story,' the rat leader sniffed. 'A thin rationalization for bloodthirsty cruelty. Why are you down here in the Kingdom Beneath at all, squirrel? To kill more rats? You came down here to kill, didn't you, to murder more helpless rats and call it vengeance!'

'I did not!' Patch protested. 'I came down here to save my mother's life! Because Lord Snout poisoned her with the blackblood disease and took her away!'

A silence fell over the chamber.

'Oh dear,' the rat leader said. 'Oh, goodness me. Lord Snout. The blackblood disease. I am sorry.'

'Who are you?' Patch demanded.

'Who am I?' the rat leader repeated, perplexed. 'Oh. Oh, I see. No, I don't have a name. We don't all have names like you squirrels. Only our lords.'

'Oh. Well. What do you know about the blackblood disease?'

The rat leader paused, then said softly, 'They try to infect squirrels with it. Then they are fed to the King Beneath. The king loves blackblood squirrels.'

'How do you know so much about the King Beneath, if you don't serve him?' White asked suspiciously.

serve him. All of us did before we escaped.'

you escape?'

oked at one another uncertainly.

mething wrong with us,' their leader said sadly. 'We

being ordered around. We don't even like bullying

rats. I think we're sick, we have some kind of disease. She' – he pointed – 'thinks we were born this way. It doesn't matter. It's the way we are. So we ran away, all of us, separately. It's this human that brought us together. We're lucky to have him.'

As if to punctuate the point, the human reached out and began gently stroking the lead rat's fur. Patch watched, amazed, as the rat arched its back with pleasure.

'I'm sorry about your mother, squirrel,' the rat leader said. 'I'm sorry I called you a killer.'

'I'm sorry I thought you were like all the other rats.' Patch couldn't believe he was feeling sympathy for rats, but he was; even fellowship, of a kind, with these misfits unable to find any real home or solace in their own kin's society. He was glad that at least they had found each other.

A silence fell.

'Happy together,' the human said cheerfully.

'Do you know where they've taken her?' Patch asked the rats. 'My mother?'

'Of course. To the chamber of the King Beneath.'

'Where is that? Can you tell me?'

The rat leader looked at Patch and White for a long time.

Then he said, 'I can show you the road.'

CROTON

he human watched curiously as the rat led the two squirrels back to the underworld ravine. They turned left and followed the ravine for a considerable distance. Every time a train thundered past Patch found himself shivering at its sheer speed and immensity; every time he feared the ravaging wind of the train's slipstream might lift him off his feet and fling him like a leaf against the ravine wall. He didn't think he would ever get used to trains.

The rat kept to the shadows, while the squirrels stayed in the light from above as much as possible. They passed hordes of beetles and cockroaches, a few grubs and spiders, the shredded bodies of animals caught on the rails by passing trains, many human footprints, and countless rat-tracks. The smell of rat was everywhere, but none were audible or visible except the one they followed.

'I shouldn't have done this,' the rat said nervously. 'It's dangerous. If the other rats come back –' He left the sentence incomplete.

'What other rats?' Patch asked.

'Usually this place is crawling with us, but Snout called them all to him to fight some war. Most followed his summons. But there are still plenty here, don't be fooled, these walls are full of them. Deserters like us, who do what they like, not what they're commanded. They won't come after us. They're killers, savage, vicious, but they won't come after us. I don't think so. Probably not. They don't like coming into the light. Squirrel doesn't even taste good. But hurry. Let's hurry. Let's run.'

The rat broke into a scamper, and Patch and White had to do the same to follow. Then, just as Patch's legs were beginning to grow weary, it slowed, sniffed the air, and halted. 'Here,' it said, and crossed over the train rails. They followed it to a dark hole in the wall just big enough for Patch.

'That goes to the Croton Road,' the rat said, low-voiced. 'Once you're there, turn left, and just keep going. The King Beneath lives in the first big chamber on the way.'

'Are there rats between here and the road?' White asked.

'No. You'll see why when you get there.' The rat looked around furtively. 'I should go. I shouldn't have come. Somebody might have seen me with you. They might stop me on the way back and ask why. What do I do then? What am I supposed to say? I shouldn't have left the human. You shouldn't have made me sorry for you.'

'It'll be fine,' Patch assured the rat, hoping he was right. 'Thank you. We owe you a favor. I am Patch son of Silver, and this is White daughter of Streak. Remember that. Maybe one day we can help you.'

'Maybe,' the rat said doubtfully. It sighed. 'I envy you your names. I wish I had a name.'

White suggested, 'Why don't you give yourself a name?'

The rat stared at her.

'That's a good idea,' Patch agreed. 'You and all your friends. Just name yourselves.'

'We can't do that!' the rat said, shocked. 'You can't just give yourself a name! Names have to come from somewhere!'

'All right,' Patch said, 'I'll give you a name. I name you ...' He thought for a moment, shrugged, and said, 'Nervous. From now on you're Nervous the rat.'

White choked down laughter. Fortunately the rat didn't notice.

'Nervous,' the rat said thoughtfully. 'Nervous. I like the sound of that. That's me all over. I'm Nervous. My name is Nervous. Pleased to meet you. I'm Nervous the rat.' He looked at Patch with fervent eyes. 'You mean it? I can keep it?'

'Of course,' Patch said, a little bewildered by the question.

'Nervous. Oh, it's wonderful! Thank you, Patch. Thank you, White. I, Nervous, thank you! I'm Nervous the rat! But – but I should go now,' Nervous said nervously, his joy in eponymy dampened by remembered fear. 'There are other rats. They might see me. I should go.'

He turned and ran.

'Good-bye, Nervous,' Patch said thoughtfully. 'I hope you like your name.'

After a moment he turned and followed White into the little hole.

Patch didn't like this tiny tunnel at all. It was lightless and claustrophobically small, and it wound its erratic way up and down and side to side. In some places they had to force their way through freshly-fallen dirt and pebbles, and he was nervously aware that the whole thing could easily collapse. It was so small there was nowhere to turn around. It felt like being buried alive. At least there was air, but it smelled wet and stagnant. He closed his eyes and felt his way forward, guiltily glad that White was in the lead.

'Patch,' White whispered. 'I think I see something.'

Patch stopped and opened his eyes. At first he saw no difference

– but slowly, as his eyes adjusted, he became aware of a dim and distant glow. He couldn't make out shapes, but he saw amorphous motion as White scurried ahead. The tunnel began to ramp downward, toward the glow, and Patch was able to make out flickers of her white tail. Then she came to a sudden stop.

'What is it?' he asked.

'I think it's water. In a cave. Below us.'

'Where's the light coming from?'

White paused. 'It's hard to say. It's a long way down. I think … I think we have to jump into the water. And we won't be able to climb back up.'

Patch winced. That was why Nervous had known there were no rats en route. This tunnel was one-way. He didn't say anything. There was nothing to say. It wasn't like they had a choice.

'All right,' White said. She took a deep breath, and stepped forward; she was gone; and a splash came from below.

Patch advanced to the faint glowing hole in the tunnel floor. It was just big enough for a squirrel to dive through. The sides of the hole were brick, not dirt, the hole was a missing brick in a human-made roof. That chilling scent from the tunnel that had taken them into the Kingdom Beneath emanated from below, stronger than ever, alien and dreadful.

He could see ripples in the water below. Something bobbed to the surface. The light was so dim he couldn't see what, but it was pale, it had to be White. Patch closed his eyes and jumped.

The water was so cold that he surfaced gasping with shock.

'Are you okay?' White asked.

Patch looked toward her voice. She was only a squirrel-length away, but all he could see was a pale blob floating in darkness.

'I think so,' he said.

'It's so cold! We have to get out!'

She was right. This icy water would suck the life from them if they stayed too long. Patch looked around, squinting into the shadow.

He couldn't see much, but he could see that the tunnel they were in was enormous, big enough that a half-dozen humans could have walked it side-by-side and without stooping. The brick walls on either side curved and met in a smooth continuous arch high above the water. It was the walls themselves that glowed in patches; they were occupied by some kind of faintly luminous mold. This light was just enough to see the brick ledges running along the walls on both sides, a squirrel-length above the water. Those ledges, rather than this deep river between them, must have been what Nervous had meant by the Croton Road.

'Maybe we can climb up the sides,' Patch said.

They swam over to the sheer brick walls of the river – but they were too crumbly and slippery; neither Patch nor White could get more than a few steps up without falling back into the water followed by a shower of brick dust. The attempts were exhausting, and the cold water was already beginning to tell.

'This isn't going to work,' Patch said, growing increasingly worried. The water would kill them if they stayed in it too long.

'No,' White said. 'Let's swim. Maybe we'll find a better place.'

They swam in what they hoped was the direction Nervous had given them. There was no current, as far as Patch could tell, but the water was fresh. The smooth rhythm of swimming loosened and warmed his muscles, and he began to breathe more normally.

The Croton Road continued in an absolutely straight line for what seemed to be forever. In places, tree-roots had fought their way through its brick ceiling and dangled in thick clusters, soaking up the wet air. In others the ceiling was shrouded by massive curtains of spiderwebs. From time to time Patch felt other creatures moving in the water beneath him; each time he nervously swam away. Once, something long and slender surfaced right in front of them, and Patch almost screamed with horror. It was one of the Legless, and it glistened as if covered with slime, and it had no eyes at all, no features but two nose-holes and a huge mouth full of teeth like needles. He froze with panic. The thing submerged and did not come back.

'We have to get out of this water!' Patch said, his voice fraught with near-panic.

'Easy,' White panted. 'We'll find a way.'

But he didn't see how. The walls were crumbling, but everywhere sheer. His legs were growing tired, a faint cramp was beginning to flicker in his right hindleg, and he knew that once they slowed down, the water would slowly leach all the life from them. They would shiver and grow numb and slowly die.

'Wait,' White whispered. 'There's something.'

Patch squinted. She was right. Something floating in the water. They approached and discovered it was a hulk of rotting wood, human-carved planks joined together into a strange and angular shape. It was crawling with wood-beetles.

'Maybe we can climb on top of it,' White suggested.

Patch tried. It wasn't easy, his strength was worryingly low. He managed briefly – but the wooden hulk was too unstable, it overturned and sent him pitching back into the water.

'No good,' he panted. 'The air's even colder than the water. We have to get out soon, or we'll freeze to death before we get dry!'

'How?'

Patch had no answer.

'Wait,' she said. 'We'll push it!'

'What?'

'We'll push it to the side, and then we'll use it to climb up. Like it's a stepping stone.'

Patch gasped. 'That's brilliant!'

'Only if it works.'

They put their noses against the side of the wooden hulk and propelled it to the side of the river. Patch scrambled up to its top again, and as it again began to topple and overturn, he leapt through the air with all his strength, and landed on the dry brick of the Croton Road.

White followed his example, and on the third try succeeded.

'We m-m-made it,' she said, teeth chattering from the cold.

'Come on,' Patch said. 'We have to keep moving.'

They trotted shivering along the Croton Road, toward the icy, bitter alien scent that they had followed when they first entered the underworld. A scent growing so powerful that it almost drowned out the omnipresent stink of rat.

They were not yet dry when they came unexpectedly upon the chamber of the King Beneath.

ust as Patch was beginning to wonder why they had seen no rats, even though their stink made it clear that the Croton Road was a rat highway, the walls began to curve and bend outward, expanding into a vast circular space. On the other side of this disk-shaped pool, the walls narrowed back into a tunnel and the Croton Road continued. The ceiling above rose into a dome, and there was enough luminescent mold on its walls that Patch could see the stone bridge that spanned the chamber crosswise, level with the ledges on either side. On either side of the stone bridge, smaller dog-sized tunnels continued into darkness.

A vast and tangled forest of roots dangled from the dome like willow branches, like an upside-down tree. The deepest tendrils almost brushed against the stone bridge. In their shadow, the things lying in a ragged line across the very center of the bridge were difficult to see, and their smell was drowned in the invasive maelstrom of rat and that other, terrible, nameless scent; but Patch and White knew them the moment they saw them. The things on the bridge were the limp and lifeless bodies of more than a dozen squirrels. And there was something moving among them.

Patch didn't hesitate. He ran along the Croton Road and onto the stone bridge.

The figure among the fallen squirrels was a lone and shadowed rat who had stopped moving and now faced down into the water as if staring at its own reflection. It didn't seem to have heard Patch's approach. The fur of one of the squirrels seemed a little brighter than the others. Patch caught his breath – Silver! He crouched, ready to charge.

'The King Beneath is here,' the rat said coolly, without looking up at Patch. 'It is death to look upon the King Beneath.'

Patch said, 'I don't care if you're king of the whole world.'

The rat laughed with genuine mirth, then took a few steps toward Patch, coming close enough to recognize. Patch blinked with surprise. It was Lord Snout.

'Oh, this is too delicious,' Snout chortled. 'You actually thought I was the King Beneath. You really have no idea.'

Patch hesitated, uneasy. That terrible nameless scent was intensifying.

'Where is Sniffer?' he demanded.

'Sniffer is dead,' Snout said. 'His usefulness ended, and he died as you will die. You should have died thrice already. What shadow fell over your destiny, squirrel? Who sent you to find the Queen of All Cats? What brought you to the Kingdom Beneath? ... It doesn't matter. The King Beneath laughs at destiny. The King Beneath is the killer of fate. I hope you don't think you've won the war. I would hate for you to die with such a wrongheaded belief. Cats can't save your kingdom. Too many of you have died already. You are too weak to survive what comes next. All creatures of darkness serve the King Beneath. *All of them.* And when he comes, all will flock to his command.'

The water beneath the bridge began to shimmer and ripple. There was something moving in it, something pale and enormous, drifting through darkness toward the stone bridge. Patch took an involuntary step back.

'You are greatly honored to die in the jaws of the King Beneath,' Snout whispered. 'He is *caiman.*'

The pale reptilian thing in the water was bigger than any human. Its scaly and sinuous tail, as long as a large dog, widened from a sharp tip into a thick, flat torso armored in pebbled white scales, from which four stubby limbs protruded, topped by claws the size of Patch's paws. Its broad snout was mostly mouth: flat and triangular, big enough to swallow a raccoon whole, adorned by vast, barbed, serrated yellow teeth. Behind and above this gigantic maw, two dark protruding eyes lay half-concealed behind a bony ridge.

Patch stared, frozen with absolute horror, as the King Beneath rose toward him. He couldn't move. He felt rooted to the bridge. He heard Snout speaking in a hissing, slithering language that was neither Mammal nor Bird. He saw the king's maw open wide, saw its enormous muscles coil and tense, ready to lunge and devour. Its eyes were like black abysses, and Patch couldn't look away from them. He felt dizzy, about to topple and fall into those black pits that were eyes, fall into them and keep falling forever ...

White screamed, 'Patch, run!'

Her shout broke the spell. The King Beneath leapt from the

water like a lightning bolt; but its gargantuan jaws clashed together on empty air as Patch jumped away, back onto the brick ledge that surrounded the room.

The monster fell back into the pool. Dark water fountained up, soaking Patch where he stood. The resulting wave rippled across the pool – and as it did, Patch thought he saw something else moving in the water; something white and scaly, something much like the King Beneath, only much smaller, or perhaps younger.

'Run!' White insisted.

'Oh, no, it's much too late for running,' Snout gloated. 'There's nothing left for you now but dying.'

The water erupted again; and this time, to Patch's horror, the King Beneath launched itself completely out of the water and onto the stone bridge. It flailed clumsily with its stubby limbs for a moment before righting itself and turning its massive body toward Patch. Its white scales and yellow fangs dripped with water.

ROOTS

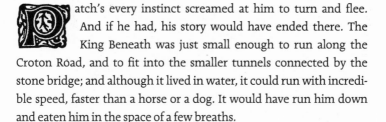 atch's every instinct screamed at him to turn and flee. And if he had, his story would have ended there. The King Beneath was just small enough to run along the Croton Road, and to fit into the smaller tunnels connected by the stone bridge; and although it lived in water, it could run with incredible speed, faster than a horse or a dog. It would have run him down and eaten him in the space of a few breaths.

But Patch did not run. His mother lay on that stone bridge behind that monster, lay poisoned and motionless but not dead, and he would not abandon her. Instead, as the King Beneath charged toward him with the speed of a diving hawk, Patch ran *toward* it; and in the moment it wavered with surprise, he jumped with all his might, leapt over its fanged and slavering maw, and landed on its stubby neck.

He almost skidded off and fell into the pool. The white scales of the King Beneath were slippery with water and harder than bark, and its enormous muscles squirmed beneath him. Patch kept moving, knowing that only momentum kept him upright. He sprinted down the length of the King Beneath, halfway along its curving tail, and leapt onto the stone bridge behind, only a few squirrel-lengths away from Lord Snout's stunned and aghast expression.

Patch didn't stop. He kept running, straight at Snout. His fangs were bared and he was snarling with rage. Snout went still for an instant, frozen by sheer astonishment. Then he scurried toward the edge of the bridge, ready to flee into the dark water – but he was too slow; his moment of surprise had lasted too long. Patch charged headfirst into the huge rat, sending them both tumbling across the stone bridge. Snout's fangs tore into Patch's shoulder. Patch's teeth met in Snout's throat. Rat-blood spurted. Lord Snout shuddered a moment. Then he lay still.

Patch straightened and turned around, fully expecting to see the King Beneath's jaws closing in on him. But the monster was nowhere to be seen. Its charge had taken it past Patch into the small cross-tunnel; and while the King Beneath could run like the wind, and swim like a fish, and kill almost anything its jaws closed upon, one thing it could not do was move backward quickly. Instead of the fanged maw of the King Beneath, Patch saw only the tip of its tail laboriously retreating from that tunnel – and White, greatly daring, racing past that flickering tail to join him on the bridge.

He also saw, in the dark water, another creature like the King Beneath, this one the size of a dog.

'Hurry!' Patch cried.

He and White rushed to Silver's fallen form.

'Cure her,' Patch said urgently.

'I can't!'

Patch stared at White. 'You said you could save her!'

'I can – I think – but I will need you both, and it will take time!'

'We don't have any time!'

'I'm sorry, I *can't*,' White repeated. 'We have to get her out of here.'

Patch nodded and looked nervously at the King Beneath, slowly emerging from the tunnel. 'All right. Hurry.'

But they couldn't hurry. They had enough strength to take Patch's mother's limbs gently in their jaws and push her along the stone bridge toward the other small tunnel, but the process was slow.

They had only gotten Silver to the mouth of the tunnel when the King Beneath finally freed itself from the opposite tunnel and turned to face them.

When it saw Snout's fallen form, its dark eyes fixed on Patch, and its throat began to hiss and rattle with murderous growls. The monster advanced across the stone bridge, moving slowly, stalking Patch carefully. This time there would be no mistakes.

'Get her out of here,' Patch said grimly to White, and turned to face the King Beneath. He knew he had only one chance.

Patch waited for a moment.

Then he ran straight at the white monster on the stone bridge.

The monster reared back, ready for another jump-over; but this time Patch leapt before he reached the King Beneath, caught hold of the tangled roots that dangled almost onto the bridge, and began to climb them.

To his terror his momentum carried him swinging onward, along the bridge, toward the King Beneath's open mouth. He hadn't expected that. The monster leapt up at him – and snapped its jaws together just as Patch let go of the root and caught another with one paw. The King Beneath's teeth barely missed him as they crunched together.

The root Patch barely held began to spin crazily as it swung from side to side, slapping him into a thick cluster of roots. Patch grabbed blindly at that tangled cluster and hung on. He was no longer spinning, but he was still dizzy, the world seemed to be whirling around him at a sickening speed. He caught a blurry glimpse of the monster beneath him, crouching to leap.

Patch made himself race up this branch-thick tangle of roots without thinking, as if he were running up a tree. The King Beneath leapt again. This time its massive jaws snapped together on Patch's tail, cutting it in two.

The monster fell back to the stone bridge, but landed awkwardly and slipped back into the pool of dark water beneath. Patch howled with shock and pain. Blood fell in a red rivulet from the stump of his severed tail as he climbed the damp tangle of roots, and kept climbing until he reached the ceiling.

At that height Patch was surrounded by a cloud of roots, he

could barely make out anything when he squinted downward, but he was sure he would have seen White or Silver if they were still on the bridge. White had dragged his mother out of the chamber of the King Beneath and into the small cross-tunnel. It was something.

His tail, what was left of it, throbbed with agony, and without its full length his balance felt all wrong; Patch almost fell when he began to make his way back down for a better view. He couldn't hang on to these slippery roots forever. He had to try to ignore the mind-swallowing pain of his tail, at least until he escaped.

The chamber appeared empty. The King Beneath and the smaller monster seemed to have departed. But Patch didn't trust his eyes. He watched very carefully as he descended toward the bridge, and as he emerged from the thick cloud of roots in the heart of the domed roof, he saw a tiny ripple in the water beside the bridge, and he knew that dark eyes were watching him carefully.

Patch hung on those roots for what felt like a long time. He knew if he dropped to the bridge the monster would take him. He could try to outwait it – but he knew that would never succeed. The King Beneath was ancient and cold-blooded. It would wait as long as it needed to catch its prey, and it wouldn't need to wait long; these roots were slippery, Patch was bleeding badly from his tail, and his shoulder ached where Snout had bitten it – that foreleg was losing strength.

He had to do something soon or he would fall involuntarily. But what?

He remembered how his momentum had unexpectedly swung him toward the enemy when he had first leapt up into the roots. Patch began to rock his body back and forth, experimentally at first, to see if anything happened; and when it did, when the root he hung on began to move in wide curving arcs, he threw himself into it, swung himself with all his might up and down the length of the stone bridge. There was only one chance. Not yet – not yet – *now* –

Patch let go of the root and soared through the air. It felt like falling off a high branch. He curled himself into a ball just before he flew into the mouth of the cross-tunnel where White had gone. The impact of landing rattled his bones and mind, and for a moment he lay there senseless; but then he heard showering water as something enormous surged out of the dark pool and onto the bridge, and sheer panic brought him to his feet and set him running.

This tunnel was circular, made of corrugated metal hoops. There was a little water in it and Patch splashed loudly as he ran up its dark length. There was just enough light to see that it divided into two similar but smaller tunnels not far from the Croton Road. As he reached that junction, Patch heard something lumbering up the tunnel toward him with incredible speed; but his heart soared, and he actually smiled. The King Beneath was much too large for these smaller tunnels, and he could smell which direction White had gone. He pelted and skidded down the right-hand fork, which bent down and around, running parallel to the Croton Road, until suddenly he shot into a small chamber with a concrete floor.

THE CHAMBER OF BONES

atch cried out with pain. He hadn't fallen far, but he had fallen onto the searing agony of his severed tail.

'Patch!' White gasped, not far away. 'Are you all right?'

He groaned. 'I think so.'

He made his way slowly toward her through the eyeless darkness. The concrete floor was wet and cracked. He could hear water trickling and dripping behind him in the tunnel he had entered, and in several places to his right.

White sniffed the air. 'Is that blood? Are you hurt?'

'My tail,' Patch groaned.

'Oh, no. Oh, Patch, I'm so sorry.'

His nose touched White's side. 'Never mind me. Did you get Silver here too?'

'Yes. She's right here.'

'Can you save her?'

'I don't know. Maybe. There's one way –'

Both of them fell silent. There was a scuttling noise coming toward them, the scrabbling of claws on metal, something coming down the metal tunnel. Patch suddenly envisioned the smaller monster in the dark water. Could it fit through that tunnel? He was terrified that it could.

'The little one's coming!' he said. 'Hurry!'

He grabbed Silver's leg with his mouth and began to drag her toward the trickling sounds behind them. White hesitated a moment before joining him. The thing in the tunnel rattled closer. Patch pulled harder, moving as fast as he could.

The bleeding stump of his tail brushed against something metal and he groaned before turning to investigate. There was another metal tunnel here, this one barely big enough for a squirrel. It ramped down so sharply that if it was long enough the fall might kill them.

Something big and wet squelched out of the larger tunnel and onto the chamber's concrete floor. The little monster was in the room with them. They had no choice. Patch dragged Silver back with one final desperate push, and then they were falling, sliding through a hinged metal flap and skidding steeply down along corrugated metal walls.

Patch screamed when he hit bottom. They hadn't fallen far, less than a squirrel's length, but he had landed severed-tail-first on a carpet of sharp little things like sticks, and Silver's weight was on top of him. Then White landed on them both and agony exploded through his body. He had no breath or strength with which to scream again.

'I'm sorry, Patch, I'm sorry!' White gasped, as he wept and choked with the pain.

'No,' he managed. 'Don't be sorry. We're alive. We're safe.'

He pulled himself away from White and Silver. This chamber was if anything even darker than the last. A thick layer of dry and hard twiglike things covered its concrete floor like dead leaves in late autumn. They shifted and rustled as he stepped on them. It wasn't until he slipped on something smooth and rounded that he began to understand what they were. He had slipped on a skull. These were rat-bones, hundreds of them.

'What is this place?' he asked.

White had no answer. Something above was moving about, hissing and snuffling, and Patch smelled something very like the King Beneath. The other *caiman*. But little as it was compared to the King Beneath, it was much too large to fit into this chamber. They were safe – from it, at least.

'Never mind,' Patch said. He decided to worry about whatever had killed these hundreds of rats if and when the time came. 'How do we help Silver?'

He returned to where his mother's apparently lifeless form lay limp amid the heaped rat-bones.

'Blood,' White said. 'It's your blood that makes you immune. She needs your blood.'

'But – how?'

'Patch, you're already bleeding. This might kill you. It might kill you both.'

'I don't care,' he said. 'What do I need to do?'

White was silent for some time. Then she moved, first to Silver, and then to Patch. He felt her head against his, nuzzling his neck softly.

'Hold very still,' she said softly, and bit him hard on the side of his neck.

Patch yowled with pain and surprise.

'Hurry!' she said urgently. 'Lie down next to her, put your wound against hers. You have to share your blood with her. It's her only chance.'

Patch obeyed. His mother's fur felt cold and dead, and her blood ran cool, and smelled of rot and decay. He pressed his bleeding neck against hers and kept up as much pressure as he could.

'How long?' he asked.

'I don't know,' White said. 'A long time.'

Patch began to grow a little dizzy, and then weak. His neck began to throb, and then his head began to pound, joining the stabbing hurt of his severed tail in a symphony of agony. The darkness around him seemed somehow to be blurring, and he began to shiver with cold. He remembered dimly that this was what the blackblood disease had been like. He was absorbing it from Silver, as she was absorbing his blood. And he was not immune. It was worse this time than last. The pain and weakness were so great that he almost didn't feel Silver beginning to shudder against him.

White said something, but Patch could no longer comprehend her. All his senses were smeared into a gray blur. He felt himself being moved, but he did not understand how or where or why. He had never felt so awful in all his life. He was sick, dizzy, confused, helpless, full of pain. He seemed frozen in an eternity of suffering. He wanted to die. Anything that would make this all-devouring misery go away would be a blessing.

Eventually he became aware that something had changed, something was different. The dizziness was going away. The headache was diminishing. The nausea was fading. He was slowly getting better, but he was still helplessly weak, desperately thirsty, ravenously hungry.

'Water ...' he groaned, barely able to speak at all.

Something nudged against him. An empty rat-skull full of water. Patch drank. It helped a little.

'Is he going to be all right?' a voice asked that sounded almost as weak as his own.

'I think so,' White said. 'If only there was some food!'

The other voice said, sighing, 'I'm so hungry.'

Patch agreed with that sentiment. He had never been so hungry in all his life, not even on that winter day when he had gone into the mountains for food. That day seemed so long ago its memory was like something that had happened to a different squirrel, like a story he had once been told.

TUNNELS

ere,' White said. 'Eat this.'

Something damp and floppy brushed against Patch's face. It had a rich, earthy scent, like a mushroom. He was so hungry he bit into it without asking what it was, and so weak he could barely break off a piece to chew. It was fibrous and tasteless, like eating spongy bark, but it was better than nothing. Patch ate until it was gone.

'What was that?' he asked.

'A fungus. It grows in the corners. I don't think it's poisonous.'

White brought him some more. After devouring this second chunk of fungus Patch tried to stand up. He swayed but succeeded.

'I feel better,' he said.

'So do I,' Silver said softly, in the darkness.

Patch's eyes widened and his whole body stiffened with wonder and delight. 'Silver! You're alive!'

'I'm alive. Only because you came to the underworld to save me,' his mother said, as if she did not quite believe it. 'From the very jaws of the King Beneath.'

Patch wanted to run to her, but – 'We're not safe yet. Is there any way out of here?'

'No,' White said. 'Only where we came from. That … thing … is still up there.'

'We can just wait for it to leave,' Silver suggested.

White hesitated. 'I don't know. All these bones … this chamber, the floor is brick, but the walls are old wood, rotted, and one of the long walls is full of little holes. The holes … they don't smell right. I think something lives in them. Something bad.'

The three of them were silent. Patch heard something thumping and snuffling around the chamber above. The little monster. It made hissing, rasping grunts as it moved.

'Wait,' White said. 'Where are we?'

Patch turned and stared with disbelief through the darkness toward White's voice. Had she gone mad?

'We're in the Kingdom Beneath,' Silver said gently, 'in an ancient human tunnel.'

'That's not what I mean,' White said, exasperated. 'I mean, how far from here to the Croton Road?'

Patch said, 'Not far, but she – it – we can't go up there.' He could hear the rough breaths of the smaller monster as it waited for them in the chamber above.

'That's not what I mean either. I mean, how far the other way?'

'The other way?' Patch asked, befuddled. 'But there's a wall –'

'Not really. That's hardly a wall at all. It's soft and rotten.'

'But there's still …'

Silver caught her breath as if she had just realized something. 'Dirt. That's all that's behind the walls here. We can dig.'

Patch gasped as he understood. She was right, they could dig through the wall and the dirt behind, not to bury a nut, but to open a passage back to the Croton Road.

He tried to calculate where they were. He had run from the King Beneath down the tunnel; after a short distance, he had taken the right-hand fork, which had bent until it ran approximately parallel with the road, before entering the chamber where the smaller *caiman* now waited; then he taken the little tunnel down and to the right, back toward the Croton Road, to this long and narrow wooden chamber. And from the end of this chamber to the bricks of the Croton Road was ...

'Maybe not very far at all,' he said doubtfully. 'I'm not sure. We just might be a few squirrel-lengths away. But there's a brick wall on the other end.'

'We might not make it,' White agreed. 'But we can try. And I don't think we should stay here.'

The acid smell had swelled during this brief conversation, and Patch was now beginning to fervently hope he was just imagining some kind of soft scuttling and faint clicking in the distance.

'You're right,' he said. 'Let's dig.'

White led the digging. Her claws tore through the rotting wood more easily than through the thick, claylike dirt beyond. Silver followed White into the newly dug tunnel. The acid smell grew rank and biting. Patch was not quite fully in the tunnel when a cacophony of soft scurrying and rustling noises swelled toward where the three squirrels huddled at the end of the chamber – and crawling things began to swarm slowly out of the long wooden wall to their left, and into the chamber of bones.

'Hurry!' Patch gasped.

'Turn around!' Silver instructed him. 'Block them off!'

It took him a heartbeat to understand: then he backed out of the tunnel, turned around, and backed into it again. White dug at the tunnel end, and Silver propelled the dirt farther back, and Patch swept it clumsily forward with his paws into the chamber of bones. As the crawling things approached, slowly but inexorably, he found himself able to back a little farther into the tunnel, and a little farther, and a little farther – until he could begin to stopper the tunnel end with fresh dirt, building a wall between their excavation and the chamber of bones.

Soon the tunnel was sealed on both ends. They had buried

themselves alive. But at least they were safe from the crawling things, and still alive.

'Up,' Patch said. 'We want to go up, to the ledge, to the Croton Road.'

Silver passed the idea on to White, who began to angle the tunnel upward as best she could. Patch hoped she had a good sense of direction. It was easy to imagine them trying to tunnel in circles until they died. This wasn't so much a tunnel as a moving bubble, and its air was already beginning to feel thick and lifeless. If they made any mistake they would suffocate and die. And even if they didn't –

'There's something here!' White said, half-triumphant, half-nervous. A few scrabbling breaths later. 'A brick! This is it, the Croton Road!'

'Now we have to go through a brick wall,' Silver muttered. 'How –'

'It's very old,' White said. 'The stuff between the bricks, it's crumbling already.'

She worked for a long time. All Patch heard was a rhythmic scratching. He closed his eyes, tried to breathe as slowly and shallowly as possible, and tried to ignore his multifarious pains. The scratching seemed to go on forever as White bit and clawed at the ancient mortar around the bricks. The thick air was making Patch sleepy. He tried to stay awake, but his eyelids felt so heavy –

'That's it,' White said, exhausted. 'That's as far as I can reach.'

'Is it free?' Silver asked.

A moment passed. 'No!' White exclaimed with despair. 'It trembles a little, but it's not free. It won't move! We can't get out!'

'Don't give up hope,' Silver said, calmly but sternly. 'We must work together. Patch will push against me, I against you, and you against the brick. We must all push as hard as we can. Ready?'

At his mother's command Patch roused himself one final time and squeezed himself backward, pressing himself as hard against her as he could. The pain in his tail was immense, and he moaned a little with every breath.

'Breathe in, then breathe out as we push,' Silver commanded. 'One, two – now!'

Patch strained with all his might. Nothing happened. He sagged, dejected.

'Again,' Silver ordered.

'It's not going to work,' Patch said hopelessly.

'Again.'

He gritted his teeth against the pain, took a deep breath, breathed out, strained –

– and the brick broke free, and fell with a loud *clunk,* and light and lifegiving air from the Croton Road flooded the tunnel. White scrambled out. She had to descend only three bricks to the ledge that ran above the water. Silver followed her, and then Patch backed awkwardly out. He fell onto his tail and groaned loudly.

'Quiet,' Silver whispered. 'I'm sorry, Patch. But the King Beneath is somewhere in this water. I know you're weak. So am I. But we have to run.'

'I know,' he said, struggling to his feet. 'Which way?'

They looked up and down the dimly lit Croton Road.

'This way,' Silver said, and she led the way into the unknown.

ENDLESS ESCAPE

The Croton Road seemed to go on forever, an unbroken highway of brick stretching endlessly through the underworld in a perfectly straight line. In some places daylight peered through cracks in its ceiling; in others, no luminescent fungus lined its walls, and the road was as dark as a wild and moonless night. Sometimes it widened into circular chambers like that where they had encountered the King Beneath, although only a very few of those boasted a stone bridge across the waters. The walls of the road were riddled with countless tunnels, some too small for any squirrel, others big enough for a human to walk without stooping, but the squirrels avoided them all. They stank of rat.

Despite their omnipresent scent, there were almost no rats to be found along the Croton Road. Patch supposed most had been recruited into the huge rat army that had invaded the Center Kingdom. On the two occasions they did hear rats squeaking and scurrying in the distance, the squirrels were able to backtrack to where roots hung thickly from the ceiling, cross the water on those sky-roads, and hide tense and breathless in the dark mouths of side-tunnels until the rat-sounds were gone.

Whenever they saw rippling movement in the water, they fled for a side tunnel, but they never found what swam in that darkness, and never again encountered either the King Beneath or the smaller caiman. They encountered a horrifying legless reptile once, and fled across the water by root-road, sprinting as if pursued, although it was motionless; only its scent showed that it was alive. They encountered any number of other underworld scents that they could not name at all. A few smelled warm and welcoming. Most made their fur stand on end and their teeth chatter.

There were several places where the ledges ramped down into dark pools, and they had to swim across. On one paw, this was welcome, as the only other sources of water were the damp and fungal bricks; on the other, the water was cold and terrifying, and they twice had to swim into utter darkness without knowing what, if anything, waited for them on the other side, or if this might be an underwater sea in which they would freeze and drown. Both times, fortunately, they discovered ramps that led back to the road.

There was almost no food. There was no edible fungus along the road. They tried to nibble at a dead frog they found, but its flesh tasted sour and poisonous, and they gave up. What saved them was that some of the roots hanging from the ceiling were edible, if bitter and chalky. Patch had to be careful when he climbed to eat; he had to relearn his whole sense of balance, now that half his tail was missing.

At one point, after their second sleep, the entire Croton Road turned into a gigantic metal tunnel. They splashed their way along its corrugated length, and then the previous architecture resumed, and they climbed up onto the ledges and continued beneath the arched brick ceiling. It was at this point, where the road began to descend even deeper into the earth, that Patch gave up hope of ever seeing the outside world again. He saw no reason that the Croton Road should not continue forever. He kept moving in a daze, only vaguely aware of his weary paws and legs, and of the countless wounds turning to scars throughout his body. He hardly spoke. Nor did White or

Silver. Conversation consumed valuable energy. They needed their strength to keep moving.

It was well after the third sleep – indeed Patch was on the verge of suggesting a fourth – when they reached a thick metal grate that walled off the entirety of the Croton Road. The squirrels halted before this discontinuity. The grate did not stop or even slow their journey, the gaps between its rusting bars were easily big enough for a squirrel, but beyond it the arching roof of the Croton Road descended suddenly toward the water. On this side of the grate, a human could have walked on the road; on the other, one might barely have crawled.

Patch became aware that there was no glowing fungus on the walls; and yet the total darkness through which they had been traveling had diminished, lit by a dim and distant light far away on the other side of that grate. And the air – it wasn't full of the usual wet and fungal smells of the Croton Road. It smelled, however faintly, of oak trees, and grasses, and the north wind.

They did not dare breathe a word of hope. Instead they moved silently on, slipping through the grate, along this low room … and toward a glowing square of open light in the distance.

But they did not reach that light. They did not have to. A tree-length before, a side tunnel full of water led off from the Croton Road. This was not unusual. What was unusual was the fresh air that burst from that side tunnel like a flower in bloom.

Silver was in the lead. She looked back at White and Patch, and smiled. Then she leapt into the water, and swam down the side tunnel. White followed, and then Patch. The tunnel led to and through an arch that seemed full of white light. Patch's eyes were so accustomed to the underworld that this light was as blinding as pure darkness, he could see nothing at all.

He felt dry stones under his paws, and scrabbled up a dry gully. It took a good dozen breaths before his eyes began to adjust, and he realized that the light was the sun, and the blue canopy above him was a cloudless sky, and they stood outside a ruined, crumbling human building in the midst of high and dense forest. They had escaped the Kingdom Beneath.

VIII. THE END OF WAR

THE ENDLESS EMPIRE

here are we?' White asked, wonder in her voice, after they had feasted on grubs and wildflowers, and drunk from the stream that flowed out of the underworld.

'I don't know. Not the Center Kingdom.' Patch was sure of that much. The air tasted different here, and the trees were taller, and the human trail that led alongside the ruined building was dirt rather than concrete. It felt so good to be beneath the sky again. Even his tail and his many wounds felt better.

'We're north,' Silver said, looking at the sun as it soared toward its apex, and the direction from which they had emerged. 'Far north. We traveled a long time beneath. I think for days.'

Patch called to mind his recollection of how the world had looked when he had soared far above the Center Kingdom in Karmerruk's claws. North, past the island of the Center Kingdom, rivers thrust their way into an expanse of land that continued all the way into the dim horizon. They must have emerged into one of the green patches in that memory landscape. Silver was right: it was a long, long way back home. They would have to cross a river and traverse uncountable miles of forbidding mountains.

The three squirrels drifted south along the human trail, avoiding the thick sky-road above for fear that other squirrels lived there and might view them as interlopers. They soon reached a place where the dirt had fallen away into a narrow gulch, revealing a curving brick slope beneath.

'That's it,' Silver said softly. 'That's where we were.'

It was a dizzying thought, that they were now witnessing from the outside the same Croton Road that they had traveled within for days; that the Kingdom Beneath, which had felt like a different world, was in some places separated from daylight only by the thickness of a brick.

'I smell squirrel,' White said sharply.

Patch sniffed. She was right. And rustling sounds were coming from beside the path. The three squirrels turned, stopped dead with amazement, and stared. The two night-black squirrels that had been scampering through the undergrowth came to an equally nonplussed halt.

'Who are you?' the female black squirrel demanded.

'*What* are you?' asked the male.

'We're squirrels!' Patch said, outraged.

The male black squirrel looked at him skeptically. 'I've seen a lot of other squirrels, and none of them looked anything like you three.'

'Don't you have albinos here?' White asked.

'Albinos?' the male asked, repeating the word without comprehension. 'We don't even know what that is.'

'I heard once there are gray squirrels to the south, in the Archipelago,' the female said thoughtfully. 'Is that where you're from?'

Patch wasn't sure how to answer that question, so he decided to fall back on basics. 'I am Patch son of Silver, of the Seeker clan, of the Treetops tribe. This is my mother Silver daughter of Strongtail, of the Watcher clan, and White daughter of Streak, of the Runner clan. We are all of the Center Kingdom.'

'The Center Kingdom!' the male exclaimed. 'I've heard of that. You're right, it's in the Archipelago.'

'I told you so,' the female scolded him. 'You never believe me.'

'Pardon me,' Silver said, 'but with whom do we have the honor of speaking?'

'Oh,' the female said, embarrassed. 'I am Dizzy daughter of Silent, and this is my mate Leafcutter son of Tallclimber, we're both Gobbler clan.'

'Of what tribe?' Silver asked.

Dizzy and Leafcutter exchanged looks. 'It's not like your Archipelago here,' Leafcutter said. 'This is the Endless Empire.'

Explanations soon ensued, from both sides. According to Dizzy and Leafcutter, the Endless Empire had no tribes, like the Hidden Kingdom, although for the opposite reason. The Hidden Kingdom was tribeless because there were not enough trees for squirrels to congregate in those numbers; the Endless Empire because its expanses were too vast and borderless for tribes to make any sense.

Squirrels simply moved on if they had any trouble with their neighbors, so no tribes had ever formed. Some squirrels clustered in loose little clan-groups, but many just lived with their families or even alone.

It didn't sound dangerous. There were owls and raccoons and foxes at night, and occasionally dogs by day, but according to Dizzy and Leafcutter, this corner of the Endless Empire was a safe and easy place to live. They doubted any other squirrel would trouble Patch, White and Silver as they traveled south to the Archipelago, although many would stop them from curiosity.

'It sounds better than the Center Kingdom,' White said wistfully, watching Dizzy and Leafcutter scramble away through the underbrush toward their drey after saying their good-byes.

Patch looked at her. 'What do you mean?'

'It's safe here. And they don't think I'm cursed by the moon. They don't even know what albinos are.'

'Do you want to stay?' Silver asked.

White looked at Patch, then looked away. She did not answer.

The uncomfortable silence was broken by a totally unexpected voice from above.

'Good heavens,' a voice said in Bird. 'I think I know you, squirrel. You with the little white patch on your forehead. Do you remember me? Do you know where my home is? I'm looking for my home, and I can't find it!'

BIRDS IN THE WIND

It's very strange,' Daffa the pigeon said, as he drifted down and landed on the ground before Patch. 'I remember exactly where I met you before, and it was very far away. I don't think I've ever known any animal that wasn't a bird to travel so far. Do you remember me? Was it a long time ago? I'm not good with time.'

He waited anxiously.

'Not so long ago,' Patch said slowly, 'not so long.'

Daffa winced, deflated. 'Then you don't know where my home is?'

'I'm sorry.'

'Oh well. It has to be somewhere. It can't just have disappeared.' The pigeon sighed and made ready to fly away.

'Wait!' Patch said. 'Wait, Daffa, the three of us, we're all from the Center Kingdom, and we don't know how to get home.'

The bird hesitated. 'I suppose you can't just fly.'

'No. We can't. But maybe, I was thinking, if I told you where the nest of my friend Toro was, he's a bluejay, maybe you could bring him to us, and he could help us get home?'

'I'm not very good with messages.'

Patch thought a moment. 'You wouldn't have to bring him a message. Just tell him my name, and bring him back here. You could do that, right?'

'Oh, of course. I know exactly anywhere I've been. Exactly. But it's a long way to the Center Kingdom ...'

'Do you have anywhere else to be going?' Patch asked gently.

Daffa sighed. 'No. Not until I find my home.'

'Then ...'

'Oh, all right. What was your name again?'

'My name is Patch.' He left out the rest of his usual introduction; no sense taxing Daffa's mind unnecessarily. 'Do you know the place in the Center Kingdom where the human-carved animals go around and around, while their music plays?'

'I know the place.'

'Toro's nest is on top of that building. He's a bluejay. Just tell him my name and bring him here.'

'And your name is Pitch?' Daffa said doubtfully.

'Patch! Listen, Daffa. This is so important. We'll never get home without help. Keep saying my name the whole way there. Patch, Patch, Patch.'

'Patch, Patch, Patch,' Daffa repeated. 'All right. I'll try. I'll try to be back soon. Patch, Patch, Patch, Patch, Patch!'

The pigeon rose chanting into the sky and soared southward. Patch waited hopefully. With Toro's help, scouting the territory, watching them from above, they would have a much better chance of making it back to the Center Kingdom.

'Do you want to stay here in the Endless Empire?' Silver asked

White, for the second time. Patch twitched; he had forgotten the exchange that Daffa had interrupted.

This time nothing prevented White from answering. But it took her a long and awkward time before she finally answered, in a low voice, while staring at the ground, 'I don't want to go back to the squirrels of the Center Kingdom. But I want to go wherever your son goes.'

It took Patch a moment to realize *your son* meant him.

Silver looked at Patch and said, almost accusingly, 'What do you think of this?'

He blinked. 'I think it's stupid the way all the other squirrels treat her. I think she's the bravest, smartest squirrel I know. She went into the Kingdom Beneath to help save your life, and she didn't even know you.'

'Yes,' Silver said, 'but what do you think of her?'

Patch didn't understand the question. 'She's my friend.'

In the long silence that followed White muttered something under her breath and turned away from him. Patch looked at her, bewildered, and said, 'What's wrong?'

'I can't believe you even have to ask!' White sniffled.

'She doesn't only want to be your friend,' Silver said softly. 'She wants to be your mate. And I agree with you, Patch, it doesn't matter that she's albino. She's a hero. I can think of no better mate for my son. But if it is not what you want –'

'My mate? But – but it's not even chasing season!'

'There's more to sharing a drey than just chasing,' Silver said dryly.

'Oh. Well.' Patch hesitated. He had always liked being alone. But he didn't want White to go away. He thought he would miss her if she did. 'Okay then. We can share a drey when we get back, if she likes.'

White turned and stared at him, her eyes alight.

'Other squirrels might say terrible things about you living with an albino,' Silver warned.

Patch shrugged. 'I don't care what other squirrels say.'

And that was that. White walked slowly over to lie very close to Patch's side as they waited. Silver sat a little distance from them. It occurred to Patch as he looked over to White that she was now his mate. It seemed odd that the word applied to him, when he had always chosen to live alone. But the thought of sharing his drey with White made him feel happy. He lay quietly beside her for a long time.

'Patch!' a voice cried out in Bird.

It was quickly followed by a second voice. 'I told you I knew where he was. You see, I knew *exactly!*'

Daffa and Toro landed on the dirt path before Patch, Silver, and White.

'Patch, I can't believe it!' his bluejay friend exclaimed. 'I heard you went into the Kingdom Beneath. I thought you must be dead!'

Patch smiled. 'Almost. Many times.' His smile faded. 'You can see my tail. But I'm alive. We need to get home, back to the Center Kingdom. Can you help us?'

Toro hesitated. 'I don't think you want to do that.'

'What? Why not?'

'Bad things are happening in the Center Kingdom right now, Patch. Terrible things, worse than the rats, worse than you can imagine. I think it's best to stay away. I don't know if there'll be any kingdom for you to go back to.'

A MURDER OF CROWS

t's the crows,' Toro said. 'They're attacking every mammal in the kingdom. Cats, dogs, even horses, I've seen them go after *humans.* But most of all they attack squirrels. Flocks of a hundred, sometimes more, the biggest flocks I've ever seen, they look like swarms of big black bees. They leave other birds alone. But anything with fur that walks or crawls is a victim.'

'They just started attacking? Out of nowhere?' Patch asked, aghast.

'No. They started a few days ago.' Toro paused. 'After the coming of the King Beneath.'

The three squirrels stared at the bluejay. Daffa covered his face with a wing.

'It's true!' Toro insisted. 'He's not a myth, he's real, I've seen him! I saw him last night, in the Northern Sea. He's bigger than a horse, and he's covered with scales like a lizard, and he's all white, and he's got fangs like you've never seen. He comes out at night and devours everything he comes near. He's so fast. Last night I saw him kill and eat a sleeping human! He's real, Patch, I saw him!'

'You don't have to convince us,' Patch said quietly. 'We've seen him too.'

'Oh. Good. Well, not good, but … He's risen from the underworld. He's the reason the crows are attacking. He's made an alliance with them. I've heard they're moon-sworn to him. And between them they're killing every mammal in the Center Kingdom.'

As Patch relayed this awful news to White and Silver, he thought of what Lord Snout had said to him. *I hope you don't think you've won the war … All creatures of darkness serve the King Beneath. And when he comes, all will flock to his command.*

'So many crows,' Silver breathed. 'There were hundreds of them, no, thousands, remember how they covered the trees, how they clouded the sun? We can't stand against them. Nothing can. They'll drive us from the trees.'

'And then the rats and the King Beneath will take us,' White said. She smiled darkly as something occurred to her. 'It's funny, I never thought of the Center Kingdom as "us" until now. Now that it's too late.'

'It isn't too late,' Patch said hollowly, but it felt like a lie, and White and Silver only looked sadly at him.

'I'm sorry,' Toro said.

'Oh, I am too,' Daffa agreed, sounding even more heartsick than the bluejay. 'I know what it's like to lose your home, Patch. It's like a hole in your heart that will never heal.'

'It can't be lost!' Patch exclaimed. 'There has to be something we can do!' It wasn't right, not after what they had been through in the Kingdom Beneath, that they finally emerged into the world only to discover that they had become homeless refugees from a doomed and faraway land.

'It would take us days just to get there, Patch,' Silver said quietly. 'If we were very lucky. And even if we succeeded, what could we do? Three squirrels against a caiman monster and thousands of crows?'

'The crows must be moon-sworn to him, they must owe him

some kind of debt, or they wouldn't be flying at night and attacking squirrels,' Patch argued. 'If we could just deal with the King Beneath –'

'Is that all?' White's laugh held no mirth in it. 'You've seen him, Patch. Every squirrel in the Center Kingdom could go after the King Beneath, and I doubt between us we could so much as scratch one of his scales before he killed us all. Your friend Zelina can't help, he'd do the same to cats.'

'I'm sorry, but she's right,' Silver said. 'There's nothing we can do. Survival is our victory. Nothing more.'

Patch paced angrily along the dirt path, as the two squirrels and two birds watched him with concern. They were right. Of course they were right. Of course there was nothing a little squirrel like him could do to defeat the King Beneath. Patch turned, ready to admit defeat.

He caught a momentary whiff of a rich, feral scent.

Patch stopped in his tracks and looked around. There was nothing moving, no other creature in sight. But there was something gleaming by the side of the path. He walked over and discovered a small glass ball, half-buried in the dirt, with a strange patterned and multicolored double helix trapped within.

Patch had discovered such things before, in the Center Kingdom. Human children played with them, and sometimes lost them. It was nothing of consequence. But it sparked a memory.

Patch stood and stared at that glass ball. Thoughts and ideas churned in his mind for what felt like a long time but was probably no more than a few heartbeats. Then he turned and raced back up the path.

'Toro! Daffa!' he said.

The birds looked at him quizzically. 'Bring Karmerruk here.' Both birds flinched at the mention of the hawk's name, but Patch carried on. 'Both of you. I need all three of you.'

Toro peered at Patch carefully. 'Are you mad? Do you rave?'

'No.'

'What in the good sky do you need Karmerruk for?'

Patch said, 'I need him to carry me to the Hidden Kingdom.'

fail to see why the whimsical desires of a ragamuffin squirrel should have anything whatsoever to do with my chosen course of action,' the Prince of the Air said haughtily. 'You presumed greatly on our acquaintance even in requesting my presence. I will have you know I came here only because the hunting is excellent.'

Patch nodded. He had expected the hawk's reluctance. 'Where do you live?'

Karmerruk's stare grew even harder. 'What business is it of yours where I nest?'

'It's near the Center Kingdom, isn't it?' Patch asked. 'Somewhere in the mountains. You have children, don't you? You mentioned your nestlings once.'

'My personal life is none of your concern –'

'But the Center Kingdom is. You know what's going on there, don't you? You know the King Beneath is no myth.'

Karmerruk beat his wings once, and the dust flew. Patch feared that the Prince of the Air would fly away but the hawk let his wings lapse back down to his sides, and admitted, 'I have seen the King Beneath.'

'And you've seen the crows.'

'I would have to be blind not to have seen them.'

'If they win, they'll eat every mammal in the Center Kingdom, and then what will you do for food?'

Karmerruk shrugged. 'There will still be pigeons and bluejays.'

Daffa and Toro backed surreptitiously away from the hawk.

'Is that good enough for your nestlings?' Patch asked. 'No mice? No chipmunks?'

The hawk thought a moment, then sighed. 'I do like mice ... I see your point, groundling. What is it you want of me?'

'I want you to carry me to a particular place in the Hidden Kingdom.'

'What particular place?'

Patch said, 'Daffa knows where.'

Daffa blinked with surprise, then wilted backward as Karmerruk

turned his penetrating gaze upon the pigeon. 'I don't know anything!' Daffa squawked nervously.

'Sure you do,' Patch said. 'You told me once you met a big cat that knew how to speak Bird. And you can go right back to that big cat anytime you want.'

'Oh, the big cat, yes, of course, I can take you there exactly,' Daffa said, relieved.

'Big cat?' Karmerruk asked suspiciously. 'Does this have anything to do with the Queen of All Cats?'

'No,' Patch answered truthfully.

'Hmm.' Karmerruk looked around as if seeking some excuse. 'It's a long way to the Hidden Kingdom.'

'That's why we need to leave as soon as possible.'

The hawk considered for some time. Then he sighed, long and loudly, tilted his head toward the sky, and said, as if musing about the weather, 'I cannot help but to think, Patch son of Silver, in retrospect, my life would have been considerably simpler if I had just eaten you on first acquaintance.'

Patch said nothing.

'All right. Let us fly.'

'Stay here,' Patch said to White and Silver. 'He can't carry more than one of us. I'll be back as soon as I can.'

'You still haven't explained what you're doing!' Silver exclaimed. 'Where are you going?'

'I have an idea,' Patch said vaguely. He didn't want to explain what he was doing. He had a notion that any such explanation might sound completely insane. 'Don't worry. I won't be in any danger. I won't be long – oh!'

This last expostulation was one of pain and surprise, as Karmerruk's talons dug into his flesh and lifted him away from the ground. Patch winced with pain as he watched White and Silver dwindle from squirrels with alarmed expressions into pale blurs and dots, until finally they were invisible, all he could see was the trees of the Endless Empire like a field of grass beneath them, and the mountains and great waters to the south, and the clouds and setting sun in the sky around them. In his paws Patch carried the glass ball he had found half-buried in the dirt path above the Croton Road.

Daffa and Toro flew beside and behind Karmerruk. The strange and improvised flock of three birds and a squirrel made their way first above the human buildings, and then, as the buildings grew from houses into mountains, between them. The journey was no more comfortable than the last time Patch had traveled by hawk, but in a strange way, the talons digging into his bleeding back made him feel safe; they were so sharp, and Karmerruk so strong, that he knew he ran no risk of falling. Patch watched the approaching Island of the Center Kingdom spread out below him as if it were no more than a single little patch of earth, lit by the rays of the falling sun. He committed the sight to memory. He wondered if perhaps he was the only squirrel ever to have seen the world like this more than once.

The rhythm of Karmerruk's wingbeats began to grow ragged, his movements more spasmodic and less smooth.

'You're too heavy,' the hawk gasped. 'I can't take you all the way to the Hidden Kingdom. I'll have to leave you in the Center Kingdom overnight, while I rest.'

Patch winced. That wasn't part of his plan – but there seemed no choice. 'All right.' He thought a moment. 'Can you take me to the middle of the western frontier?'

'Yes.'

'Toro, can you meet me at my drey tomorrow? And bring Daffa. Keep an eye on him. He forgets things.'

'It's true,' Daffa admitted, ashamed. 'In fact I've completely forgotten what I'm doing with the three of you. Have I gone mad?'

'Of course not,' Patch assured him. 'Just stay with Toro here and you'll be fine.'

Daffa looked unconvinced, but didn't argue, as Toro led him south toward the bluejay's nest, and Karmerruk swooped down toward what had once been the territory of the Treetops tribe, when such a tribe had existed. The trees of the North were so covered with crows they seemed to have been infected by some awful blackening disease, but to Patch's relief, the trees near his drey seemed empty of crows – and of all other living things.

'Be careful,' Karmerruk warned, as he deposited Patch on a particular oak tree. 'The crows roost mostly in the North, but by night, when the King Beneath emerges, they fly all over the kingdom. They can see in the dark, not like owls, but well enough. I'll be back here at dawn. Good luck.'

And the hawk flew away, leaving Patch on his home tree. He had not stood on it since the day he had first ventured into the mountains. So many things had changed since then that this sturdy oak now felt alien to Patch, so strange and foreign that he half-thought it was the wrong tree; but no, his drey was still there, in the hollowed-out stump of a big branch, just as he had left it. As the sun set behind the mountains he curled up in his own home. He felt safe: surely no crow could find and attack him here.

It occurred to Patch as he fell asleep that for a long time he had never expected to see his drey again, and despite his desperate mission, he smiled.

He did not sleep long. When darkness fell, the King Beneath rose, and the crows began to fly.

A DESPERATE NIGHT

atch shivered to hear the cawing of thousands of crows in the night. Crows, like squirrels, were normally active by day and roosted in trees by night. He hoped the owls were feasting on the black birds. He stiffened as the caws grew louder, and he heard sudden flapping sounds followed by silence, very near. Crows had landed on his tree.

He breathed as silently as he could. He could easily defend himself in this drey, no more than one crow at a time could squeeze through its narrow entry, but if they learned of his presence they might wait to ambush him in the morning –

Suddenly all the crows on his tree took off, cawing as if to summon the end of the world. There were so many that the oak tree actually shuddered as if with a great wind. Patch heard pawsteps of something – somethings – racing across the ground. He hoped it wasn't squirrels; but it sounded like it was, yes, he heard squirrels crying with rage and pain, barely audible over a cacophony of harsh caws. There was a battle going on outside, and the squirrels were losing. Worse: from their gurgling screams it sounded like they were dying.

229

Patch wanted to go and help, but he knew that if he emerged from his drey all he would do was die with the others. He heard the sounds of claws on bark, almost drowned out by cawing sounds, and as both grew louder his mind drew a picture of a squirrel climbing the oak tree, covered by a murderous knot of pecking crows –

Something forced itself into the entry of Patch's drey. Patch leapt to his feet, ready to defend himself; but it was a squirrel, a huge squirrel covered with wounds. In the moonlight Patch saw that one of its eyes had been pierced by a beak and was now only a half-empty sac dripping pale fluid onto the squirrel's cheek. Patch could hardly smell the other squirrel under the stench of fresh blood. But this squirrel he would have known anywhere.

'Twitch!' Patch gasped, horror in his voice.

'Patch?' Twitch asked with dull amazement as he shoved himself all the way into the drey. It was barely big enough for both of them and their bodies were pressed together. Twitch's flank was wet with his blood, and his breath was ragged. He was facing away from the entrance, and there was no room to turn around. A crow tried to follow him in, pecked at Twitch's tail. Patch lunged forward, enraged, and tore a tuft of feathers from the crow's neck before it pulled itself free and fluttered unevenly into the night. Other crows settled watchfully around the drey's entrance.

'Is that really you, Patch?' Twitch asked. His voice was rasping and thick with pain. 'Am I dreaming? Is this the afterlife? It hurts so much. I thought it wouldn't hurt anymore in the afterlife. Is it always like this? Does it get better?'

'This isn't the afterlife, Twitch,' Patch said grimly, watching the entrance. 'This is really me. You're not dead. You're not going to die.'

'I killed a lot of them, Patch. A whole lot.'

'I bet you did.'

'I'm hungry.'

Patch winced. There was no food in his drey.

'What happened?' he asked.

'We were going south. The south was safer, it has to be, the King Beneath is in the Northern Sea. We heard the humans were spraying trees with something to keep the crows away. I guess we didn't get far enough. I think they killed Stardancer. It was hard to see, there's not much moon, but I saw him for a moment, it looked like he stopped fighting and they were eating him. I don't know who's king now. The King Beneath took Sharpclaw. I saw him. Isn't that strange? I actually saw the King Beneath. I'm hungry. The crows almost killed me too. If I hadn't remembered your drey was here … I never thought you'd be in it. My right eye, I can't see out of it at all. Maybe, maybe it will get better. I'll get better, Patch. I always get better.'

By the time Twitch finished his voice was so weak he was almost whispering. Patch said nothing.

'You were looking for Silver,' Twitch said, barely audible. 'Did you find her?'

'Yes,' Patch said, glad to have some good news for his friend. 'Yes, she's fine, she's far away, she's safe.'

'Oh, good. Maybe she's the new king. I'm tired, Patch. I'll see you in the morning.'

Twitch shuddered twice and then lay silent. For a moment Patch feared the worst – but he could feel his friend's strong heart still beating within his torn body, faint and fast, but regularly; could feel his battered body swell with ragged breaths.

Patch hardly slept that night. It seemed that every time his eyes closed, another crow tried to enter his drey, and he had to fight it off. He suffered a half-dozen pecks to the snout that night. Eventually, exasperated, he shouted at one attacking crow, 'Why are you doing this?'

The crow leapt back to the threshold of the drey, surprised that Patch spoke Bird. Motionless, the crow was so black that it looked less like a thing and more like an absence in the night.

Eventually it said, gruffly, 'I don't know, groundling. I'm just a crow. It's what the flock-lord commands. I don't even know why we came here in the first place, much less why now we have to kill you ourselves. All I know is the King of Crows made some kind of bargain.'

'What bargain?'

'I'm just a crow,' the bird repeated. 'I don't like it either. I don't like the night, we can hardly see. Hundreds of us have died. The owls are terrible. But we can't go home until you're dead. I'm sorry.'

Then the crow retreated, disappearing into darkness. It did not return; and for the rest of the night no more crows tried to force their way into Patch's drey.

Patch must have eventually fallen asleep; he was awoken by the dawn. Twitch lay beside him, unconscious. Patch wormed his way forward and poked his head gingerly outside the entrance of his drey. There were still crows outside, roosting on the branches of his oak tree, covering them like leaves: dozens of them, hundreds. Patch hesitated, not sure what to do.

Then a mighty avian cry came from above, as if the sky itself was screaming, and the crows on his tree all came to life at once and fled panicked into the western sky, as Karmerruk came soaring down. One crow was too slow; Karmerruk caught it, tore it in two, landed on the branch that included Patch's drey, and began to feast.

'Ready, squirrel?' the hawk asked between bites, as Toro and Daffa fluttered to landings on branches a safe and respectful distance away from him.

'Just a moment,' Patch said.

He dashed to the ground and filled his mouth with tulip bulbs from across the nearest concrete path. He returned to his drey, opened his mouth, and left the bulbs there for Twitch. Then he took the glass ball back into his paws.

'I have to go, Twitch,' he said to his friend's unconscious form. 'I'm sorry. I'll be back as soon as I can.'

Patch emerged from the drey to the branch. He groaned with pain as once again Karmerruk's talons dug into his back, and the hawk beat his enormous wings, and once again they rose into the sky. They followed Daffa and Toro eastward.

As they passed out of the Center Kingdom, into the eastern mountains, Patch craned his neck to look behind him, at his home. To his alarm he saw a black cloud of crows rising into the sky and soaring after them.

'Behind us!' he cried out. 'Crows! They're chasing us!'

Daffa and Toro accelerated forward and away from the pursuing mob. Karmerruk strained to do the same; but he was so slowed by Patch's weight that he could not match their pace. The hundred black birds in howling pursuit were bound to catch them before they reached their destination.

ou're too heavy,' Karmerruk gasped. 'I'm going to put you down.'

'They'll kill me!'

'Stay in the metal cave. You'll be safe there.'

'The what? No, not the water!' Patch exclaimed as they reached the wide, churning river that divided the island of the Center Kingdom from the Hidden Kingdom. He knew this water was cold and violent, and he could easily envision crows perching on his back and pecking his eyes out as he tried to swim ...

'Not the water,' Karmerruk agreed. The fastest crows were almost upon them.

The hawk swooped into a southward dive, heading toward one of the huge bridges that spanned the river. For a moment Patch thought he would be dropped like a rock on the bridge's metal arch. Then he saw, parallel to and just north of the bridge, a metal-and-glass cage the size of a large automobile, suspended from a massive wire by what looked like two giant metal feet. This cage was actually somehow crawling through the sky. Karmerruk pulled up just above it, and in the instant of least motion, his talons released, and Patch fell with a gentle thump to the cage's metal roof.

By the time he rolled back to his feet and took stock of his surroundings the crows were almost upon them. He dashed beneath the metal feet that held up the cage. This space was like a low and narrow cave of metal, as Karmerruk had said. Any crows who followed him would be easy to kill, unable to fly, unable to gang up on Patch.

But this safety was a moot point. For when Karmerruk had slowed to release Patch safely, he had made himself vulnerable. All the crows hurled themselves at the hawk. For a breath the Prince of the Air was invisible, somewhere inside a whirling, tearing knot of crows; then the knot began to plummet downward, toward the cold river. Patch stared aghast, thinking that Karmerruk had sacrificed himself to save him.

Then the cloud of crows exploded outward, and a gray streak erupted from it, leaving a shower of black and gray feathers in its wake, and two lifeless crows who fell until they hit water. Karmerruk dived faster than his pursuers could follow, pulled up at the last moment, skidded a hairbreadth over the water, and then began to climb steadily into the sky. The crows strained to follow him, but they could not match his power. Patch thought the hawk had escaped.

But escape was not his intention. Karmerruk suddenly turned in a dizzyingly tight circle and dived back down, straight into the pursuing crows. There was a frenzy of slashing as he passed through them. Three more crows toppled from the sky and splashed into the river; two more tried to fly to safety, but their wings were torn, and they scudded in ragged descending spirals until they too fell into the water and disappeared beneath its waves. Karmerruk was already climbing again. When he reached the apogee of his flight, he screamed, a noise so terrible that the mob of crows wavered; and then he dived through them again, rending and tearing with beak and claws, and six more of his enemies fell into the water and died.

The cloud of crows dissipated and fled singly back toward the Center Kingdom. Patch stared in awe at the Prince of the Air as he landed neatly atop the still-moving cage. His feathers were ragged in patches, and the side of his head was bleeding, but Karmerruk seemed not to notice. The hawk's eyes were alight with triumph and delight.

'They dared think they could match me in the open sky,' he said, and his laugh made Patch shudder. 'Let all of them come, here where there are no trees to hide in. Let every crow in the world come and I'll kill every one of them, I'll turn them into a sea of blood and feathers, I'll stop this river with their bodies. Oh, that was good hunting, little squirrel, the finest I've had in years. I'm glad you brought me here. It's such joy to have prey who don't run away immediately. I only wish they had stayed longer.'

Patch didn't dare meet Karmerruk's gaze. He looked up and saw Toro and Daffa, circling high above. They did not seem inclined to come any lower. Patch couldn't blame them. He had grown so accustomed to the hawk's presence, he had almost forgotten how deadly a killer he was; and he had never known until now the joy and exultation that Karmerruk took in killing.

'You can come out,' Karmerruk said, amused. 'It's safe.'

Patch made himself waddle out into the open air. The hawk

snatched him up and carried him east, following Daffa and Toro up a smaller river, to a metal bridge, and then to one of a series of low, enormous buildings. Karmerruk deposited Patch on the roof, then settled down himself.

'I'd best return, lest they follow me here,' he said. 'But I must confess to a certain curiosity. What exactly is your plan?'

'You wouldn't believe me,' Patch said honestly.

Karmerruk nodded, unoffended. 'Perhaps later I will see for myself. Good luck, Patch son of Silver. I salute you. You have the heart of a hawk.'

He flew off. Toro and Daffa breathed mutual sighs of relief and hopped over to stand close to Patch.

'What is your idea?' Toro asked. 'What's here?'

Patch said, smiling grimly, 'You better come inside with me. You won't believe me until you see him for yourself.'

BURNING BRIGHT

un and moon and stars,' Toro breathed, awed.

Patch could hardly hear the bluejay over the homicidal howling of dogs. They had flown and climbed through a broken window into this vast and empty space covered with bloodstains. On one side of this enormous chamber, scores of small animals lay trapped in stacked metal cages that Patch knew all too well. On the other, a dozen huge dogs snarled murderously and clawed frantically at the insides of their cages, trying to get to Patch; and at the end of the line of dogs, in the largest cage in the room, a cage with bars as thick as branches, sealed by three mysterious devices, stood Siva the tiger.

'Kill you and eat you!' the dogs roared, but Patch and the birds ignored them.

'I dared to hope,' Siva said softly to Patch. 'I dared, and my hope has flowered. You have come to me, little squirrel. Do you bring my human brother? Has he come to free me from this terror?'

'Not yet,' Patch admitted. 'That's next. Daffa! Toro! Come here.'

The pigeon and bluejay flapped over to stand next to him.

'Take this,' Patch said to Toro, and gave him the glass ball he had carried all the way from the Endless Empire. It fit perfectly into the bluejay's claws. 'Daffa, take him to where you first met me. Find the *kabooti* man. He speaks to animals. I think he can speak Bird.'

'He can,' Siva interjected.

'Bring him back here. As soon as you can. Hurry.'

Toro, his eyes wide with wonder, nodded his understanding; and Daffa led him out of the chamber's one shattered window, into the sky, and toward the Ocean Kingdom.

'When do the other humans come?' Patch asked the tiger. 'The ones who keep you here?'

'The war-drinkers,' Siva said softly. 'The blood-feasters. They will not come tonight. Tomorrow there will be killing, so tonight they starve us, they try to steep us in hate. It would be so easy to hate them. But I will not. I will pity them. They are lost and starveling creatures themselves, and their cages are of their own making, impossible to escape.'

'Do you think your human brother can get you out of here?' Patch asked.

'I don't know,' Siva said. 'I hope.'

They waited. The sun set, and the colossal chamber was lit only by a single red light above a door. Patch and Siva spoke for a long time. Eventually Patch fell asleep, curled up beside the tiger's cage.

He was awoken by a shattering of glass, and came tensely to his feet, ready for battle and disaster. There was a new smell, a human smell – but not *entirely* human –

'Do not be afraid,' Siva said. 'My brother has come.'

A small adult male human dressed in rags appeared in the main doorway. Its dark skin was stained red by the light above. The dogs began to bark again; but this time they sounded more unnerved than enraged. 'Who's there? What's that? Is it human? Kill it? Eat it? What is it?'

'Siva!' the human cried out, in Bird, and the tiger growled softly in reply.

The human raced to the cage, thrust its arms fearlessly between the bars, and the tiger pressed himself against the bars and allowed himself to be stroked.

'I thought you lost,' the human said. The Bird it spoke was heavily accented but understandable. 'I thought you dead!'

'They set many dogs to kill me. I had to kill to live.'

'Patch!' Toro said, fluttering into the room. 'The human brought me here! The human speaks Bird! The human hid me and took me in an underground cage, and then in a death machine! Patch, I rode in a death machine! Can you believe it?'

'You are Patch,' the human said, stooping. 'You sent me the glass ball.'

Patch shuddered, warring with his instincts, as the human reached out its hand and gently stroked his fur.

'I am in your debt forever, noble squirrel,' the human said. 'My name is Vijay.'

'Hello,' Patch said awkwardly.

'The squirrel needs my aid,' Siva said gravely. 'And I would grant it to him. But first I must escape from this cage. Can you free me, Vijay? It is sealed, it is solid steel.'

Vijay stood, and reached into his rags, and Patch recoiled as a bright light winked into being. The human aimed the light at the cage and examined it carefully, paying particular attention to its three steel seals. Then he shone it at the wall behind the tiger.

'Brick,' he mused aloud. 'Much weaker than steel, but still too strong.'

Then he shone it at the floor, and his eyes lit up, and he said, 'Wood.'

Patch looked down at the wide bloodstained planks that made up the floor. They disappeared into darkness as Vijay turned and explored the rest of this killing place, muttering to himself in human language. A cry of discovery came from a distant corner; and then Vijay returned, holding a metal bar that was very thin at one end, and thick and curved at the other. He inserted the thin end between two planks that protruded beneath the wall of the cage; then he pushed on the thick end, pushed with all his might; Patch could smell his sweat, and hear his thudding heart – and suddenly one of the planks sprang from the ground like a startled chipmunk.

Vijay pulled the plank free and aimed the light downward. The space beneath was deep and laced with pipes and cables. It stank of rat, and Patch saw a half-dozen scurrying things race away from the pool of light as it stabbed into the darkness.

'Yes,' Vijay said, pleased. 'They built this cage to keep you in, Siva, not to keep a determined human out.'

He pried another plank free, and another – and soon there was a tiger-sized hole in the floor of the cage, and Siva simply stepped down into the darkness, then leapt up into the open chamber, free. Vijay wrapped his arms around Siva and held him tightly for some time as Siva licked tears from Vijay's face with his rough tongue.

'Come,' the human eventually said. 'Come outside, and then help this squirrel with what he needs. Whatever he needs. Anything I can do for you, Patch, name it, and it is yours.'

Patch and Vijay climbed carefully through the shattered window and out into the night. Toro flew through, and Siva simply jumped through the open space with a single bound. Once outside the tiger took a deep breath and looked up at the stars.

'It has been so long since I have seen the open sky,' he said, his voice trembling. 'So long. I owe you a debt immeasurable, Patch son of Silver. What would you of me?'

Patch said, 'I need you to come to the Center Kingdom and fight for me.'

Siva only nodded. 'Show me the way.'

'Follow me,' Patch said, and began to run westward – but was stopped by Siva's low and throaty laugh.

'I think you will find, my little friend, that we will go considerably faster at my speed,' the tiger said, amused. 'Climb onto my neck and ride. Don't worry about your claws. I've suffered much worse in the pit from which you just freed me.'

Patch took a moment to digest the offer. Then, hesitantly, trying not to draw blood, he leapt up and used his claws to climb up the tiger's flank to his back, and settled in on the bulge of bone just behind Siva's neck.

'Toro,' Vijay said, 'can you follow them, and then return to me and tell me where they went?'

Patch hardly heard the bluejay's assent. He could not believe he was riding a tiger.

'Tell me the way,' Siva said, 'and hold on as tight as you can.'

iding a tiger was like running and flying at the same time. Siva loped with incredible speed down shadowed human streets, staying in the dark as much as possible, avoiding automobiles, keeping away from the human lights that stitched lines into the night sky, while Patch, calling to mind his memory picture of the world as seen from the sky, directed their journey with urgent whispers into Siva's ears. They passed a few humans dozing in doorways or staggering through the streets. All stopped and cried out with surprise and dismay as the tiger flashed past: up stairs and over the metal bridge across the little river, through the low buildings and wide streets of the district just north, and finally to the massive concrete ramp that curled up to the enormous bridge that stretched across the great eastern river.

Even in this quietest and darkest hour of the night, the city thrummed with life, and the bridge was busy with automobiles. All of them screeched and skewed to sudden halts when they came within sighting distance of the tiger. There were several collisions as Siva sprinted across the bridge, and once he had to leap over two automobiles that had just violently intertwined and spun to a halt in his path. He cleared both with space to spare. In the distance, far ahead of them, Patch heard high-pitched sounds like the mating call of crazed and gargantuan birds, and saw whirling and flashing lights approach; but the tiger reached the island of the Center Kingdom before those lights arrived, and Patch whispered in his ear, and the tiger zigged north before zagging west again.

They passed the Great Avenue, very near where Patch had once emerged from the underworld with Zelina and her feline court. There were a few more humans walking the streets here, singly and in small groups, and Siva left a wake of shouts and screams and disbelieving expostulations behind him as he crossed the last avenue, leapt casually over the subsequent stone wall, and landed on the grass and soil of the Center Kingdom.

'North,' Patch whispered into the tiger's ear, and Siva turned and pelted along the kingdom's wall, moving so fast that tears streamed from Patch's eyes.

'It's wonderful here.' Siva's whole chest rumbled when he spoke, and Patch shivered with it. 'I never imagined this city of blood might have a green and growing heart. Is this your home, Patch son of Silver?'

'Yes.'

'You are a lucky creature.'

Patch said, 'Not if we don't save it.'

Siva bared his fangs. 'I will do my best – what is *that*?'

The big cat stopped so suddenly that Patch very nearly somersaulted through the air and fell into the dirt, and only saved himself by clawing hard in the last second. Siva seemed not to notice. The tiger was busy staring up at a tall stone spire that jutted toward the stars. At night, to animal eyes, it seemed almost lit from within.

'This is where I met Coyote,' Patch said, without thinking.

'Coyote,' Siva echoed, and the tiger roiled beneath Patch, and all Siva's fur stood up on end. 'Yes, of course, I should have known, I should have smelled this as his work ...'

'You know him?' Patch asked, astonished.

'By reputation.' Siva hesitated. 'But I suppose it no longer matters who set us on this course, or when. We must save this glorious home of yours.'

Siva leapt once more into the night and the shadows. He raced to and then along the Great Sea, and through the meadows and tree-laden hills just north of it, until he reached the hills of jumbled rock that walled the southern edge of the Northern Sea. Above and around them, the crows were flying. Patch could hear their wing-beats, and their panicked caws as they flew around the tiger. He feared they would descend in a dark and unstoppable whirlwind; and if they had, they might well have killed Patch and Siva both, albeit at the cost of half their number. But Siva was a nightmare figure for those birds who carried nightmares. No crow, not even the King of Crows himself, could muster enough courage to be the first to attack a cat nearly as big as a horse. Instead they awaited their champion.

Patch directed Siva to the Northern Sea and then along its edge, until they reached a place where a tiny bay protruded between a sloping face of solid rock and a grassy hill in which human steps were set. Here there was no fence between land and water; and here Patch smelled a cold and ancient and reptilian scent.

'He's near,' Patch whispered. 'He's very near.'

'Dismount,' Siva said.

It was not a suggestion. Patch obeyed and scurried a little way up the dirt slope. Siva did not watch him go. The tiger stood crouching, coiled, ready to pounce, staring into the dark and silent water of the Northern Sea.

The only light came from a single glass globe across the sea, and the mountain lights beyond. Patch blinked. Was there something moving near the water's edge? Or were those only ripples from the night wind on its calm surface? In the darkness he couldn't be sure.

Above them, crows circled, clouds of them, a whole sky full, an opaque curtain of crows that blotted out the stars.

For a long moment nothing happened.

Then Siva uncoiled, uncrouched, braced himself, and roared.

Patch thought the sound might tear his ears off. The tiger's roar was like the breaking of the moon. It was a challenge, a warning, a war cry, a keening lament of a year lost in a blood-soaked chamber of killing, a howling celebration of the glory of life and the courage of death, and a roar for the pure and simple sake of roaring. The crows above scattered in all directions as if by a thunderclap. The roar echoed across the Northern Sea, and lights began to wink on in two massive octagonal mountains past the northeast corner of the Center Kingdom, as humans were torn untimely from their dreams by this howl of a savage beast.

Before the echoes had even diminished the King Beneath erupted from the waters, moving with transcendent power and terrible speed. It launched itself like a pale-scaled lightning bolt at the tiger, its great maw open for the single killing bite that was all it needed, while Siva stood apparently stiff-limbed and unready –

But Siva was no longer there. The tiger, born in jungle, veteran of a year of lethal battles, somehow found the time and strength, in the eyeblink of the King Beneath's deadly attack, to leap straight up, above the caiman's killing blow.

The tiger landed clawing atop the caiman's hindquarters; the caiman knocked the tiger sprawling with a lashing blow from its massive tail; then caiman and tiger leapt at one another in the same moment – and Siva twisted his head and caught the King Beneath's lower jaw between his own fangs – and the two huge beasts, one white and one golden, slammed together belly to belly, fur against scales, and began to thrash about on the sand and grass, raking at one another with their vicious and massive claws. Dark blood flowed from both. Both snarled and howled with rage and pain.

The King Beneath had an extra appendage: its powerful tail. It used that for leverage, to anchor itself on top of the tiger, and its great weight pressed into Siva, splaying the tiger's limbs out, making Siva more vulnerable to the caiman's stubby but incredibly powerful claws. The King Beneath bore down on Siva, snarling and clawing, until it was between Siva's limbs, and the tiger was no longer able to attack the caiman's belly –

And Siva reached out almost casually with his long, limber forelegs, and clawed out the eyes of the King Beneath.

The caiman's body convulsed with shock; and in that moment Siva released its jaw and dipped his fangs into the caiman's throat. Black blood showered out, covering the tiger. The King Beneath twitched once, twice, a third time; and then it died.

Siva crawled painfully out from beneath the caiman's corpse.

'Your debt is paid, Patch son of Silver,' the tiger wheezed. 'All debts are paid.'

By the time Vijay and Toro reached them, the crows were already feeding on the broken body of the King Beneath.

IX. EPILOGUE

o few,' Patch said, aghast. 'So few.'

He and White stood near the entrance to Silver's drey and looked around. The new queen of the Center Kingdom had called all of her subjects to her, and they had come. They were barely enough to occupy the medium-sized spruce tree that was home to their queen's drey.

'More than fifty,' Queen Silver said, emerging from her drey with its adornments of glittering glass. 'It is said the Forever Winter reduced us to fewer than twenty. We have enough to prosper, to thrive. The crows are gone, and the rats will not bother us again, not with the cats as our allies. Ten years, a few generations, and we will be a proper kingdom again.'

'How many dead?' Patch asked.

Silver shook her head and would not answer.

Patch looked back to the squirrels of the Center Kingdom. Most were scarred, or limping, or both – but their eyes were stony with resilience. These were survivors, every one of them; battered, wounded, but also hardened strong as metal.

Standing there, surrounded by his tribe, it seemed to Patch that he was in the presence of something great and terrible, as if he had just sworn a moon-oath, as if all of them had. He felt like the lives of those around him were part of his own, and his own was part of theirs. It made him feel stronger and more vulnerable at the same time.

He looked at one-eyed Twitch, and winced. The war seemed to have burned away almost everything in Twitch that could enjoy the world. He seemed almost to have been replaced by another squirrel, one whose words were mostly grim prophecies of disaster, one filled with despair. But the last time they had met, Patch had brought him a tulip bulb to eat; and when he had seen the momentary flicker in Twitch's eye when he first saw the treat, Patch had dared to hope that even though his once-joyous friend had been burned by war and buried within his scarred and one-eyed body, the old Twitch still stood some chance of being one day unearthed.

Patch looked back to Silver, who was observing him closely.

'What is it?' The careful intensity of her gaze made him feel like he had done something wrong.

After a moment she said to him, thoughtfully, 'You will be king one day, Patch, when I am gone.'

Patch stared at her. He didn't want to think about Silver ever being gone, and he couldn't imagine ever being king. But there was no trace of humor in her voice.

'You should go back to your drey now,' she said. 'I believe you have a visitor.'

Patch wondered how she knew, but did not doubt her. Silver seemed different now that she was queen: more remote, and yet aware of everything happening in her kingdom.

White led the way from Silver's spruce to Patch's oak. He was still getting used to running the sky-road without his tail-weight for balance. He already had a vague idea of who his visitor might be; and to his delight, when he saw the figure waiting beneath his oak tree, he was proved right.

'Zelina!' Patch cried out.

'Patch! Oh, I'm so very glad to see you. And White, a pleasure as always. Am I to understand that you're officially mated? Congratulations!' exclaimed the Queen of All Cats.

Patch looked around. 'No Alabast?'

'No. Just me. No other cat knows where I am. If they did, they would come to me and draw me back to the court. It isn't all sushi and cream being the Queen of All Cats, you know. I have so many duties, so many worries – lately, it's the humans, it seems there's something terribly wrong with them – and so many affairs of state, little dignitaries to entertain, so many little treacheries and rivalries and territorial turf wars to deal with, you have *no* idea how byzantine and backstabbing the cats of my court can be. And all the protocol, the titles, the ceremonies – oh, sometimes they're wonderful, but honestly, Patch, sometimes I think of those days we went wandering through the Ocean Kingdom, nothing to us but our names, not knowing what we'd eat or where we'd sleep next, and I wish I could be there again. And so. You told me once to visit you in the Center Kingdom. And there was the small matter of a poisoning, and a war, and an attempt to exterminate your entire people, and an underworld quest, and a tiger – and before you ask, no, I don't know what happened to Siva and his attendant – but the point I am trying to attain is, finally, here I am. Would you like to show me around?'

Patch looked at White; and his mate smiled back at him; and Patch said, 'Zelina, I'd be delighted.'

A long time ago, on a glorious mid-spring day, a young squirrel named Patch led his new mate, White, and his best friend, Zelina, on a tour of discovery, an exploration of the delights of the Center Kingdom, in which he lived. They paused often for laughter and stories and reminiscences. The sky above was blue, and the wind was clear and rich with life, and the trees and bushes were thick with flowers and berries, and the days of blood and terror seemed already long forgotten, and this day and all days beyond seemed to stretch into a warm and golden forever.

X. CODA

hid under that bush right there,' Patch reminisced, 'I could hardly walk, my leg really felt like it was going to fall off. The spire's right on the other –'

He fell silent, stopped walking, and sat back on his hindlegs to sniff the air.

Zelina, startled, turned to face him.

'What is it?'

For a moment Patch wondered if the hint of a rich, feral scent in the air was only a trick played by his mind and memory.

Then the branches of the very bush under which he had sheltered parted; and the dog-thing with golden eyes called Coyote emerged. Zelina stiffened, and arched her back, and her fur rose.

'Zelina, Queen of All Cats, Patch son of Silver,' Coyote said. 'Breathe easy, my little queen. I am not your enemy today. Tomorrow, who knows? For tomorrow has always its own mind and madness. But today I am your friend, and today I say, well met.'

'Do you live here?' Patch asked.

'I live in the Kingdom of Madness,' Coyote said. 'As do you all, as do we all, and yet so few of us know it, for that is the madness. The Old One knows. And some humans, perhaps, but too few, too few.' His grin seemed to reveal too many sharp teeth. 'And fewer every day, now.'

'The humans,' Zelina said. 'Do you know what's gone wrong with them?'

Coyote's grin widened. 'I cannot say I know, my queen, for who can truly know anything? But if forced, if pressed, if cornered, well, then I might have a guess or two. I might guess that it is something not unlike the blackblood disease. I might guess that when the King Beneath came Above – and how did that happen, some might wonder? What voice sent whispers to his scaly ear, telling him of the blood and glories that awaited him Above? Who ensured that the fortunes of war left him devoid of any other option? Who arranged for the desperate finale? Ah, who indeed. I certainly can't imagine.' His predator's grin grew even wider and toothier, and his golden eyes shone. 'The King Beneath came, is the important thing, and he died, and the crows feasted on him. And. Well. I would guess that when his black blood mingled with theirs, with that other sickness already growing within them, then something else was born. Something new. Something dreadfully deadly to our two-legged friends. Something that will spread its seed wherever birds fly.'

His words stirred a remembrance in Patch: a remembrance of the turtle's words, the Old One. *Birds fly to these marshes ... even from empires across the great mountains, even from empires across the ocean ... a sickness that spreads among all the birds of the world.*

'You,' Zelina said slowly. 'You did all this. You made it all happen.'

Patch blinked with surprise at this astonishing accusation.

'Oh, no, my little queen,' Coyote said. 'I don't control the great game. But it is true I do play, from time to time. I do like to ensure that it continues. I may perhaps have nudged here, nipped there, made some suggestions to some with sharp noses, whispered into the ears of some with sharp teeth. But I make no claim of authorship. That title belongs to humans themselves. For from where did the blackblood disease come? From human poisons that seeped and festered, drop by drop, year by year, into the Kingdom Beneath. Where the seed falls, there the tree grows. Any animal can tell you that.'

'The humans are sick,' Patch said slowly, thinking of the two humans he had met who spoke Mammal, and wondering if they too were dying of this new disease. 'Because of what we did? Because of what we helped you do?'

'Don't listen to him,' Zelina said to Patch. 'I've heard of him. He's a trickster. A troublemaker. We saved the Center Kingdom. And Silver. We did something good. Something wonderful.'

'Is that regret I smell, Patch?' Coyote sneered at him. 'Is that *remorse*? Waste it not on humans. Look around you. Once this whole island belonged to us. Now we have only a little patch of it, walled by human mountains, covered by human highways, riddled by human tunnels. Why should that be? Why should humans have all the world as their plaything, and leave us only their scraps?'

Patch considered the question. He had to admit that it had no good answer.

'Do you remember when first we met, Patch?' Coyote asked. 'Not here. Outside your drey, near the end of winter.' Patch started, amazed, remembering the dog-thing he had encountered on that morning when he had been so hungry, the morning he had first gone into the mountains. 'I chose you because you were a survivor. I could smell that about you. But you have a good heart, too, generous and kind, I could smell that too. That was what worried me, what worries me yet. It may yet be too good a heart for your own good. I wonder if one day you will have to choose between the two.'

Patch shivered and looked away from Coyote's golden eyes.

'Take care, Patch, and be careful. Watch the skies. And you, Zelina, Queen of All Cats, do take a little look at what lies behind this bush. I think you'll find it very interesting indeed.' Coyote stretched lazily. 'And now I must be gone. A friend is waiting for me. My oldest friend, my most ancient adversary. We have much to discuss. A whole new world, indeed. Enjoy it while you can, Patch son of Silver. For one thing I have learned about worlds, in my time, is that they never last for very long.'

AFTERWORD

In 1935, the New York Times reported the discovery of an eight-foot alligator in a manhole on East 123rd Street. In 2001, a five-foot caiman was captured in the Harlem Meer in Central Park. Deer have been seen on Staten Island. Tigers have lived in Harlem high-rises. In October 2007, a seven-foot python was discovered emerging from a Brooklyn toilet. And a coyote was found in Central Park in the summer of 2005.

One could, if so inclined, inspect many of the places Patch visited during his adventures. His drey is on the tree-covered hills near West 83rd Street, the highest point in Central Park. Karmerruk flew him to the overgrown beaches near Fort Tilden. From there, he and Zelina traversed the Cross Bay Bridge to the Jamaica Bay Wildlife Preserve.

After being captured and caged, they escaped from a Brooklyn warehouse near the Pulaski Bridge over Newtown Creek, rode a bus across the Brooklyn Bridge, disembarked in lower Manhattan, and headed north. Patch found Sniffer at the 8th Street/NYU subway station. He and the cats rode the N/R to the 59th Street station, and followed Zelina to Park Avenue, before Patch returned to his home in Central Park. White's tree is near the park's southeast corner. The Dungeon is the Central Park Zoo; the Great Sea is the Onassis Reservoir; and the Labyrinth is the Conservatory Garden. The stone spire where Patch meets Coyote for the second time is Cleopatra's Needle, and the Northern Sea is the Harlem Meer.

As for the Kingdom Beneath, the Amtrak tunnel where Patch speaks to a robin runs up the west side of Manhattan, beneath Riverside Park; and the long-disused Croton Aqueduct stretches for 41 miles from Central Park, north across the abandoned High Bridge into the Bronx, and along the Aqueduct Trail in Van Cortlandt Park. It is there, at an abandoned way station that still stands, where the squirrels finally emerged into daylight. All of these places lie within the five boroughs of magnificent New York City.

ACKNOWLEDGMENTS

My sincere thanks go to the following: Deborah Schneider, my agent extraordinaire; Chelsea Watt, for the New York City apartment in which I started the book; Elisa Korenne, for the New York City apartment in which I finished the book; Linda Tom, for designing beastsofnewyork.com; Sarah Langan, for exploring the Croton Road with me; Maggie Cino and my sisters, Alison and Jennifer, for reading early versions; Elizabeth Bear, Charles Stross, and David Wellington, for their advice; Simon Law, for his unflagging assistance; Kate Ward, for her support and belief; Julia Solis, for her book *New York Underground*; L.B. Deyo and David Leibowitz, for their book *Invisible Frontier*; Temple Grandin, for her book *Animals in Translation*; Robert Sullivan, for his book *Rats: Observations on the History and Habitat of the City's Most Unwanted Inhabitants*; Edwin G. Burrows and Mike Wallace, for their book *Gotham: A History of New York City to 1898*; Michelle Walker and Caleigh Minshall, for helping to get the word out; Michael Worek, for turning a pretty good story into a much better one; Chandra Wohleber, for copyediting above and beyond the call of duty; Jim Westergard, for reasons that are already apparent; and, especially, thanks to Tim and Elke Inkster, for taking a chance on my weird little squirrel book when no one else would.

ABOUT THE AUTHOR

Born and raised in Waterloo, Ontario, Jon Evans is the son of a Rhodesian expatriate father and a tenth-generation Canadian mother. He studied electrical and computer engineering at the University of Waterloo, graduated in 1996, and promptly moved to California to work in the burgeoning software industry. Evans spent the next fourteen years working, writing, and traveling far and wide around the globe before returning to Canada in 2010.

Evans is the author of four thrillers, one graphic novel, and one dark urban fantasy. His journalism has been published in *Wired, The Guardian, Reader's Digest* and *The Globe and Mail.* His first novel, *Dark Places,* won the 2005 Arthur Ellis Award for Best First Novel. Evans currently lives in Toronto and at www.rezendi.com.

ABOUT THE ARTIST

Jim Westergard was born in Ogden, Utah. He was educated at a variety of colleges and universities in California, Arizona and Utah where he completed his BFA and MFA at Utah State. He moved to Red Deer in 1975 and taught at Red Deer College until his retirement in 1999. He became a Canadian citizen in 1980.

Jim Westergard has been creating prints from wood engravings since his university days in the late '60s. His first book-length collection, *Mother Goose Eggs,* was a limited deluxe letterpress edition bound and released in 2003. The Porcupine's Quill published a paperback reprint of *Mother Goose Eggs* in 2005. Westergard continues to create wood engravings on his cantankerous old VanderCook SP-15 proofpress, which he has affectionately named the 'Spanish Fly'.